"I WOULD PREFER A FRIEND," SHE SAID.

"A friend?" He looked at her.

"Life can be tedious," she said, "for a widow who chooses not to burden herself with another husband. You are an interesting man. You have more to talk of than health and the weather and horses."

"I am, I believe, a tolerably well-educated man, ma'am," he said.

She looked at him measuringly. "You are not perfect after all, are you?" she said. "You are sensitive about your origins. Take me somewhere tomorrow," she said. "I shall decide where between now and then. Let me have someone intelligent with whom to share my observations."

He was tempted. How was he to say no? He must say no. He did not want a thirty-six-year-old mistress. *Rationally* he did not want her. Irrationally, of course, he wanted her very much indeed. He was a rational being. He chose to want a wife who was below the age of thirty, a wife who would give him children for his contentment, a son for Mobley Abbey.

"I am sorry," he said.

A Christmas Bride

Mary Balogh

A SIGNET BOOK

SIGNET
Published by the Penguin Group
Penguin Putnam Inc., 375 Hudson Street,
New York, New York 10014, U.S.A.
Penguin Books Ltd, 27 Wrights Lane,
London W8 5TZ, England
Penguin Books Australia Ltd,
Ringwood, Victoria, Australia
Penguin Books Canada Ltd, 10 Alcorn Avenue,
Toronto, Ontario, Canada M4V 3B2
Penguin Books (N.Z.) Ltd, 182-190 Wairau Road,
Auckland 10, New Zealand

Penguin Books Ltd, Registered Offices:
Harmondsworth, Middlesex, England

First published by Signet, an imprint of Dutton Signet,
a member of Penguin Putnam Inc.

First Printing, November, 1997
10 9 8 7 6 5 4 3 2 1

Chapter 1

Mr. Edgar Downes had decided to take a bride.

Doubtless he should have made up his mind to do so long before he did, since he was six-and-thirty years old and had both a high respect for matrimony and a fondness for family life. But the truth was that he had procrastinated. He had felt caught between two worlds. He was not a gentleman. He was the son of a Bristol merchant who had grown enormously wealthy over the years and had eventually purchased and renovated a grand mansion and estate near Bristol and retired to live there like a gentleman. Edgar had been educated at the best schools, had become a respected and successful lawyer, and then had taken over his father's business.

He was hugely wealthy in his own right. He had received a gentleman's education. He spoke and dressed as a gentleman. He would inherit Mobley Abbey on his father's death. He was extremely eligible. But he was not a gentleman by birth, and in certain circles that fact made all the difference in the world.

He had thought about marrying someone of his own kind. At various points during his adulthood he had even singled out a few daughters or sisters of his middle-class acquaintances as possible wives. But he had never felt that he quite belonged in their world—not when it came to something as personal and intimate as marriage. He would have been hard put to it to explain exactly why that was so. There were certain almost puritanical attitudes in the class, perhaps, or a certain vulgar preoccupation with money and possessions for their own sake. Though neither explanation quite accounted for his discomfort.

He had thought of marrying a lady. But there had been obvious arguments against that. And they all narrowed down to one simple fact—he was not a gentleman. It was true that Cora, his sister and only sibling, had married a younger son of a duke seven years before and had become Lady Francis Kneller as a result. It was true too that Edgar got along remarkably well with his exceedingly elegant brother-in-law and with those of their aristocratic friends he had met. But though Cora's marriage appeared to be bowling along very nicely indeed and had produced four bouncing children, Lord Francis would not in the normal course of events have wed her. It was her disastrous tendency to play heroine without pausing for one hundredth part of a second to consider the wisdom of her actions that had forced him on more than one occasion to her rescue and to compromising circumstances at the same time. Finally, poor fellow, he had had no choice—as a *gentleman*—but to take on a leg shackle and Cora all at the same time.

Lord Francis Kneller and his friends—the Earl of Thornhill, for example, or the Marquess of Carew or the Duke of Bridgwater—might be quite prepared to treat Mr. Edgar Downes, Lady Francis's brother, as a friendly acquaintance. But would they be happy to watch him woo and wed their sisters or cousins if he so chose, and if there were any such females available? It was a question Edgar could not answer with any certainty since he had never posed it to any of the gentlemen concerned, but he could make an educated guess.

Some lesser gentleman with a daughter difficult to fire off in a more acceptable manner—due to impoverishment or lack of beauty or a shrewish nature, perhaps—might be very willing to ally her to a cit, to a lawyer-turned-merchant who also happened to be as wealthy as all but a few of the bluest-blooded lords in the land and with as much more wealth again to inherit on the death of his father. That lesser gentleman, however, would believe in his heart—and all the genteel world would believe with him—that he had stooped low indeed for the mere satisfaction of seeing his daughter wed.

But at the age of six-and-thirty Edgar Downes had decided to take a bride. A bride of good birth. A lady, no less. And he was going to do it soon. By Christmastime he would either be betrothed or have fixed his choice firmly and confidently enough that he would invite the woman and her family to Mobley Abbey for the holiday and a celebration of the betrothal. It was a promise he had made his father, and he always kept his promises.

The elder Mr. Downes celebrated his sixtieth birthday at the beginning of September. And though it would be difficult to find a healthier, more robust, more mentally agile man of his age anywhere in the kingdom, he had chosen on that occasion to remember his mortality and to declare himself an old man. An old man with a dying wish. Cora had shrieked when he had put it thus, doubtless imagining all sorts of hidden and deadly ailments, and Lord Francis had pursed his lips. Edgar had rocked back on his chair. The dying wish was to see his son wed. Perhaps he would even be spared long enough to see a grandson in the nursery—not that he had any objection in the world to granddaughters, but in the nature of things a man longed for at least one grandson.

And since Mr. Downes had achieved almost every goal that any man could possibly set himself in the course of his lifetime—including a lamentably short but blissfully happy marriage, the birth and survival of the best son and daughter a man ever had, not to mention a challenging and successful career and the acquisition of the abbey—he had only one more thing to wish for, apart from the marriage of his son, of course, and that was the birth of a grandson. He could wish that his son would marry well, that he would finally ally the Downes name to one of undoubted gentility.

"You are a gentleman, my son," he said, nodding his head in Edgar's direction, his eyes beaming with pride and affection. "Your dear mother was a lady in every sense that mattered to me. But for my son I want a lady by birth. You have deserved such a wife."

Edgar felt embarrassed, especially since these words had been spoken in the presence of Lord Francis Kneller. He also felt suspiciously damp-eyed. His father meant more to him than almost anyone else in this world.

"And it is high time you married, Edgar," Cora said. "It is all very well for the children to have an uncle who spoils them dreadfully every time he crosses paths with them, but cousins would be of more practical value to them. And an aunt."

Lord Francis chuckled. "You must confess, Edgar," he said, "you have had a good run of it. You are six-and-thirty and only now is your family laying siege to your single state."

"That is quite unfair, Francis," Cora said. "You know that every time Edgar has come to Sidley since our marriage I have thrown the most eligible young ladies in his way. You know that I have tried my very best."

Lord Francis chuckled again. "You are as successful as a matchmaker, my love," he said, "as you are at your swimming lessons."

"Well," she said crossly, "whoever says that the human person—*my* human person anyway—is not heavier than water and will not sink like a stone when laid out on top of it must have windmills in his head and that is all I have to say."

"For which mercy may the Lord be praised," Edgar said, provoking outright laughter from his brother-in-law and a glare followed by a rueful chuckle from his sister.

But his father was not to be diverted from what he had clearly planned as the mission of his sixtieth birthday. Edgar was to marry and to marry a lady. A duke's daughter could not be too good for his son, he remarked.

"What a pity it is that Francis's sisters are married," Cora commented. "Is it not, Francis?"

"Quite so, my love," he agreed.

But any lady of breeding would do nicely, Mr. Downes continued after the interruption. Provided Edgar could like and respect her—and feel an affection for her. That, it seemed, was of greater importance than almost anything else.

"She does not have to be a lady of fortune, my boy," Mr. Downes said. "She can come to you penniless, provided she has the birth and breeding and can love you."

A penniless lady of *ton* would probably love his money a great deal, Edgar thought cynically. But he could not argue with his father, who looked as if he would live until the age of one hundred with all his energies and faculties intact, but who was, when all was said and done, sixty and aging. It was understandable that his father should need the assurance that all he had worked for through his life would descend to more than just an unmarried son.

And so Edgar found himself agreeing that it was indeed time he took it upon himself to find a bride and that if it would please his father he would choose one who had some distinction of birth. And there was nothing to be served by delaying, he suggested without waiting to be prompted by his father. He had some business in London, a city he hated and avoided whenever it was possible to do so. He had a few connections there who would effect some introductions. He would undertake to choose himself a bride, perhaps even to be affianced to her by Christmas. He would bring her down to Mobley Abbey for Christmas—or at least invite her parents to bring her. By his father's sixty-first birthday he would be married and be in a fair way to getting his first child into the nursery.

Cora shrieked and clasped her hands to her bosom.

"You are conceiving an idea, my love?" Lord Francis asked, sounding amused. He was frequently amused, having decided long ago, it seemed, that it would be far more comfortable to laugh his way through life with Cora than to grimace his way through all her excesses and disasters. Wise man.

"Francis was not able to have his month in London during the Season this year," she said. "First we were in the north with Jennifer and Gabriel and then we went with them to Stephanie and Alistair's, and we were all having such a marvelous time and so were the children—were they not, Francis?—and Stephanie has the most *adorable* baby, Papa. He even had me dreaming of number five, but Francis insists in that most odious voice he uses when he wants to pretend to be lord and master that four is quite enough, thank you very much. What was it I set out to say?"

"That since I was not obliged to spend a month of the Season in town," Lord Francis said, "I should be encouraged to take you and the children there for the autumn. I do believe that was where your verbal destination lay, my love."

She favored him with a dazzling smile. "What a splendid idea, Francis," she said. "Jennifer and Gabriel and Samantha and Hartley were talking about going there for a month or so after the heat of the summer was over. We could have a wonderful time. And we could take Edgar about with us and see to it that he meets the right people."

"With all due respect, my love," Lord Francis said, "I do not believe Edgar is a puppy who needs our patronage. But certainly we will give him the comfort of having some familiar faces to greet at whatever entertainments are to be found during the autumn. And you will stay with us if you please, Edgar. The Pulteney Hotel may close its doors and go into a permanent decline when they discover that they are not to have your business, but we can offer some rowdy nephews and a niece for your entertainment. Who could possibly resist?"

"Edgar will spoil them and make them quite unmanageable," Cora said.

"Their maternal grandfather has spoiled them for the past two weeks as well as their uncle. *We* spoil them, my love," her husband said. "Yet we manage them perfectly well when it is necessary that they be managed. Their rowdiness and exuberance do not denote lack of all manners and discipline."

Between them they sealed Edgar's fate. He was to go to town by the end of September, it seemed, and stay at his brother-in-law's town house. He was to involve himself in the social life of the capital as it was lived in the autumn. There would not be all the balls and huge squeezes for which the spring Season was so renowned, but there would be enough people in residence in the grand houses of Mayfair to allow for a fair sprinkling of social entertainments. Lord Francis would see to it that Edgar was invited to a goodly number of them, and Cora would undertake to introduce him to some likely matrimonial prospects.

He needed their help. Despite the courteous tact of his brother-in-law's words, Edgar felt no doubt about that. He might have managed it himself, but with far more effort than would be needed if he simply relied upon the fact that Francis was a member of the upper echelons of the *ton.* Edgar was resigned to forcing his way into ranks from which his birth would normally exclude him. He was prepared for some coolness, even some rejection. But he knew enough about the world to believe that his wealth and his prospects would open a number of doors to him, especially those of people who felt themselves in need of sharing in his wealth.

He did not doubt that it was within his power to win himself a bride by Christmas. Someone of birth and breeding. Someone who would not look upon his own origins with contempt or condescension. Someone pretty and personable. Someone of whom he could be fond, it was to be hoped. He came from a family that set much store by that elusive something called love. He loved his father and his sister and was loved by them in return. His parents had enjoyed a love match. So did Cora and Francis, though the marriage had not appeared too promising at the start. Edgar rather thought that he would like to make a love match, too, or at least a match of affection.

He had until Christmas. Three months.

He was going to choose himself a bride. He traveled up to London at the end of the month, a little chilled by the thought, a little exhilarated by it.

After all, he was enough his father's son to find a challenge stimulating.

Lord Francis Kneller's friends were indeed in London. The Earl and Countess of Thornhill and the Marquess and Marchioness of Carew had come down together from Yorkshire with their six children for the purpose of shopping and seeing the sights and socializing at a somewhat less frantic pace than the Season would have allowed. Even the Duke and Duchess of Bridgwater had come up with their new son, mainly because their other friends were to be there. The duke's sister and Cora's special friend, the Countess of Greenwald, was also in residence with her husband and family. And they all decided to be kind to Cora's brother and to take him under their collective wing.

It was all somewhat daunting. And rather embarrassing. And not a little humbling to a man who was accustomed to commanding other men and to thinking himself very much master of his own life and affairs. His first social invitation, to what was termed an intimate soirée, came from the Countess of Greenwald. The affair was termed "intimate," Edgar guessed, to excuse its lack of numbers in comparison with what might have been expected during the Season.

But when his sister informed him that quite one hundred people had been invited and that surely all but a very few would make an appearance, Edgar felt absurdly nervous. He had never forgotten how the other boys at school had made him suffer for his birth. He had never complained to his father, or to any of the masters, who had undoubtedly shared the sentiments of the bulk of their pupils anyway. He had learned how to use his fists and his tongue, too, with blistering effect. He had learned endurance and pride and self-respect. He had learned that there was an invisible barrier between those men—and boys—who were gentlemen and those who were not. He had vowed to himself that he would never try to cross that barrier.

As a very young man he had scorned even to want to cross it. He had been proud of who he was and of what he had made of himself and what his father had made of *him*self. But Cora had married Francis. And the bridge had been set in place. And then his father had expressed his dying wish—surely thirty years before he was likely to die.

Edgar dressed carefully for the soirée. He wore a plain blue evening coat with gray knee breeches and white linen. He directed his valet to tie his neckcloth in a simple knot rather than fashion one of the more elaborate and artistic creations his man favored. His only jewelry was a diamond pin in the folds of the neckcloth. His clothes were expensive and expertly tailored. He would allow the tailoring to speak for itself. He would not try to put on any show of wealth. He certainly would not wear anything that might suggest dandyism. The very thought made him shudder.

Cora and her friends would doubtless introduce him to some young ladies. Indeed, he had been quite aware of them going into a huddle after dinner at the Carews' the evening before.

He had been painfully aware from the enthusiastic tone of their murmurings and the occasional furtive and interested glance thrown his way by one and another of them that he had been the subject of their conversation.

He hoped they would not introduce him to very young ladies. He was thirty-six. It would be most unfair to expect a young girl straight from the schoolroom to take him on. And he did not believe he would find appealing a girl almost young enough to be his daughter. He should have told Cora that he wanted someone significantly past the age of one-and-twenty. Such ladies were deemed to be on the shelf, of course. There had to be something wrong with them if they had not snared a husband by the age of twenty. And perhaps it really was so. How would he know?

"I would lead you in the direction of a congenial game of cards, old chap," Lord Francis said to him as they arrived at the Greenwalds' town house. He clapped a hand on his brother-in-law's shoulder and grinned. "But Cora would have my head and your purpose in coming to town would not be served. I shall allow her to go to work as soon as she emerges from the ladies' room. But no, you will not have to wait that long. Here comes our hostess herself and from the look in her eye, Edgar, I would guess she means business."

And sure enough, after greeting them both with a gracious smile, Lady Greenwald linked one arm through Edgar's and bore him off to introduce him to a few people he might find interesting.

"Everyone is starved for the sight of a new face and the sound of new conversation, Mr. Downes," she said, "especially at this time of year when there are so few people in town."

It seemed to Edgar that there was a vast number of people in Lady Greenwald's drawing room, but the fact that almost all of them were strangers might have contributed to the impression.

He was introduced to a number of people and conversed briefly with them about the weather and other such general topics until Lady Greenwald finally led him to where he guessed she had been leading him from the start. Sir Webster Grainger shook him heartily by the hand instead of merely bowing, and laughed just as heartily for no apparent reason. Lady Grainger swept him a curtsy that looked deferential enough to have been made in the queen's drawing room. And Miss Fanny Grainger, small, slight of figure, fair of hair, rather pretty, blushed rosily and directed her gaze at the floor somewhere in the vicinity of Edgar's shoes.

It had been planned, he thought. As both an experienced lawyer and a businessman he was canny at interpreting tone and atmosphere and the language of the body. Words were not always necessary for the assessment of a situation. It was very clear to him from the first moment that Sir Webster Grainger and his lady were in search of a husband for their daughter, that they had heard of his availability, and that they had determined to fix his interest. He did not doubt that Lady Greenwald would have done her job well. The Graingers would be well aware of his social status.

"You are familiar with Bristol, I understand, Mr. Downes," Sir Webster said as Lady Greenwald excused herself to greet some new arrival at the drawing room door.

"I live there and conduct my business there, sir," Edgar said very deliberately. Let there be no possible mistake.

"We invariably spend a day in Bristol whenever we go to Bath for Lady Grainger to take the waters," Sir Webster said. "She has an aunt living there. At Bristol, that is."

"It is an agreeable place in which to have one's residence," Edgar said. Good Lord, the girl could be no more than eighteen. He must have been her present age when she was born. Her mother must be of an age with him.

"Fanny always particularly enjoys the days we spend in Bristol," Lady Grainger said. "You must tell Mr. Downes what you like best about Bristol, Fanny, to see if he agrees with you."

There could have been no suggestion better calculated to tie the girl's tongue in knots, Edgar could see. She lifted her eyes to his chest, tried to raise them higher, failed, and blushed again. Poor child.

"Whenever I have been to London and return home," he said, "I am invariably asked what I liked best about town. I am never able to answer. I could, I suppose, describe the Tower of London or Hyde Park or a dozen other places, but I can never think of a single one when confronted. In my experience, one either likes a place or not. Do you like Bristol, Miss Grainger?"

She shot him a brief and grateful glance. She had fine gray eyes in a rather thin face. "I like it very well, sir," she said. "Because my great-aunt lives there, I believe, and I like her."

It was not a profound answer, but it was an endearingly honest one.

"It is the best reason of all for liking a place," he said. "I grew up in Bristol with a father and a sister whom I loved and still love, and so for me Bristol will always be a more pleasant place than London."

The child had almost relaxed. She even smiled briefly. "Is your mother d— Is she not living, sir?"

"She died giving birth to my sister," he said. "But I remember her as a loving presence in my life."

"And your sister is Lady Francis Kneller, Mr. Downes," Sir Webster announced, just as if Edgar did not know it for himself. He rubbed his hands together. "A fine lady. I remember the time—it was before her marriage, I do believe—when she saved Lady Kellington's poodles from being trampled in Hyde Park."

"Ah, yes." Edgar smiled. "My sister has a habit of rushing to the rescue."

"She saved some dogs from being *trampled*?" Miss Grainger's eyes were directed full at him now.

It needed Francis to tell the story in all its mock-heroic glory. But Edgar did his best. It appeared, though, as if he failed to convey the humor of Cora's heroism in endangering her life to save some dogs who had been in no danger except from her rescue. Miss Grainger looked earnestly at him, her mouth forming a little O of concern. A very kissable little mouth—in rather the way that Cora's children's mouths were kissable when they lifted them to him on his visits to the nursery.

He must be getting old, he thought. Too old to be in search of a bride.

And then he glanced across to the doorway, where another new arrival stood. A woman alone, dressed fashionably and elegantly in a high-waisted, low-bosomed dress of pure scarlet silk. A woman whose magnificent bosom more than did justice to the gown. Her whole figure, in fact, was generous. It might even be described as voluptuous more than slender. But then it was a mature woman's figure. She was not a young woman, but well past her thirtieth year if Edgar's guess was correct. Her dark hair was piled high and dressed in smooth curls rather than in more youthful ringlets. She looked about her with bold eyes in a handsome face, a half smile on her lips, which might denote confidence or contempt or mere mocking irony. It was difficult to tell which.

Before Edgar could realize that he was staring and proving himself to be indeed less than a gentleman—Sir Webster was saying something complimentary about Cora—the woman's eyes alit on him, held his own for a moment, and then moved deliberately down his body and back up again. She lifted one mocking eyebrow as her eyes met his once more and pursed her lips into something like the O that had just made Miss Grainger's lips look kissable. Except that there was nothing this time to remind him of his niece and nephews. He felt heated, as if there had been a hot hand at the end of her eyebeams that had scorched its way down the length of his body and back up again.

If he had not been standing in the Earl of Greenwald's drawing room, he would have been convinced that he was surely in the presence of one of London's more experienced and celebrated courtesans.

"Ah, yes, indeed," he said to Sir Webster, feeling that it was the correct response to what had just been said, though he was not at all sure.

Sir Webster seemed satisfied with his answer. Lady

Grainger smiled and Miss Grainger lowered her gaze to the floor again.

The scarlet lady had moved into the room and was being greeted by the Earl of Greenwald, who was bowing over her hand.

Chapter 2

Helena Stapleton was invited everywhere. She was quite respectable even though the general feeling seemed to be that she was only just so. She had been a widow for ten years, yet apart from the first four of those years, when she had gone to stay with cousins in Scotland, she had adopted neither of the two courses that were expected of widows. She had not retired to live quietly as a dowager on the estate of her dead husband's son, and she had not shown any interest in remarrying.

She had gone traveling. Her husband, more than thirty years her senior, had been besotted with her and had left her a very generous legacy. This she had conserved and increased through careful investments. She traveled to every corner of the British Isles and to every country of Europe, the wars being long over. She had even been to Greece and to Egypt, though she would tell anyone who cared to ask that she thought too highly of her creature comforts to repeat either of those two experiences. Sometimes she rested from her travels and took up temporary residence in London, where she proceeded to amuse herself with whatever entertainments were available. This was one of those occasions. She almost always avoided the crush of the spring Season.

She was always careful to travel with companions, with congenial female acquaintances and with gentlemen to serve as escorts. She always set up house in London with a female companion, usually an aunt, whom she sent into the country to visit a nephew and a brood of great-nephews and great-nieces as soon as respectability had been established. And so she almost always arrived alone at entertainments, making her aunt's excuses to her hosts. There never had been such a sickly aunt.

Ladies—even those of six-and-thirty with independent means—were not expected to move about town or about *ton* parties alone, even when they had the misfortune to have female companions who were always catching chills or suffering from headaches. And ladies of six-and-thirty were not expected to dress as they pleased, unless it pleased them to wear such colors as purple or mulberry and to cover their hair with large turbans decked out with waving plumes. They were certainly not expected to favor scarlet gowns or emerald green or sunshine-yellow ones—or to go bareheaded into society.

Lady Stapleton did all that a lady of six-and-thirty was not expected to do. But there was a confidence and a self-assurance about her that seemed excuse enough for the absence of escorts or companions. And she had a beauty and arrogance of bearing, coupled with an impeccable taste for design and elegance, that made one hesitate about describing her appearance as vulgar or even inappropriate to her age.

She had few, if any, close friends. There was an air of aloofness, even of mystery, about her, even though she conversed quite freely about her travels and experiences. Everyone knew who she was—the daughter of a respectable but impoverished Scottish gentleman, the widow of Sir Christian Stapleton of Brookhurst. She was amiable, charming, sociable—and yet she gave the impression that there was a great deal more to be known about her than she had ever revealed.

She was invited everywhere. Gentlemen found her fascinating despite the fact that she was long past her youth. Ladies were secretly envious of her, though her age protected her from their jealousy. Yet the feeling was—though no one could quite explain it—that she hovered dangerously close to the edge of respectability.

She knew it. And cared not the snap of two fingers. She had decided long ago—six years ago to be precise—that life was to be lived and enjoyed, and live it and enjoy it she would. She had earned her enjoyment. She had been snatched from the love of her life—or so she had thought with the foolish sensibilities to which very young people were so prone—at the age of nineteen in order to be forced into marriage with the wealthy, fifty-four-year old Sir Christian Stapleton. She had lived through seven years of marriage to him with bright smiles and determined affection and feigned eagerness in the marriage bed. She had lived through— but she would not remember what else she had lived through during those years. She had punished herself after her husband's death for her widowhood and her youth and her human frailties by retiring to a quiet life in Scotland, where she had seen her former love himself married with five children and an eagerness to begin an affair with her. Although she had longed to give in, she had resisted and had in general become a dull and abject creature, as if she believed that she deserved no better.

She deserved better. She deserved to live. Everyone deserved to live. No one owed anyone else anything. She owed no one anything. And if she did, then she had more than paid with eleven years of her life—seven with Christian and four after his death.

At the age of thirty—perhaps it was the nasty shock of that particular number—she had thrown off the shackles. And though she was always careful to cling to the semblance of respectability, she did not care that she hovered close to its edge. Indeed, she rather enjoyed the feeling of being almost, but not quite, notorious.

Helena arrived rather late at Lady Greenwald's soirée, as was customary with her. She liked to arrive after everyone else so that she could look about her and choose the group to which she wished to attach herself. She hated to be caught among people who had no conversation beyond the weather and the state of their health. She liked to be with interesting people.

She was acquainted with most of the people, she saw, standing in the doorway, looking about her. But then one usually was at *ton* events in London. And it was even more true of events outside of the Season. There were not a great many families in residence at this time of the year. Inevitably, all who were, were invited everywhere. Equally inevitably, all who were invited attended every function.

The Marquess of Carew was there, she saw, in the midst of a group of his particular friends. She had met the marquess for the first time just the week before. She had not sought out the introduction since he was a very ordinary-looking man with a slightly crippled hand and foot and a smiling placidity of manner that usually denoted dullness. He had spoken to her about his passion, landscape gardening, a dull topic indeed. And unexpectedly he had held her fascinated attention. The extremely elegant, almost foppish Lord Francis Kneller was part of the same group. Whenever she saw him, Helena felt regret that he was a married man. He had married a cit's daughter, who went with him almost wherever he went. She was with him now, laughing with quite ungenteel amusement at something someone had said. What a waste of a perfectly lovely man.

And then her eyes, moving on to another group, alit on a man whom she did not know—and paused on him. At first she looked only because he presented the novelty of being a stranger. And then she looked because he looked back and she would not glance away hastily and in apparent confusion. Though in reality there was more reason to look at him than stubbornness. He was a very tall and very large gentleman. Large not in the sense of fatness. She doubted that there was one spare ounce of fat on his frame. But he was certainly not a slender man. It was a perfectly proportioned frame—she looked it down and up again in leisurely fashion, noting at the same time the simple yet very expensive elegance of his clothing. And he had a head and face worthy of such a body. His brown hair was short but expertly styled. His face was strikingly handsome. He gave an impression of strength and power, she thought. Not just physical power. He looked like a man who knew exactly who he was and what he was and was well satisfied with both. Like a man who knew his own mind and was comfortable with his own decisions and would not be easily moved by anyone who opposed him.

She felt a wave of pure lust before he looked away to pay attention to the Graingers, with whom he stood, and the Earl of

Greenwald arrived almost simultaneously to greet her. She explained that her aunt had been persuaded to stay at home to nurse a persistent cough.

Who was he? she wondered. She would not ask, of course. It was not her way to signal so direct an interest in a man. But she set about maneuvering matters slowly—there was no hurry—so that she would find out. And not only find out who he was. She was going to meet him. It was quite soon obvious to her that the man was not married, even though he must be very close to her own age. There was no strange lady in the Greenwalds' drawing room. And it was unlikely that he had a wife who was absent. The Graingers took much of his time, and it was an open secret that they had brought their daughter to town in the hope of finding her a husband before Christmas. They were not wealthy. They could not afford to bring their daughter to town during the Season, when there would be the exorbitant expenses of a court dress and innumerable ball and party gowns. And so they had come now, hoping that there would be a single gentleman of sufficient means to be snared. The girl was twenty and perilously close to being on the shelf.

The unknown gentleman must be both single and rich. He certainly *looked* rich—wealthy and self-assured enough not to have to make an obvious display of his wealth. He was not bedecked with jewels and fobs and lace. But his tailor doubtless charged him a minor fortune to fashion coats such as the one he wore tonight.

She talked with Lord Carew and Lord Francis Kneller and their wives for a while, and then sat with elderly Lord Holmes during a musical presentation. She told Mr. and Mrs. Prothero and a growing gathering of other people about some of her more uncomfortable experiences in Egypt while they all refreshed themselves with a drink together afterward and then accepted Sir Eric Mumford's invitation to join him at the supper table. He did not even realize that she led him rather than submitting to being led once they were inside the dining room. She seated herself beside the still-unknown gentleman, but turned her head immediately away from him to speak with her partner.

She was an expert at maneuvering matters to her own liking. Especially where men were concerned. Men were so easily manipulated. She laughed with amusement at something Sir Eric said.

Her low laugh shivered down his spine. It came straight from the bedchamber, even though she was sitting in a crowded dining room beneath brightly lighted chandeliers.

She had seated herself in the empty chair beside his and was reacting to something her supper companion had said to her. She was totally unaware of him, of course, Edgar thought, as she had been all evening after that first assessing glance. She had not once looked his way after that. She was Lady Stapleton, widow of Sir Christian Stapleton of Brookhurst. Brookhurst was not so very far from Mobley Abbey—not above twenty-five or thirty miles. But she did not live there now. Sir Gerald Stapleton, the present owner, was only her stepson.

Edgar had been introduced to three marriageable ladies during the course of the evening, all of whose parents had clearly been informed of his own possible interest and had acquiesced in allowing their daughters to be presented to a man whose immense wealth would perhaps compensate for the fact that he was not a gentleman. All three ladies were amiable, genteel, pretty. All three knew that he was a prospective bridegroom and they appeared docile and accepting. His sister and her cohorts had done a superlative job in so short a time, he thought. They had gone about things in the correct way, choosing with care, preparing the way with care, and leaving him choices.

There was only one problem—well, two actually, but the second was not in the nature of a real problem, only of an annoyance. The problem was that all three ladies appeared impossibly young to him. It struck him that any one of them would be a perfect choice for just that reason. All three had any number of breeding years ahead, and breeding was one of his main inducements to marry. But they seemed alarmingly young to him. Or rather, perhaps, he felt alarmingly old. Did he want a wife only so that he might breed her? He wanted more than that, of course. Far more.

And the problem that was not a problem was his constant awareness—an uncomfortable, purely physical awareness—of the lady in scarlet. Lady Stapleton. His mouth had turned dry as soon as she seated herself beside him and he smelled her perfume—something subtle and feminine and obviously very expensive.

And then she turned his way, leaned forward slightly, ignored him completely, and spoke to the young lady at his other side.

"How do you do, Miss Grainger?" she said. "Allow me to tell you how pretty you look in blue. It is your color."

Her bosom brushed the top of the table as she spoke. And her voice was pure warm velvet. Edgar could see now that he was close, that the red highlights he had noticed in her dark hair were no reflection of her gown. They were real. He could not make up his mind whether her eyes were hazel or green. They had elements of both colors.

"Why, thank you," Miss Grainger said, blushing and gratified. "It is my favorite color. But I sometimes wish I could wear vivid colors as you do."

Again that low bedroom laugh.

"Oh," Miss Grainger said, "may I present Mr. Downes? Lady Stapleton, sir."

Her eyes came to his. She did not move back, even though she was still leaning forward and was very close to him. He resisted the urge to move back himself. She looked very directly at him, a faint mockery or amusement or both in the depths of her glance.

"Ma'am," he said, inclining his head.

"Mr. Downes." She gazed at him. "Ah, now I remember. Lady Francis Kneller was a Downes before her marriage, was she not?"

"She is my sister," he said.

"Ah." She made no immediate attempt to say anything else. He could almost sense her remembering that Cora was the daughter of a Bristol merchant and realizing that he was no gentleman. That half-smile deepened for a moment. "You are from the west country, sir?"

"From Bristol, ma'am," he said. And lest she was not quite clear on the matter, "I have lived there all my life and have worked there all my adult life, first as a lawyer and more recently as a merchant."

"How fascinating," she murmured, her eyes moving to his lips for a disconcerting moment. He was not sure if it was sincerity or mockery he heard in her voice. "Pardon me. I am neglecting Sir Eric quite shamefully."

She turned back to her companion. Obviously it had been mockery. Lady Stapleton had found herself seated beside a cit and conversing with him before realizing who he was. She would not repeat the mistake.

He set himself to making Miss Grainger feel comfortable again. He felt quite protective of her. She so clearly knew why she was in London, why she was here tonight, and why she was spending a significant portion of the evening in his company. The Graingers, he guessed, were going to be more persistent in their attentions to him than either of the other two couples. Miss Grainger's pretty blue gown, he noticed, was neither new nor costly. Nor was it in the first stare of fashion.

Helena sat with Mr. Hendy and a few other guests after supper. The others mainly listened while the two of them exchanged stories and opinions about the land-crossing from Switzerland to Italy. They both agreed that they were fortunate indeed to have lived to tell of it.

"I admire mountains," Mr. Hendy said, "but more as a spectator than as a traveler crawling along a narrow icy track directly above a sheer precipice at least a mile high."

"I do believe I could endure crawling with some equanimity," Helena said. "It is riding on the back of one of those infernal mountain donkeys that had me gabbling my prayers with pious fervency."

Their audience laughed.

Mr. Downes had left his group in order to cross to a sideboard to replenish the contents of his glass. There was no one else there. Helena got to her feet and excused herself. She strolled toward the sideboard, her own empty glass in hand.

"Mr. Downes," she said when she was close, "do fill my glass with whatever is in that decanter, if you please. One becomes mortally sick of drinking ratafia merely because one is female. I would prefer even the lemonade at Almack's."

"Madeira, ma'am?" He looked uncertainly at the decanter and then at her with raised eyebrows.

"Madeira, sir," she said, holding out her glass. "I suppose you do not know about the lemonade at Almack's."

"I have never been there, ma'am," he said.

"You have not missed anything," she told him. "It is an insipid place and the balls there are insipid occasions and the lemonade served there is insipid fare. Yet people would kill or do worse to acquire vouchers during the Season."

He half filled her glass and looked into her eyes. She had the distinct feeling that if she ordered him to fill her glass he would refuse. She did not issue the order. He was a lawyer and a merchant. He had freely admitted as much. A prosperous merchant if her guess was correct. But a cit for all that. If his sister had not had the good fortune to snare Lord Francis Kneller, he would never have gained entry to such a place as the Earl of Greenwald's drawing room. But she understood now the aura of confidence and power he exuded. He was a wealthy, powerful, self-made man. She found the idea infinitely exciting. She found *him* exciting.

Sexually exciting.

"I am tired of this party, Mr. Downes," she said. "But I am a single woman alone, alas. My aunt, my usual companion, is indisposed, my manservant and maid walked home rather than stay in the kitchen with my coachman, and will not return for another hour at the earliest. Yet I will be scolded by aunt and servants alike if I return unaccompanied."

He was not sure he understood her. His eyes shrewdly regarding her told her that. She raised her eyebrows, half smiled at him, and sipped her madeira. It was a vast improvement on ratafia.

"I would offer my escort, ma'am, if I thought it would be welcomed," he said.

"How kind you are, Mr. Downes," she said, mocking him with her eyes. "It would be accepted."

"Shall I have your carriage called around, then?" he asked. "Shall I have a maid accompany us?"

She allowed herself to laugh softly. "That will be quite unnecessary, Mr. Downes," she said, "unless you are afraid of me. We are both adults."

He inclined his head to her without removing his eyes from hers, set down his glass, and slipped quietly from the room.

She found flirtations exhilarating, Helena admitted to herself as she sipped from her glass and looked about the room without making any attempt to rejoin any group. She indulged in them whenever she felt so inclined—always in private. She scorned the appearance of propriety for its own sake, but how could one conduct a satisfactory flirtation in the sight of others? She did not care if people noticed her disappearing alone with a certain gentleman and thought her promiscuous.

She was not. She had never desired the distastefulness of full physical intimacy—she had endured enough of that during her seven-year marriage. Though of course there had been a time during that marriage . . . no! She shuddered inwardly. She would not think of that now—or ever if she could help it.

She had never sought to enliven her widowhood with affairs—or even with *an* affair. But then she had rarely met a man of greater physical appeal then Mr. Downes.

She would take him home and lure him up to her drawing room. She would find out more about him. She suspected that he might be a fascinating man—perhaps he could fascinate her for an hour or more of the night. Nights were always interminably long. She would flirt with him. Perhaps she would even allow him to steal a kiss—there was definite appeal in the thought, though she normally avoided even kisses.

Perhaps he would not be satisfied with a mere kiss. But she was not afraid. She had never found herself unable to deal with amorous men, though she had known her fair share.

She smiled as her eyes found the Countess of Greenwald.

She set her glass down in order to go bid her hostess a good night.

And perhaps *she* would not be satisfied with a mere kiss, she thought a few minutes later as she allowed Mr. Downes to hand her into her carriage and climb in beside her.

She had never felt quite so tempted.

How would it *feel* with him? she wondered, turning her head to smile half scornfully at her companion, though he was not necessarily the object of her scorn. With a handsome, virile, powerful, doubtless very experienced man.

She felt a twinge of alarm at the direction her thoughts had taken. And more than a twinge of desire.

She would talk sense into herself before she arrived home, she told herself. She might even dismiss him on the pavement outside her door and send him back to the soirée.

But she knew she would not do that.

Sometimes loneliness was almost a tangible thing.

Chapter 3

Edgar was not really sure he understood the situation. Or believed her story. Why would two servants have walked home after accompanying her to the Greenwalds'? And she did not seem the sort of person to tire early when she was at a party. She had been the center of attention in every group gathered about her all evening.

And why him?

He sat beside her as close to his side of her carriage as he could so that she would not think he was taking advantage of the situation. She sat with her back half across the corner at her side, looking at him in the near-darkness, talking easily and quite without malice about the people who had attended the party. She spoke in that low, velvety voice, the half-smile of mockery or something else on her lips every time a street lamp lit her face.

He would help her to alight at her door, he thought, see her safely inside her home, and then walk back to Greenwald's house. It was not very far. He would refuse the offer—if she made it—of a ride back in her carriage. He would go back to the soirée rather than straight home. He had not told Cora he was leaving.

But when the lady had stepped down from the carriage to the pavement and had removed her hand from his, she did not lift her skirt with it the more easily to ascend the four steps to the front door. She slipped it through his arm.

"You must come inside, Mr. Downes," she told him, "and have a drink before returning."

Presumably the aunt she had mentioned was inside the house. But was it likely that an ailing lady would be out of her bed at this time of night—it must be well past midnight—and sitting in the drawing room with her embroidery on the chance that she would be called upon to play chaperone? He was not being naive. He was merely unwilling to accept the evidence of his own reasoning powers.

A manservant had opened the front door even before the steps of the carriage had been set down. He took Edgar's hat and cloak from him, after favoring him with a level, measuring look—he was as tall as Edgar and even broader, and as bald as a polished egg. He looked more like a pugilist than a butler, an impression enhanced by his crooked, flattened nose.

"You need not wait up, Hobbes," Lady Stapleton said, taking Edgar's arm and turning him in the direction of the stairs.

"Very well, my lady," the servant said in a voice one might expect a man to use if he had a handful of gravel lodged in his throat.

The lady paused on the first landing as if in thought, appeared to come to some decision, and climbed on to the second. Edgar would have had to be an innocent indeed if he had expected to find a drawing room beyond the door at which she stopped, indicating with an inclination of the head that he might open it. This was not the living floor of the house. Even so it was something of a shock to find himself entering a very cozy bedchamber. There was a soft carpet underfoot. The curtains were looped back from the large canopied bed. The bedcovers were neatly turned back. There were lit candles on the dressing table and bedside table. A fire burned in the hearth.

Edgar closed the door behind his back and stayed where he was. It was a very feminine room, warm and comfortable and clean. That subtle perfume she wore clung to it. It was, he thought, the room of a very expensive courtesan. He found himself wondering if he would be presented later with a quite exorbitant bill. He did not much care.

"Well, Mr. Downes." She had walked into the room and turned to him now, one hand resting on the dressing table. There was a look almost of defiance on her face. She raised one mocking eyebrow. "Shall I ring for tea?"

"That seems hardly necessary." He walked toward her until

he was a foot away from her. But why him? he wondered. Because of her discovery that he was not a gentleman? Would a gentleman have offered his escort? Would he have come inside the house with her? Ascended that second flight of stairs with her?

To hell with what gentlemen would have done or would do. She had made her choice. She would live with it for tonight. He set his hands on either side of her waist—not a slender waist, but an undeniably shapely one. He drew her against him, angled his head to one side, parted his lips, closed his eyes, and kissed her.

And felt that he had landed in the very midst of a fireworks display—not as a spectator but as one of the fireworks.

She moved against him. Not just to bring herself closer to him but to—move against him. He became hotly aware of everything—her warm and shapely thighs, her generous hips, her abdomen rubbing against his almost instant erection, her breasts, her shoulders. One of her arms had come about his waist, beneath his coat. The fingers of the other hand twined themselves in his hair. Her mouth opened beneath his own and moved against it. He found himself doing what he had not done since his youth, having found it distasteful then. He pressed his tongue deep into her mouth.

And then she withdrew and he withdrew and they stood gazing at each other, still touching from the waist down, their breathing labored. That strange smile lingered about her lips. But her eyes were heavy with passion and excitement.

"I do hope you live up to early promise, Mr. Downes," she said.

"I shall do my very best, ma'am," he said.

And then she turned and presented him with a row of tiny pearl buttons down the back of her gown. He undid them one at a time while she lifted her arms and withdrew the pins from her hair. She held it up until he was finished and then let it fall, long and dark and wavy, with its enticing reddish tints. He nudged the gown off her shoulders with the straps of her shift and she let them fall to the floor before turning and removing her undergarments and her stockings while he watched.

She had a mature figure—firm, ample, voluptuous. She was incredibly beautiful. He felt his mouth go dry again as he shrugged out of his coat and reached for the buttons of his waistcoat.

"Ah, no," she said, brushing his hands aside and laughing at him with that throaty laugh that now seemed to be in its proper setting. "You have had the pleasure of unclothing me, Mr. Downes. You will not deny me the pleasure of doing the like for you."

She undressed him while he listened to his heartbeat hammering against his eardrums and concentrated on controlling and mastering the urge to tumble her back onto the bed so that he might the sooner explode into ease. She took her time. She was in no hurry at all.

Not until they were finally on the bed. Then she became passion unleashed. There was no shyness, no shrinking, no ladylike modesty, no taboos. Her hands explored him with frank interest and wild demand while his did the like to her. Her mouth participated in the exploration, moving over him, kissing, licking, sucking, biting. He devoured her with his own mouth, tasting perfume and sweat and woman.

He had never been a man for rough sex. Perhaps because of his size he had always been careful to leash his passions, to touch gently, to mount slowly, to pump with control. But he had never before been with a woman whose passion could equal his own—and perhaps even outstrip it. When he rolled her nipples between his thumbs and the bases of his forefingers, she spoke to him.

"Harder," she begged him. "Harder."

And when he squeezed and she gasped with pain and he would have desisted, her hands came up to cover his, to press his thumbs and forefingers together again. She gasped with pain once more.

"Come to me," she was saying then, her body in frenzied motion. "Give it to me. Give it to me."

He moved between her thighs, felt her legs lift to twine about his, felt her hands spread hard over his buttocks, positioned himself, and thrust hard and deep. She cried out. He settled his weight on her—his full weight. He knew what she wanted and what he wanted. Neither of them would have it if he allowed her to buck and gyrate beneath him. And he was very aware that she had led the way thus far. It was not in his nature to allow a woman to dictate his every action and reaction.

She urged him on with frenzied words and clawing hands and with the muscles of her thighs and the muscles inside, where he worked. But he took her without frenzy, with deep, methodical, rhythmic strokes. His heart felt as if it must burst. With every inward thrust he felt as if he must surely explode into release. But he would not let a woman master him.

She was pleading with him. She was swearing at him, he realized in some surprise. And then she lost her own control and came shuddering and shattering about him. He continued to stroke her while it happened and then, when she began to relax, he drove to his own release, growling out his pleasure into her hair.

He was not quite sure he was going to survive, he thought foolishly, relaxing downward onto her damp and heated flesh. He felt her legs untwine themselves from about his and somehow found the energy to lift himself off her and draw her against him before closing his eyes and sinking into sleep.

She did not sleep. She lay relaxed against the heat of his body. She tried to summon the energy to wake him and dismiss him. She would have to dismiss him. She needed to be alone.

She needed to digest what had just happened—what *she* had caused to happen. She had not even taken him as far as the drawing room. She had scarcely even paused on the first landing.

She had seemed to be led by a power quite beyond her will to control. A ridiculous notion—*though it had happened before. She* had chosen to bring him to her bed, just as she had chosen that other time. . . .

She breathed in slowly—a mistake. She breathed in the smells of his sweat and his cologne, of his maleness.

Her earlier curiosity at least had been satisfied. She knew now how it felt with him.

It had felt frightening. The pleasure—oh, yes, there had been an overabundance of that—had got far beyond her control. It had been in his control and he had held it from her—quite deliberately, she would swear—with his weight holding her immobile and with his insistence on setting the pace himself. Having made the decision she had made, she had at least wanted to command the situation. She had wanted to protect something of herself. He had not allowed it.

She had been frightened. All she had was herself.

He had the most magnificent body she could ever have imagined. It seemed all massive, solid muscle. And that part of him . . . She closed her eyes and inhaled slowly. She had been stretched and filled. For one foolish moment she had felt the terror of a virgin that there could not possibly be room. She rather believed she had screamed.

He was a man who expected and got his own way. He was a businessman. Clearly a very successful and wealthy one. A man did not achieve success in the business world unless he was firm and controlled and even ruthless, unless he was well able to make himself undisputed master of any situation. She had sensed that on her first sight of him, of course. It was not his looks alone that had prompted that rush of lust and the growing temptation. And then she had had her intuition confirmed at supper when he had told her, a look of cool defiance on his face, that he had been a lawyer and was a merchant. Lustful words. She wondered if he had realized that she found them so.

She should not have chosen to break her own—and society's—rules with him of all people.

She wanted him again, she thought after a while. She could feel her breasts, her womb, her inner thighs begin to throb with need. She wanted his weight, his mastery. No, she did not. She wanted to be on top. She wanted to master him. She wanted to ride him at her own speed, to drive him mad with desire, to have him shatter past climax so that she could feel she had avenged what he had done to her.

She wondered if she would be able to master this man if she woke him and aroused him and got on top of him. Would she win this time? Or would he merely resume that alarmingly controlled stroking and endure long enough to send her headlong again into release and happiness—and weakness? It would be humiliating to have that happen twice.

And wonderful beyond belief.

She did not want anything wonderful beyond belief.

And then, while she was still at war with herself, the decision was taken out of her hands. She had not noticed that he was awake again. And aroused again. He turned her onto her back and came on top of her. She found herself opening her legs to him, lifting to him, letting her breath out on a sighing moan as he came, hard and thick and long, sliding into her wetness. And she found that she had his full and not inconsiderable weight on her again and that she did not fight either it or him. She lay under him rather as she had always lain beneath Christian—but no, there was no comparison. None whatsoever.

She observed their coupling almost like a spectator. Almost. There was, of course, the throbbing desire she had felt even while he still slept, and the crescendo of desire that built *there,* where he stroked relentlessly, and spread upward in waves, through her womb, up into her breasts, into her throat, and even behind her nose. He found her mouth with his and she opened to his tongue and did not even try to fight the total invasion of her body—or even the frightening sensation that it was her whole person that was being invaded.

She was, she thought a moment before she burst past control to another of those intense moments of something that felt deceptively like happiness, though it was not that at all—she was a little frightened of Mr. Downes, Bristol merchant and cit. And that was perhaps a large part of the attraction. She had never felt frightened of any other man. His own climax came a few moments after hers, as it had the first time. He was, then, in perfect control of himself, even in bed.

She had made a mistake. *Of course* she had made a mistake.

They lay beside each other, panting, waiting for their heartbeats to return to normal. The backs of their hands touched damply between them. She wondered if he had set out to make a fool of her, or if mastery came so naturally to him that he did not even think of her as a worthy adversary. She hated him in that moment, quite as intensely as she had earlier lusted after him.

She got off the bed, crossed the room unhurriedly on legs that shook slightly—the candles, though low, were still burning—picked up her night robe, which her maid had set out over the back of a chair, and drew it about her as she went to stand at the window, looking out on the deserted street below. She drew a deep, silent breath and released it slowly.

"Thank you, Mr. Downes," she said. "You are superlatively good. A master of the art, one might say. But I daresay you know that."

"I can hardly be expected to reply to such a compliment," he said.

She looked over her shoulder at him. He was lying on the bed, the covers up to his waist, his hands clasped behind his head. Even now, sated as she was, he looked magnificent.

"It is time for you to leave, sir," she said.

"Past time, I believe," he said, throwing back the covers and coming off the bed with remarkable grace for such a big man. "It would not do for me to be seen slinking from your house at dawn, wearing evening clothes."

"No, indeed," she agreed. And she stood watching him dress. She had never thought of any other man as beautiful—*oh, yes, she had.* Yes, she had. She clenched her hands unconsciously at her sides. But he had been youthful, slender, sweet. . . .

She turned back to the window.

She shrugged her shoulders when his hands came to rest there, and he removed them.

"Thank you," he said. "It was a great pleasure."

"I daresay you can see yourself out, Mr. Downes," she said. "Good night."

"Good night, ma'am," he said.

She heard the door of her bedchamber open and close again

quietly. A minute or so later she watched him emerge from the front door and turn right to walk with long, firm strides along the street. She watched him until he was out of sight, a man quite unafraid of the dark, empty streets of London. But then he had probably known a great deal worse in Bristol if his work took him near the dock area. She would pity the poor footpad who decided to accost Mr. Downes.

What was his first name? she wondered. But she did not want to know.

She stood at the window, staring down into the empty street. Now, she thought, her degradation was complete. She had brought home a complete stranger, had taken him to her bed, and had had her pleasure of him. She had given in to lust, to loneliness, to the illusion that there was happiness somewhere in this life to be grasped and to be drawn into herself.

And she was to be justly punished. She already knew it. Her bedchamber already seemed unnaturally quiet and empty. She could still smell him and guessed that the enticing, erotic smell, imaginary though it doubtless was, would linger accusingly for as long as she remained in this house.

Now she was truly promiscuous. As she always had been, though she had never lain with any man except Christian—until tonight. Now her true nature had shown itself. She closed her eyes and rested her forehead against the cold glass of the window.

And she had enjoyed it. Oh, how she had enjoyed it! Sex with a stranger. She heard herself moan and clamped her teeth hard together.

She was awash with the familiar feeling, though it was stronger, rawer than usual—self-loathing. And then hatred, the dull aching hatred of the one man who might have allowed her to redeem herself and to have avoided this. For years she had waited patiently—and impatiently—for him to release her from the terrible burden of her own guilt. But finally, just a year ago, he had plunged her into an inescapable, eternal hell. She felt hatred of a man who had done nothing—ever—to deserve her hatred or anyone else's.

A hatred that turned outward because she had saturated herself with self-hatred.

She could feel the rawness in her throat that sought release through tears. But she scorned to weep. She would not give herself that release, that comfort.

She hated Mr. Downes. Why had he come to London? Why had he come to Lady Greenwald's soirée? He had no business there, even if his sister was married to a member of the *ton*, even if he was something of a nabob. He was not a gentleman. He had stepped out of his own world, upsetting hers.

But how unfair it was to hate him. None of what had happened had been his fault. She had seduced him. His only fault had been to allow himself to be seduced.

For one moment—no, for two separate moments—the loneliness had been pushed back. Now it was with her again, redoubled in force, like a physical weight bowing down her shoulders.

She must never again—not even by mild flirtation—try to dislodge it. She must never again so much as see Mr. Downes.

Edgar felt shaken. What had just happened had been a thoroughly physical and erotic thing, quite outside his normal experience. He had been caught up entirely in mindless passion.

Lady Stapleton. He did not know her first name. It somehow disturbed him that he did not even know that much about her. And yet he knew every inch of her body and the inner, secret parts of her with great intimacy.

He had had women down the years. But except for his very early youth, he had never been led to them from lust alone. There had always been some sort of a relationship. He had always known their first names. He had always bedded women with the knowledge that the act would bring him more pleasure than it brought them. He had always tried to be gentle and considerate, to make it up to them in other ways.

He had never known a truly passionate woman, he realized—until tonight. He was not sure he wanted to know another—or this one again. There had been no doubt about her consent, but still he felt vaguely guilty at the way in which he had used her. He had not been gentle. Indeed, he had been decidedly rough.

He felt distaste at what he had done. He felt dislike of her. She had clearly set out to lure him to her bed. If there was a seducer in tonight's business, it was she. He did not like the idea that he had been seduced. If she had had her way she would have dictated every move of that first encounter, including, he did not doubt, the moment and manner of his climax.

He had come to London, he had gone to that soirée, in order to find himself a bride. And he had been presented with three quite eligible prospects. He would perhaps choose to pay court to one of them. He would betroth himself to her before Christmas or perhaps at Mobley Abbey during Christmas. He would wed the girl soon after and in all probability have her with child before spring had turned into summer. He had promised his father, and it was high time, even without the promise.

And yet on the very evening he had met those three young ladies, he had allowed himself to be drawn into a scene of sordid passion with a stranger, with a woman whose first name he did not know.

She was a lady, not a courtesan. A beautiful lady, who was accepted by the *ton.* Obviously tonight's behavior was not typical of her. If it were, she would be unable to keep it hidden well enough to escape the sharp eyes and gossiping tongues of the beau monde. Clearly, then, he was partly to blame for what had happened. He had stared at her when she had first appeared, and she had caught him at it. He had freely admitted his origins and present way of life to her at supper and had thus revealed to her that he was a man outside her own world.

Somehow he had tempted her. He understood that young widows—and perhaps those who were not so young, too—could feel loneliness and sexual frustration. One of his longer-lasting mistresses had been the widow of a colleague of his. He might eventually have married her himself if she had not suddenly announced to him one day that she was to marry a sea captain and take to the sea with him.

He had done Lady Stapleton a great wrong. It would not be repeated. He wondered if he owed her an apology. Perhaps not, but he owed her something. A visit tomorrow. Some sort of an explanation. He must make her aware that he did not hold her in contempt for what she had allowed tonight.

He did not look forward to the visit.

Lord Francis came out of his library as Edgar let himself into the house. He lifted the cup he held in one hand. "The chocolate is still warm in the pot," he said. "Come and have some."

Edgar had hoped everyone would be safely in bed. "Waiting up for me, Francis?" he asked, entering the library reluctantly and pouring himself a cup of chocolate.

"Not exactly," Francis said. "Waiting for Cora, actually. Annabelle woke up when we tiptoed into the nursery to kiss the children, and Cora lay down with her. I daresay she has fallen asleep. It would not be the first time. Once Andrew came to *me* for comfort and climbed into bed beside me because his mama was in his own bed fast asleep and there was no room left for him."

"That sounds like Cora," her brother said. He felt some explanation was necessary. "I escorted Lady Stapleton home because she had no other escort. And then I decided to walk about Mayfair and get some fresh air rather than return to Greenwald's. A few hours at such entertainments are enough for me."

"Quite so," Francis said. "Firm up the story for Cora by breakfast time, old chap. She will wish to know about every post and blade of grass you passed in your nocturnal rambles. You do not owe me any explanation. She is a woman extraordinarily, ah, well-endowed with charms."

"Lady Stapleton?" Edgar said carelessly, as if the idea were new to him. "Yes, I suppose she is."

Lord Francis chuckled. "Well," he said, "I am for my lonely bed. You look as if you are ready for yours, too, Edgar. Good night."

"Good night," Edgar said.

Damnation! Francis knew all right. But then he would have to be incredibly dim-witted to believe that story about the walk and fresh air.

Chapter 4

Helena was usually from home in the mornings. She liked mornings. She loved to walk in the park early, when she was unlikely to meet anyone except a few tradesmen hurrying toward their daily jobs or a few maids running early errands or walking their owners' dogs. Her own long-suffering maid trotting along behind her or, more often, the menacing figure of Hobbes, the one servant who traveled everywhere with her, made all proper. She liked to go shopping on Oxford Street or Bond Street or to go to the library to look at the papers or borrow a book. She also liked to visit the galleries.

Mornings were the best times. The world was fresh and new each morning, and she was newly released from the restlessness and bad dreams that oppressed her nights. Sometimes in the mornings she could fill her lungs with air and her body with energy and pretend that life was worth living.

But on the morning after Lady Greenwald's soirée, she was at home. She had not found the energy nor the will to go out. The clouds were low and heavy, she noticed. It might rain at any moment. And it looked chilly and raw. In reality, of course, she rarely allowed weather of any type to divert her when she wished to go abroad. This morning she was tired and listless and looking for excuses.

She would send for her aunt, she decided. Aunt Letty liked town better than the country anyway, and would be quite happy to be summoned. She was, in fact, more like a friend than an aging relative—and therein, perhaps, lay the problem. Helena had numerous friendly acquaintances and could turn several of them into close friends if she wished. She did not wish. Friends, by their very nature, knew one intimately. Friends were to be confided in. She preferred to keep her acquaintances at some distance. She certainly did not need a friend in residence. But, paradoxically, her friendless state sometimes became unbearable.

She procrastinated, however, even about writing the letter that would bring her aunt home. She stood listlessly at the drawing room window, gazing down on the gray, windblown street. She was standing there when she saw him coming, walking with confident strides toward the house just as he had walked away from it last night. He wore a greatcoat and beaver hat and Hessian boots. He looked well-groomed enough, arrogant enough to be a duke. But that firm stride belonged to a man who had all the pride of knowing that he had made his own way in his own world and was successful enough, rich enough, confident enough to encroach upon hers.

She hated him. Because seeing him again, she felt a deep stabbing of longing in her womb. What she had allowed last night—what she had initiated—was not so easily shrugged off this morning. Her hands curled into fists at her sides as she saw him turn to approach her front door. She stepped back only just in time to avoid being seen as he glanced upward.

So he thought he had acquired himself a mistress from the beau monde, did he? As a final feather in his cap? She supposed that a mistress from her class might be more satisfactory even than a wife, though perhaps he thought to acquire both. The Graingers would not have shown such interest in him last evening if they had not heard somewhere that he was both eligible and available.

He thought that because he had given her undeniable pleasure last night she would become his willing slave so that she could have more. She swallowed when she remembered the pleasure. How humiliating!

The door of the drawing room opened to admit her butler. There was a card on the silver tray he carried. She picked it up and looked at it, though it seemed an unnecessary gesture.

Mr. Edgar Downes. *Edgar.* She had not wanted to know. She thought of Viking warriors and medieval knights. *Edgar.*

"He is waiting below?" she asked. It was too much to hope, perhaps, that he had left his card as a courtesy and taken himself off.

"He is, my lady," her butler told her. "But I did inform him that I was not sure you were at home. Shall I say you are not?"

It was tempting. It was what she wished him to say, what she intended to instruct him to say until she opened her mouth and spoke. But it was not to be as simple as that, it seemed. She was on new ground. She had done more than flirt with this man.

"Show him up," she said.

She looked down at the card in her hand as she waited. Edgar. Mr. Edgar Downes.

She felt very frightened suddenly—again. What was she doing? She had resolved both last night and this morning never to see him again. He posed far too great a threat to the precarious equilibrium of her life. She had spent six years building independence and self-assurance, convincing herself that they were enough. Last night the glass house she had constructed had come smashing and tinkling down about her head. It would take a great deal of rebuilding.

Mr. Edgar Downes could not help. Not in any way at all.

She could no longer possibly deny that she wanted him. Her body was humming with the ache of emptiness. She wanted his weight, his mastery, the smell of him, his penetration. She wanted him to make her forget.

But she knew—she had discovered last night if she had been in any doubt before that—that there was no forgetting. That the more she tried to drown everything out with self-gratification, the worse she made things for herself. She should not have told Hobbes to send him up. What could she have been thinking of? She must leave the room before they came upstairs.

But the door opened again before she could take a single step toward it. She stood where she was and smiled.

At each of his professions in turn Edgar had learned that there were certain unpleasant tasks that must be performed and that there was little to be gained by trying to avoid them or put them off until a later date. He had trained himself to do promptly and firmly what must be done.

It was a little harder to do in his personal life. On this particular morning he would have preferred to go anywhere and do anything rather than return to Lady Stapleton's house. But his training stood him in good stead. It must be done, and therefore it might as well be done without delay. Though he did find himself hoping as he approached the house that she would be from home. A foolish hope—if she was out this morning, he would have to return some other time, and doubtless it would seem even harder then.

He knew that she was at home when he turned to climb the steps to her door and looked up and caught a glimpse of her at a window, ducking hastily from sight. She would not, of course, wish to appear overeager to see him again. His irrational hopes rose again when that pugilist of a manservant who answered the door informed him that he thought Lady Stapleton might be from home. Perhaps she would refuse to see him—that was something he had not considered on his way here.

But she was at home and she did not refuse to see him. He drew deep breaths as he climbed the stairs behind the servant and tried to remember his rehearsed speech. He should know as a lawyer that rehearsed speeches scarcely ever served him when it came time actually to speak.

She looked even more beautiful this morning, dressed in a pale green morning gown. The color brought out the reddish hue of her hair. It made her look younger. She was standing a little distance from the door, smiling at him—that rather mocking half-smile he remembered from the evening before. The events of the night seemed unreal.

"Good morning, Mr. Downes." She was holding his card in one hand. She looked beyond his shoulder. "Thank you, Hobbes. That will be all."

The door closed quietly. There was no sign of the aunt or of any other chaperone—an absurd thing to notice after last night. He was glad there was no one else present, necessitating a conversation about the weather or the social pages of the morning papers.

"Good morning, ma'am." He bowed to her. He would get straight to the point. She was probably as embarrassed as he. "I believe I owe you an apology."

"Indeed?" Her eyebrows shot up. "An apology, sir?"

"I treated you with—discourtesy last evening," he said. Even in his rehearsed speech he had been unable to think of a more appropriate, less lame word to describe how he had treated her.

"With discourtesy?" She looked amused. "*Discourtesy,* Mr. Downes? Are there rules of etiquette, then, in your world for—ah, for what happens between a man and a woman in bed? Ought you to have said please and did not? You are forgiven, sir."

She was laughing at him. It had been a foolish thing to say. He felt mortified.

"I took advantage of you," he said. "It was unpardonable."

She actually did laugh then, that low, throaty laugh he had heard before. "Mr. Downes," she said, "are you as naive as your words would have you appear? Do you not know when you have been seduced?"

He jerked his head back, rather as if she had hit him on the chin. Was she not going to allow him even to pretend to be a gentleman?

"I was very ready to take advantage of the situation," he said. "I regret it now. It will not be repeated."

"Do you?" Neither of them had moved since he had stepped inside the room. She moved now—she took one step toward him. Her eyes had grown languid, her smile a little more enticing. "And will it not? I could have you repeat it within the next five minutes, Mr. Downes—if I so choose."

He was angry then. Angry with her because despite her birth and position and title she was no lady. Angry with her because she was treating him with contempt. Angry with himself because what she said was near to the truth. He wanted her. Yet he scorned to want what he could not respect.

"I think not, ma'am," he said curtly. "I thank you again for your generosity last night. I apologize again for any distress or

even bodily pain I may have caused you. I must beg you to believe that whenever we meet again, as we are like to do over the next few weeks if you plan to remain in town, I shall treat you with all the formal courtesy I owe a lady of your rank."
There. He had used part of his speech after all.

She took him by surprise. She closed the gap between them, took his arm with both of hers, and drew him toward the fireplace, in which a fire crackled invitingly. "You are being tiresome, sir," she said. "Do come and sit down and allow me to ring for coffee. I am ready for a cup myself. What a dreary morning it is. Talk to me, Mr. Downes. I have been in the mopes because there is no one here to whom to talk. My aunt is on an extended visit in the country and will not be back for a couple of days at the earliest. Tell me why a Bristol merchant is in London for a few weeks. Is it for business, or is it for pleasure?"

He found himself seated in a comfortable chair to one side of the fire, watching her tug on the bell pull. He had intended to stay for only a couple of minutes. He was feeling a little out of his depth. It was not a feeling he relished.

"It is a little of both, ma'am," he said.

"Tell me about the business reasons first," she said. "I hear so little that is of interest to me, Mr. Downes. Interest me. What *is* your business? Why does it bring you to London?"

He had to wait while she gave her instructions to the crooked-nosed servant, but then she looked back at him with inquiring eyes. They were not rhetorical questions she had asked.

He told her what she wished to know and answered the numerous other questions she asked—intelligent, probing questions. The coffee was brought and poured while he talked.

"How satisfying it must be," she said at last, "to have a purpose in life, to know that one has accomplished something. Do you feel that you have vanquished life, Mr. Downes? That it has been worth living so far? That it is worth continuing with?"

Strange questions. He had not given much thought to any of them. The answers seemed, perhaps, self-evident.

"Life is a constant challenge," he said. "But one never feels that one has accomplished all that can be done. One can never arrive. The journey is everything. How dull it would be finally to arrive and to have nothing else for which to aim."

"Some people would call it heaven," she said. "Not being on the journey at all, Mr. Downes, is hell. It surely is, is it not?"

"A self-imposed hell," he said. "One that no one need encounter for any length of time. It is laziness never to reach beyond oneself for something more."

"Or realism," she said. "You must grant that, Mr. Downes. Or are you so grounded in the practicalities of a business life that you have not realized that life is ultimately not worth living at all? Realism—or despair."

He had been enjoying their lively discussion. He had almost forgotten with whom he spoke—or at least he had almost forgotten that she was last night's lover, to whom he had come this morning in some embarrassment. But he was jolted by her words. The smile on her lips, he noticed now, was tinged with bitterness. Was she talking theoretically? Or was she talking about herself?

She gave him no chance to answer. She took a sip from her cup and her expression lightened. "But you came to town for pleasure, too," she said. "Tell me about that, Mr. Downes. For what sort of pleasure did you hope when you came here?" Her smile was once more pure mockery.

To his mortification Edgar felt himself flush. "My sister and brother-in-law were to be here the same time as me," he said. "They have insisted upon taking me about with them."

"How old are you, Mr. Downes?" she asked.

She had a knack for throwing him off balance. He answered before he could consider not doing so. "I am six-and-thirty, ma'am," he said.

"Ah, the same age as me," she said. "But we will not compare birthdays. I was married at the age of nineteen, Mr. Downes, to a man of fifty-four. I was married to him for seven years. I have no wish to repeat the experience. I have earned my freedom. But it is an experience everyone should be required to have at least once in a lifetime. You have come to London in search of a wife?"

He stared at her, speechless. Did she really expect him to answer?

She laughed. "It is hardly even an educated guess," she said. "Sir Webster Grainger and his lady were determinedly courting you last evening. They are in desperate search of a wealthy husband for poor Miss Grainger. I daresay you are very rich indeed. Are you?"

He ignored the question. "*Poor* Miss Grainger?" he said. He was feeling decidedly irritable again. How dare she probe into his personal life like this? Would she be doing so if he were a gentleman? "You believe she would be pitied if she married me, ma'am?"

"Very much so," she said. "You are sixteen years her senior, sir. That may not seem a huge gap in age to you and me—we both know that you are vigorous and in your prime. But it would appear an enormous age difference to a very young lady, Mr. Downes. Especially one who has a prior attachment—but a quite ineligible one, of course."

He frowned. Was she deliberately goading him? He could not quite believe he was having this conversation with her. But was it true? Did Miss Grainger have an attachment to someone else?

"You need not look so stricken, Mr. Downes," she said. "It is a common thing, you know. Young ladies of *ton* are merely commodities, you see. Sometimes people make the mistake of thinking that they are persons, but they are not. They are commodities their fathers may use to enhance or repair their fortunes. Unfortunately young ladies have feelings and an alarming tendency to fall in love without sparing a single thought to the state of their fathers' fortunes. They soon learn. That is one thing women are good at."

This, he thought, was a bitter woman indeed. And doubtless an intelligent woman. Too intelligent for her own good, perhaps.

"Is that what happened to you?" he asked. "You loved another man?"

She smiled. "He is married now with five children," she said. "He was kind enough to offer me the position of mistress after I was widowed. I declined. I will be no man's mistress." Her eyes mocked and challenged him.

He got to his feet. "I have taken too much of your time, ma'am," he said. "I thank you for the coffee. I—"

"If you are going to apologize again for your discourtesy in bedding me without saying 'please,' Mr. Downes," she said, "I beg you to desist. I should then feel obliged to apologize for seducing you and that would be tiresome since I do not feel sorry. But you need not fear that I will do it again. I never seduce the same man twice. It is a rule I have. Besides, in my experience no man is worth a second seduction."

"Ah," he said, suddenly more amused than angry, "you will have the last word after all, will you? It was a magnificent set-down."

"I thought so, too," she said. "You are a superior lover, Mr. Downes. Take it from someone who has had some experience of lovers. But I do not want a lover, even a very good one. Especially perhaps a very good one."

He despised himself for the satisfaction her words gave him.

"I would prefer a friend," she said.

"A friend?" He looked at her.

"Life can be tedious," she said, "for a widow who chooses not to burden her relatives with the demand for a home and who chooses not to burden herself with another husband. You are an interesting man. You have more to talk of than health and the weather and horses. Many men have no knowledge of anything beyond their horses and their guns and their hunting. Do you kill, Mr. Downes?"

"I have never been involved in gentlemanly sports," he said.

She smiled. "Then you will never be properly accepted in my world, sir," she said. "Let us be friends. Shall we be? You will alleviate my tedium and I will ease you into my world. Do you enjoy wandering around galleries, admiring the paintings? Or around the British Museum, absorbing history?"

"I am, I believe, a tolerably well-educated man, ma'am," he said.

She looked at him measuringly. "You are not perfect after all, are you?" she said. "You are sensitive about your origins. I did not imply that you are a clod, sir. But you do not know London well?"

"Not well," he admitted.

"Take me somewhere tomorrow," she said. "I shall decide where between now and then. Let me have someone intelligent with whom to share my observations."

He was tempted. How was he to say no? He must say no.

"You are afraid of ruining your matrimonial chances," she said, reading his hesitation aright. "How provincial, Mr. Downes. And how bourgeois. In my world it is no matter for raised eyebrows if a gentleman escorts a lady about who is not his wife or his betrothed or his intended, even when there is such another person in existence. And no one is scandalized when a woman allows a man to escort her who is not her husband or her father or her brother—even when she is married. In my world it is considered somewhat bad *ton* to be seen exclusively in the company of one's spouse."

"I daresay, then," he said, "that my sister is bad *ton*. And Lord Francis Kneller, too."

"Oh, those two." She waved a dismissive hand as she got to her feet. "I do believe they still fancy themselves in love, sir, though they have been married forever. There are other such oddities in the beau monde, but they are in the minority, I do assure you."

"You were right," he said. "I came to London in search of a bride. I promised my father that I would make my choice by Christmas. I rather think I should concentrate upon that task."

"My offer of friendship is rejected, then?" she said. "My *plea* for friendship? How very lowering. You are no gentleman, sir."

"No," he said with slow clarity, "I am not, ma'am. In my world a man does not cultivate a friendship with one woman while courting another."

"Especially with a woman whom he has bedded," she said.

"Yes," he agreed. "Especially with such a woman."

Her smile this time was one of pure contempt. "And you

were right a minute or two ago, Mr. Downes," she said. "You have stayed overlong. I tire of your bourgeois mentality. I would not find your friendship as satisfying as I found your lovemaking. And I do not desire lovemaking. I use men for my pleasure occasionally, but only very occasionally. And never the same man twice. Men are necessary for certain functions, sir, but essentially they are a bore."

Her words, her looks, her manner were all meant to insult. He knew that and felt insulted. At the same time he sensed that he had hurt her somehow. She had asked for his friendship and he had refused. He had refused because he would not be seduced again and knew beyond a doubt that any friendship with Lady Stapleton would inevitably lead eventually back to bed. She must surely know it, too.

He did not want a thirty-six-year-old mistress. *Rationally* he did not want her. Irrationally, of course, he wanted her very much indeed. He was a rational being. He chose to want a wife who was below the age of thirty, a wife who would give him children for his contentment, a son for Mobley Abbey.

"I am sorry," he said.

"Get out, Mr. Downes," she said. "I shall be from home if you call again, as I would have been today if I had had any sense. But I daresay you will not call again."

"No," he said, "I will not call again, ma'am."

She turned away from him and crossed the room to the window. She stood looking out of it while he let himself out of the room, as she had looked from the window of her bedchamber the night before.

She was a strange woman, he thought as he left the house and made his way along the street, thankful for the chilliness of the air. Confident, independent, unconventional, she appeared to be a woman who made happiness and her own gratification her business. Other women must envy her her freedom and her wealth and her beauty. Yet there was a deep-seated bitterness in her that suggested anything but happiness.

She must have had a bad marriage, he thought, one that had soured her and made her believe that all men were as her husband had been.

He had, it seemed, been one of a long string of lovers, all of whom had been used and never reused. It was a lowering and a distasteful thought. She made no secret of her promiscuity. She even seemed proud of it. His brief involvement with her was an experience he would not easily forget. It was an experience he was very glad was in the past. He was relieved that he had found the strength to reject her offer of friendship—he had certainly been tempted.

She was not a pleasant woman. A beautiful temptress of a woman, but not a pleasant one. He did not like her.

And yet he found himself regretting that he would not see her again, or if he did, that he must view her from afar. She could have been an interesting and an intelligent friend if there had never been anything else between them.

Chapter 5

Helena summoned her aunt from the country and felt guilty when she arrived for having encouraged her to leave just a few weeks before. She was uncomfortably aware that her aunt was not a person who deserved to be used.

"How very thoughtful you are, Helena, my dear," Mrs. Cross said as she stood in the hallway, surrounded by her rather meager baggage. "You know that I find life with Clarence and his family trying, and you have invited me back here, where I am always happy. Have you been enjoying yourself?"

"When do I not?" Helena said, hugging her and linking her arm through her aunt's to draw her toward the stairs. "Hobbes will have your bags attended to. Come to the drawing room and drink some tea. There is a fire there."

She let her aunt talk about her journey, about her stay in the country, about the snippets of news and gossip she had learned there. Sometimes, she thought, it felt good to have a companion, someone who was family, someone who loved one unconditionally. Often it was annoying, confining. But sometimes it felt good. Today it felt good.

"But here I am going on and on about myself," her aunt said eventually. "What about you, Helena? Are you looking pale, or is it my imagination?"

"The wind has not stopped blowing and the sun has not once peeped through the clouds for days," Helena said. "I have stayed indoors. I *feel* pale." She smiled. "Now that you are here, I shall go out again. We will go shopping tomorrow morning. I noticed when you arrived that there was a hole in the palm of your glove. I daresay there were no shops of note in the village close to Clarence's where you might have bought new ones. I am glad of it. Now I have an excuse to buy them for you as a gift. I was still in Switzerland at the time of your birthday, was I not?"

"Oh, Helena." Her aunt was flustered. "You do not need to be buying me presents. I wore those old gloves because they are comfortable and no one would see them in the carriage."

Helena smiled. Mrs. Letitia Cross was a widow, like herself. But Mr. Cross had not left her with an independence. Her meager stipend barely enabled her to keep herself decently clothed. She had to rely on various relatives to house her and feed her and convey her from place to place.

"I need gloves, too," Helena said, "and perhaps a muff. I need a warm cloak and warm dresses for a British winter. Ugh! It seems to be upon us already. Why can no one seem to build up the fires decently in this house?" She got up and jerked on the bell pull.

"But Helena, my dear." Her aunt laughed. "It is a magnificent fire. One would need a quizzing glass to be able to detect the fires in Clarence's hearths, I do declare. Though I must not complain. They were kind to me. The children and the governess were not allowed fires in their bedchambers either."

"I shall have one built half up your chimney tonight," Helena said. And then she turned to speak irritably to Hobbes, who looked expressionlessly at the roaring fire and said he would send someone immediately with more coals.

"I think I may go to Italy for Christmas," Helena said, throwing herself restlessly back onto her chair. "It will be warmer there. And the celebrations will be less cloying, less purely hypocritical than they are here. The Povises will be going at the end of November, I daresay, and there is always a party with them. I shall make one of their number. And you will make another. You will like Italy."

"I will not put you to so much expense," Mrs. Cross said with quiet dignity. "Besides, I do not have the wardrobe for it. And I am too old to be jauntering around foreign parts."

Helena clucked her tongue. "How old *are* you?" she asked. "You speak as if you are an octogenarian."

"I am fifty-eight," her aunt replied. "I thought you planned to stay here for the winter, Helena. And for the spring. You said you longed to see an English spring again."

Helena got restlessly to her feet and walked over to the window, although it was far from the fire, which a maid had just built up. "I am bored with England," she said. "The sun never shines here. What is the point of an English spring, Aunt, and English daffodils and snowdrops and bluebells when the sun never shines on them?"

"Has something happened?" her aunt asked her. "Are you unhappy about something, Helena?"

Her niece laughed. "Of course something has happened," she said. "Many things. I have been to dinners and dances and soirées and private concerts and have seen the same faces wherever I go. Pleasant faces. People with pleasant conversation. How dull it is, Letty, to see the same faces and listen to the same conversation wherever one goes. And no one has been obliging enough to do anything even slightly scandalous to give us all something more lively to discuss. How respectable the world has become!"

"There is no special gentleman?" her aunt asked. It was always her opinion that Helena should search for another husband, though she had never done so herself in twenty years of widowhood.

Helena did not turn from the window. "There is no special gentleman, Aunt," she said. "There never will be. I have no wish for there to be. I value my freedom far too much."

The street outside was quite busy, she noticed, but there was no tall, broad gentleman striding along it as if he owned the world. It was only as the thought became conscious that she realized she had spent a good number of hours during the past five days standing just here watching for him, waiting for him to return to apologize again. Had she really been doing that without even realizing it? She was horrified.

"And yet, my dear," Mrs. Cross said, "all husbands must not be condemned because yours made you unhappy."

Helena whirled around, her eyes blazing, her heart thumping with fury. "It was *not* an unhappy marriage," she said so loudly that her aunt grimaced. "Or if it was, the fault was mine. Entirely mine. Christian was the best of husbands. He adored me. He lavished gifts and affection on me. He made me feel beautiful and charming and—and lovable. I will not hear one word against him. Do you hear me? Not one word."

"Oh, Helena." Her aunt was on her feet, looking deeply distressed. "I am so sorry. Do forgive me. What I said was unpardonable."

Helena closed her eyes and drew a deep breath. "No," she said. "The fault was mine. I did not love him, Letty, but he was good to me. Come, let me take you up to your room. It should be warm by now. I am in the mopes because I have not been out in five days." She laughed. "That must be something of a record. Can you imagine me not going out for five whole days?"

"Frankly no, dear," her aunt said. "Have there been no invitations? It is hard to believe, even if this is October."

"I have refused them," she said. "I have been suffering from a persistent chill—or so I have claimed. I do believe it is time I recovered my health. Do you fancy an informal dance at the Earl of Thornhill's tomorrow evening?"

"I always find both the earl and the countess charming," Mrs. Cross said. "They do not ignore one merely because one is past the age of forty and is wearing a gown one has worn for the past three years and more."

Helena squeezed her arm. "We are going shopping tomorrow morning," she said. "I feel extravagant. And I feel so full of energy again that I do not know quite what to do with it." She stopped at the top of the stairs and hugged her aunt impulsively. "Oh, Letty, you do not know how good it is to have you here again." She was surprised to find that she had to blink her eyes in order to clear her vision.

"And *you* do not know," Mrs. Cross said, "how good it is to be here, Helena. Ah, the room really is warm. How kind you are to me. I feel quite like a person again, I do declare. And how ungrateful that sounds to Clarence. He really was very good to me."

"Clarence," Helena said, "is a sanctimonious, parsimonious bore and I am very glad he is not *my* relative. There. I have put it into words for you so that they will not be upon your conscience. I am going to leave you to rest for a while. There is nothing more tiring than a lengthy journey."

"Thank you, dear," her aunt said with a grateful sigh.

Had she really not been out for five days? Helena thought as she made her way back downstairs. Had she really convinced herself that the weather was just too inclement? And that the company of those of the beau monde who were at present in London was too tedious to be borne?

Her lip curled with self-mockery. Was she afraid to face him? Because he had rejected her? Because he had refused her offer of friendship and declined her invitation to escort her to one of the galleries? Was she so humiliated that she could not look him in the eye?

She *was* humiliated. She was unaccustomed to rejection. No man had ever rejected her before—oh! Her stomach lurched uncomfortably. Oh, that was not true. She realized something else suddenly about the past five days. She had hardly eaten.

To have been rejected by a cit! To have been rejected by any man—but by a man who was not even a gentleman. And a man to whom she had *given* herself. She had offered to make him better acquainted with London. She had offered her—patronage, she supposed was the word she was looking for. And he had said no for the purely bourgeois reason that he was about to pay court to some young girl.

How dared he reject her! And how petulant that thought sounded—and was.

She should, of course, never have asked for his friendship. She wanted no one's friendship, especially not any man's. Most especially not his. She could not imagine what she had been thinking of. She should not even have received him. And he had not even come to beg for further favors, but to apologize for his lack of *courtesy.* If it were not so lowering, it would be funny. Hilarious.

She certainly was not going to avoid him. Or show him that his rejection had meant anything to her. The very idea that she should mope and hide away just because he had refused to give her his escort on an afternoon's outing! She wished him joy of his young girl.

She was going to the Earl of Thornhill's informal ball tomorrow evening and she was going to dance and be merry. She was going to be the belle of the ball despite her age or perhaps because of it. She was going to wear her bronze satin gown. She had never worn it in England before, having judged it far too risque for stodgy English tastes. But tomorrow night she was going to wear it.

She was going to have Mr. Edgar Downes salivating over her—if he was there. And she was going to ignore him completely.

She hoped he would be there.

Edgar was uncomfortable with Fanny Grainger's age. It seemed that she was twenty, at least two years older than she looked. But even so she seemed a child to him. Lady Stapleton had been wrong when she had said that the age gap must appear nothing to him, that it would be apparent only to the girl herself. He was uncomfortably aware that he was well past his youth, while she seemed to be just embarking upon hers.

The other two young ladies he had met at the Earl of Greenwald's appeared equally young. And less appealing in other ways. Miss Turner, whom he had met two evenings later, was noticeably older—closer to thirty than twenty at a guess—but she was dull and lethargic and totally lacking in conversation. And she had a constant dry sniff, an annoying habit that grated on his nerves when he sat beside her for half an hour.

Miss Grainger, he rather suspected, was going to be the one. He had imagined when he came to London that he would be able to look about him at his leisure for several weeks before beginning a serious courtship of any lady in particular, almost as if he had thought he would be invisible and his intentions undiscernible. Such was not the case, of course. And Sir Webster Grainger and his lady had begun to court him. They were quite determined, it seemed, to net Edgar Downes for their daughter.

She was sweet and charming in a thoroughly youthful way. If he had been ten years younger, he might have tumbled head over ears in love with her. At his age he did not. He kept remembering Lady Stapleton's saying that the girl had a previous, ineligible attachment. He did not know how she had learned that. Perhaps—probably—she had merely been trying to make him uncomfortable. She had succeeded. The thought of coming between a young lady and her lover merely because he happened to be almost indecently rich was not a pleasant one.

He wondered if the girl disliked him, was repulsed by him. Whenever he spoke with her—and her parents made sure that he often did, always in their presence—she was polite and sweet, her deeper feelings, if she had any, quite hidden from view.

Cora was pleased. "She is a pleasant young lady, Edgar," she announced at the breakfast table one morning, "and will doubtless be a good companion once she has recovered from her shyness, poor girl, and her awe at your very masterful bearing. You could try to soften your manner, you know, but then it comes naturally enough to you and soon she will realize that behind it all you are just Edgar."

"You do not think I am too old for her, Corey?" he asked, unconsciously using the old nickname he had tried to drop since her marriage.

"Oh, she will not think so when she comes to love you," his fond sister assured him. "And that is bound to happen very soon. Is it not, Francis?"

"Oh, quite so, my love," Lord Francis said. "Edgar is eminently lovable."

Which remark sent Cora off into peals of laughter and left Edgar quite unreassured.

The promise he had made to his father seemed quite rash in retrospect. Perhaps at the Thornhills' ball, he thought, he would dance with the girl and have a chance to converse with her beyond the close chaperonage of her parents. Perhaps he would be able to discover the answers to some of his questions and find out if Cora was right. Could Miss Grainger be a good companion?

Was there something in his bearing that other people, particularly young ladies who were facing his courtship, found daunting, even overbearing? Lady Stapleton had not been daunted. But he did not particularly wish to think of Lady Stapleton. He had not seen her since that ghastly morning visit. He hoped that she had left town.

He realized she had not when he was dancing with Miss Turner, feeling thankful that the intricate patterns of the dance took away the necessity of trying to hold a conversation with her. It was not a great squeeze of a ball. Lady Thornhill had been laughingly apologetic about it and had insisted on calling it a small informal dance rather than a ball. To him the ballroom seemed crowded enough, but it was true that it was possible to see almost all the guests at once when he looked about him. He looked about him—and there she was standing in the doorway.

He did not even notice the older lady standing beside her. He saw only her and found himself swallowing convulsively. She wore a gown that might have appeared indecent even in a boudoir. It was a bronze-colored sheath that shimmered in the light from the chandeliers. To say that it was cut low at the bosom was seriously to understate the case. It barely skimmed the peaks of her nipples and dipped low into her decolletage. The gown was not tightly fitted and yet it settled about her body like a second skin, revealing every shapely and generous curve. It left little if anything to the imagination. It made Edgar remember with unwilling clarity exactly how that body had looked and felt—and tasted—beyond the thin barrier of the bronze satin.

She stood proudly, looking about her with languid eyes and slightly mocking smile, apparently quite unaware of any impropriety in her appearance. But then she somehow looked too haughty to be improper. She looked plainly magnificent.

The lady beside her must be the aunt, Edgar decided, noticing the woman when she turned her head to address some remark to Lady Stapleton. She was gray-haired and pleasant looking and dressed with neat propriety.

Edgar returned his attention to the steps of the dance.

She had been late to the Greenwalds' soirée, too, he remembered. Clearly she liked entrances. But then she had the looks and the presence to bring them off brilliantly. Thornhill was hurrying toward her.

Edgar returned his partner to her mother's side at the end of the set, bowed to them both, and made his way in the direction of his sister. There was to be a waltz next. He would dance it with Cora, who was closer to him in height than almost any other lady present. He felt uncomfortable waltzing with tiny females. But the Countess of Thornhill, one of Cora's close friends, hailed him as he passed and he turned toward her with a sinking heart.

"Mr. Downes." She was smiling at him. "Have you met Lady Stapleton?" It was a rhetorical question, of course. She did not pause to allow him to say that yes, he had met the lady at Lady Greenwald's soirée the week before and had escorted her home and stayed to bed her two separate times.

"And Mrs. Cross, her aunt," Lady Thornhill continued. "Mr. Edgar Downes, ladies. He is Lady Francis Kneller's brother from Bristol."

Edgar bowed.

"I am pleased to make your acquaintance, Mr. Downes," Mrs. Cross said.

"How do you do, Mr. Downes?" He had forgotten how that velvet voice could send shivers down his spine.

"Lady Francis is a very pleasant lady," Mrs. Cross said. "She is always very jolly."

Yes, it was an apt description of Cora.

"And quite fearless," Mrs. Cross continued. "I remember the year the Duchess of Bridgwater—the dowager duchess now, of course—brought her out. The year she married Lord Francis."

"Ah, yes, ma'am," he said. "The duchess was kind enough to give my sister a Season."

"The next dance is a waltz," the Countess of Thornhill said. "I have promised to dance it with Gabriel, though it is perhaps vulgar to dance with one's own husband at one's own ball. But then this is not a real ball but merely an informal dance among friends."

"I think one need make no excuses for dancing with one's husband," Mrs. Cross said kindly.

Edgar could feel Lady Stapleton's eyes on him, even though he looked intently at her aunt. He could feel that faint and characteristic scorn of her smile like a physical touch.

"Ma'am." He turned his head to look at her. "Will you do me the honor of dancing with me?"

"A waltz, Mr. Downes?" She raised her eyebrows. "I believe I will." She reached out one hand, though there was no necessity of taking to the floor just yet, and he took it in his.

"Mrs. Cross," the countess was saying as Edgar led his partner onto the floor, "do let me find you a glass of lemonade and some congenial company. May my husband and I have the pleasure of your company at the supper table when the waltz is at an end?"

Edgar's senses were being assaulted by the heady mixture of a familiar and subtle perfume and raw femininity.

"Well, Mr. Downes," she said, turning to face him, waiting for the music to begin, "in your school for budding merchants, did they teach you how to waltz?"

"Well enough to keep me from treading on your toes, I hope, ma'am," he said. "I was educated in a gentleman's school. They allowed me in after I had promised on my honor never, under any circumstances, to drop my aitches or wipe my nose on my cuff."

"One can only hope," she said, "that you kept your promises."

She was alarmed by her reaction to him. She felt short of breath. There was a fluttering in her stomach, or perhaps lower than her stomach, and a weakness in her knees. She had vowed, of course, to ignore him completely tonight. But then she had not planned that very awkward introduction Lady Thornhill had chosen to make. Strange, that. It was just the sort of thing she would normally maneuver herself. But not tonight. She had not wanted to be this close to him again. He was wearing the same cologne. Though it seemed to be the smell of the very essence of him rather than any identifiable cologne. She had fancied even as recently as last night that there was a trace of it on the pillow next to her own.

He danced well. Of course. She might have expected it. He probably did everything well, from making love on down—or up.

"Are congratulations in order yet, Mr. Downes?" she asked to take her mind off her fluttering nerves—and to shake his cool air of command. "Have you affianced yourself to a suitably genteel and fertile young lady? Or married her? Special licenses are available, as you must know."

"Not yet, ma'am," he said, looking at her steadily. He had been looking into her face since the music began. Was he afraid to look lower? But then he had seen all there was to see on a previous occasion. "It is not like purchasing cattle, you know."

"Oh, far from it," she agreed, laughing, "if by *cattle* you mean horses, Mr. Downes. I would not have asked you so soon if I must congratulate you if it were a horse you were choosing. I would know that the choice must be made with great care over an extended period of time."

He stared at her for so long that she became uncomfortable. But she scorned to look away from him.

"Who hurt you?" he asked her, jolting her with surprise and even shock. "Was it your husband?"

The same assumption in two days by two different people. Poor Christian. She smiled at Edgar. "My husband treated me as if I were a queen, Mr. Downes," she said. "Or to be more accurate, as if I were a porcelain doll. I am merely a realist, sir. Are your riches not sufficient to lure a genteel bride?"

"I believe my financial status and my personal life are none of your concern, ma'am," he said with such icy civility that she felt a delicious shiver along her spine.

"You do that remarkably well," she said. "Did all opposing counsel crumble before you in court? Were you a very successful lawyer? No, I will not make that a question but a statement. I have no doubt you were successful. Do all your employees quiver like jelly before your every glance? I would wager they do."

"I treat my employees well and with respect," he said.

"But I will wager you demand total obedience from them," she said, "and require an explanation when you do not get it."

"Of course," he said. "How could I run a successful business otherwise?"

"And are you the same in your personal relations, Mr. Downes?" she asked. "Am I to pity your wife when you have married her—after congratulating you, of course?" With her eyes she laughed at him. Her body was horribly aroused. She had no idea why. She had never craved any man's mastery. Quite the opposite.

"You need feel nothing for my wife, ma'am," he said. "Or for me. We will be none of your concern."

She sighed audibly. "You are naive, Mr. Downes," she said. "When you marry into the *ton,* you will become the concern of the *ton.* What else do we have to talk about but one another? Where can we look for the most fascinating scandals but to those among us who have recently wed? Especially when the match is something of a misalliance. Yours will be, you know. We will all look for tyranny and vulgarity in you—and will hope that there will not be only bourgeois dullness instead. We will all look for rebellion and infidelity in her—and will be vastly disappointed if she turns out to be a docile and obedient wife. Will you insist upon docility and obedience?"

"That will be for me to decide," he said, "and the woman I will marry."

She sighed again and then laughed. "How tiresome you are, Mr. Downes," she said. "Do you not know when a quarrel is being picked with you? I wish to quarrel with you, but I cannot quarrel alone."

For the first time she saw a gleam of something that might be amusement in his eyes—for the merest moment. "But I have no wish to quarrel with you," he said softly, twirling her about one corner of the ballroom. "We are not adversaries, ma'am."

"And we are not friends either," she said. "Or lovers. Are we nothing, then? Nothing at all to each other?"

He gave her another of those long stares—even longer this time. He opened his mouth and drew breath at one moment, but said nothing. He half smiled at last—he looked younger, more human when he smiled. "We are nothing," he said. "We cannot be. Because there was that night."

She almost lost her knees. She was looking back into his eyes and unexpectedly had a shockingly vivid memory of that night—of his face this close, above hers. . . .

"Do you understand the etiquette of such sets as this, Mr. Downes?" she asked. "It is the supper dance. It would be unmannerly indeed if you did not take me in to supper and seat yourself beside me and converse with me. What shall we converse about? Let me see. Some safe topic on which people who are nothing to each other can natter quite happily. Shall I tell you about my dreadful experiences in Greece? I am an amusing story-teller, or so my listeners always assure me."

"I believe I would like that," he said gravely.

She almost believed him. And she almost wanted to cry. How absurd! She felt like crying.

She never cried.

Chapter 6

It was amazing how few choices could be left one sometimes, Edgar discovered even more forcefully over the following month. He tried very hard not to fix his choice with any finality, simply because he did not meet that one certain lady of whom he could feel confident of saying in his heart that yes, she was one he wished to have as his life's companion, as his lover, as the mother of his children.

Miss Turner was of a suitable age, but he found her dull and physically unappealing. Miss Warrington was also of suitable age, and she was livelier and prettier. But her conversation centered almost entirely upon horses, a topic that was of no particular interest to him. Miss Crawley was very young—she even lisped like a child—and had a tendency to giggle at almost any remark uttered in her hearing. Miss Avery-Hill was equally young and very pretty and appealingly vivacious. She made very clear to Edgar that she would accept his courtship. She made equally clear the fact that it would be a major condescension on her part if she stooped to marry him.

That left Miss Grainger—and the Grainger parents. He liked the girl. She was pretty, modest, quiet without being mute, pleasant-natured. She was biddable. She would doubtless be a good wife. She would surely be a good mother. She would be a good enough companion. She would be attractive enough in bed. Cora liked her. His father would, too.

There was something missing. Not love, although that was definitely missing. He did not worry about it. If he chose a bride with care, affection would grow and even love, given time. He was not sure quite what it was that was missing with

Miss Grainger. Actually there was nothing missing except fortune, and that certainly was of no concern to him. He did not need a wealthy wife. If there was something wrong, it was in himself. He was too old to be choosing a wife, perhaps. He was too set in his ways.

Perhaps he would even have considered reneging on his promise to his father if matters had not appeared to have moved beyond his control. He found that at every entertainment he attended—and they were almost daily—he was paired with Miss Grainger for at least a part of the time. At dinners and suppers he found himself seated next to her more often than not. He escorted her and her mother to the library one day because Sir Webster was to be busy at something else. He went driving in the park with the three of them on two separate occasions. He was invited one evening to dinner at the Graingers', followed by some informal musical entertainment. There were only four other guests, all of them from a generation slightly older than his own.

Cora spoke often of Christmas and began to assume that the Graingers would be coming to Mobley. She was working on persuading all her particular friends—hers and Francis's—to spend the holiday there, too.

"Papa will be delighted," she said at breakfast one morning after the topic had been introduced. "Will he not, Edgar?" Francis had just suggested to her that she write to her father before issuing myriad invitations in his name.

"He will," Edgar agreed. "But it might be a good idea to fire off a note to warn him, Cora. He might consider it somewhat disconcerting to find a whole gaggle of guests and their milling offspring descending upon him and demanding a portion of a lone Christmas goose."

Lord Francis chuckled.

"Well, of *course* I intend to inform Papa," Cora said. "The very idea that I might neglect to do so, Edgar. Do you think me quite addle-brained?"

Lord Francis was unwise enough to chuckle again.

"And everyone knows that my main function in life is to provide you with amusement, Francis," she said crossly.

"Quite so, my love," he agreed, eliciting a short bark of inelegant laughter from his spouse.

"And I daresay Miss Grainger will be more comfortable with Jennifer and Samantha and Stephanie there as well as me," Cora said. "She is familiar with them and they with her. But she *is* rather shy and may find the combination of you and Papa together rather formidable, Edgar."

"Nonsense," her brother said.

"I did, Edgar," Lord Francis said. "When I dashed down to Mobley that time to ask if I might pay my addresses to Cora, I took one look at your father and one look at you and had vivid mental images of my bones all mashed to powder. You had me shaking in my Hessians. You might have noticed the tassels swaying if you had glanced down."

"And what gives you the idea," Edgar asked his sister, "that Miss Grainger will be at Mobley for Christmas? Have I missed something? Have you *invited* her?" He had a horrid suspicion for one moment that perhaps she had and had forced his hand quite irretrievably.

"Of course, I have not," she said. "I would never do such a thing. That is for you to do, Edgar. But you will do it, will you not? She is your favorite and eligible in every way. I love her quite like a sister already. And you did promise Papa."

"And it is Edgar's life, my love," Lord Francis said, getting to his feet. "We had better go up and rescue Nurse from our offspring. They are doubtless chafing at the bit and impatiently awaiting their daily energy-letting in the park. Is it Andrew's turn to ride on my shoulders or Paul's?"

"Annabelle's," she said as they left the room.

But Cora came very close that very evening to doing what she had said she would never do. They were at a party in which she made up a group with the Graingers, Edgar, Stephanie, Duchess of Bridgwater, and the Marquess of Carew. The duchess had commented on the fact that the shops on Oxford Street and Bond Street were filled with Christmas wares already despite the fact that December had not even arrived. The marquess had added that he and his wife had been shopping for gifts that very day in the hope of avoiding any last-minute panic. Cora mentioned Mobley and hoped there would be some snow for Christmas. All their children, she declared—if she could persuade her friends to come—would be ecstatic if they could skate and ride the sleighs and engage in snowball fights.

"There are skates of all sizes," she said, "and the sleighs are large enough for adults as well as children. Do you like snow, Miss Grainger?"

Edgar felt a twinge of alarm and looked pointedly at his sister. But she was too well launched on enthusiasm to notice.

"Good," Cora said when the girl had replied that indeed she did. "Then you will have a marvelous time." She reacted quite in character when she realized that she had opened her mouth and stuffed her rather large slipper inside, Edgar noticed, wishing rather uncharitably that she might choke on it. She blushed and talked and laughed. "That is, if it snows. If it snows where you happen to be spending Christmas, that is. That is, if . . . Oh dear. Hartley, do tell me what I am trying to say."

"You are hoping there will be snow to make Christmas a more festive occasion, Cora," the Marquess of Carew said kindly. "And that it will fall all over England for everyone's delight."

"Yes," she said. "Thank you. That is exactly what I meant. How warm it is in here." She opened her fan and plied it vigorously before her face.

Sir Webster and Lady Grainger, Edgar saw, were looking very smug indeed.

And then at the very end of November, when the noose seemed to have settled quite firmly about his neck, he discovered the existence of the ineligible lover—the one Lady Stapleton had mentioned.

Edgar was walking along Oxford Street, huddled inside his heavy greatcoat, avoiding the puddles left by the rain that had just stopped, wondering if the sun would ever shine again and if he would ever find suitable gifts for everyone on his list—he had expected London to make for easier shopping than Bristol—when he ran almost headlong into Miss Grainger, who was standing quite still in the middle of the pavement, impeding pedestrian traffic.

"I do beg your pardon," he said, his hand going to the brim of his hat even before he recognized her. "Ah, Miss Grainger. Your servant." He made her a slight bow and realized two things. Neither of her parents was with her—but a young man was.

She did not behave with any wisdom. Her eyes grew wide with horror, she opened her mouth and held it open before snapping it shut again. Then she smiled broadly, though she forgot to adjust her eyes accordingly, and proceeded to chatter.

"Mr. Downes," she said. "Oh, good morning. Fancy meeting you here. Is it not a beautiful morning? I have come to change my book at the library. Mama could not come with me, but I have brought my maid—you see?" She gestured behind her with one hand to the young person standing a short distance away. "How lovely it is to see you. By a very strange coincidence I have run into another acquaintance, too. Mr. Sperling. May I present you? Mr. Sperling, sir. Jack, this is Mr. Downes. I-I m-mean *Mr. Sperling,* this is Mr. Downes."

Edgar inclined his head to the slender, good-looking, very young man, who was looking back coldly. "Sperling?" he said.

A few things were clear. This particular spot on Oxford Street was not between the Grainger lodgings and the library. The doorway to a coffee shop that sported high-backed seats and secluded booths was just to their right. The maid was not doing a very good job as watchdog. Jack Sperling was more than a chance acquaintance and the meeting between him and Miss Grainger was no coincidence. Sperling knew who he was and would put a dagger through his heart if he dared—and if he had one about his person. Miss Grainger herself was terrified. And he, Edgar, felt at least a century old.

He would have moved on and left his prospective bride to her clandestine half hour or so—he doubted they would allow themselves longer—with the slight acquaintance she happened to call by his first name. But she forestalled him.

"Jack," she said. She was still flustered. "I m-mean *Mr. Sperling,* it was pleasant to meet you. G-good morning."

And Jack Sperling, pale and murderous of countenance, had

no choice but to bow, touch the brim of his hat, bid them a good morning, and continue on his way down the street as if he had never so much as heard of coffee shops.

Fanny Grainger smiled dazzlingly at Edgar—with terrified eyes. "Was not that a happy chance?" she said. "He is a neighbor of ours. I have not seen him for years." Edgar guessed that beneath the rosy glow the cold had whipped into her cheeks she was blushing just as rosily.

"May I offer my escort?" he asked her. "Are you on your way to or from the library?"

"Oh," she said. "To." She indicated her maid, who held a book clasped against her bosom. "Y-yes, please, Mr. Downes, if it is not too much trouble."

He felt like apologizing to her. But of course he could not do so. He should be feeling sternly disapproving. He should be feeling injured proprietorship. He felt—still—a century old. She took his arm.

"Mr. Downes," she said before he had decided upon a topic of conversation, "p-please, will you—? That is, could I ask you please— Please, sir—"

He wanted to set a reassuring hand over hers. He wanted to pat it. He wanted to tell her that it was nothing to him if she chose to arrange clandestine meetings with her lover. But of course it *was* something to him. There was one month to Christmas and he had every intention—he had thought it through finally just last evening and had come to a firm decision—of inviting her and her parents to Mobley Abbey for the holiday, though he had thought he would not make his offer until they had all been there for a few days and he could be quite sure before taking the final step.

"I believe, my dear," he said, and then wished he had not called her that, as if she were a favored niece, "my size and demeanor and—age sometimes inspire awe or even fear in those who do not know me well. At least, I have been told as much by those who do know me. I have no wish either to hurt or distress you. What is it?"

He noticed that she closed her eyes briefly before answering. "Please," she said, "will you refrain from mentioning to

Mama and Papa that I ran into Mr. Sperling by chance this morning? They do not like him, you see, and perhaps would scold me for not giving him the cut direct. I could not do that. Or at least I did not think of doing it until it was too late."

"Of course," he said. "I have already forgotten the young man's name and indeed his very existence."

"Thank you." Some of the terror had waned from her eyes when she looked up at him. "Though I w-wish I had done so. It was disagreeable to have to acknowledge him. I was very relieved when you came along."

"It is a quite impossible situation?" he found himself asking when he should have been content to play along with her game.

There was fright in her eyes again. She bit her lip and tears sprang to her eyes. "I am sorry," she whispered. "Please do not be angry with me. It was the last time. That is— It will not happen again. Oh, please do not be angry with me. I am so frightened of you." And then the fright escalated to terror once more when she realized what she had said, what she had admitted, both about him and about Jack Sperling.

This time he did set his hand over hers—quite firmly. "That at least you need not be," he said. "What is the objection? Lack of fortune?"

But she was biting hard on her upper lip and fighting both tears and terror—despite his words. The library was before them.

"I shall leave you to your maid's chaperonage," he said, stopping on the pavement outside it and relinquishing her arm. "We will forget about this morning, Miss Grainger. It never happened."

But she did not immediately scurry away, as he rather expected she would. She looked earnestly into his face. "I have always been obedient to Mama and Papa," she said, "except in very little things. I will be obedient—I would be obedient to a husband, sir. I would never need to be beaten. I—Good morning." And she turned to hurry into the library, her maid behind her.

Good Lord! Did she imagine—? Did he look that formidable? And what a coil, he thought. He could not possibly marry her now, of course. But perhaps it would appear that he had gone rather too far to retreat without good cause. There was excellent cause, but nothing he could express to another living soul. He could not marry a young lady who loved another man. Or one who feared him so much that she imagined he would be a wife-beater.

Whatever was he going to do?

But he was not fated to think of an answer while he stood there on the pavement, staring at the library doors. They opened and Lady Stapleton stepped out with Mrs. Cross.

He forgot about his problem—the one that concerned Miss Grainger, anyway. He always forgot about everything and everyone whenever his eyes alighted on Lady Stapleton. They had avoided each other for the past month. They attended almost all the same social events and it was frequently necessary to be part of the same group and even to exchange a few words. But they had not been alone together since that evening when they had waltzed and then taken supper together. The evening when he had told her they could be nothing to each other because there had been that night.

That night. It stayed stubbornly in his memory, it wove itself into his dreams as none other like it had ever done. Not that there had been another night like that. Perhaps, he thought sometimes, he would forget it sooner if he tried less hard to do so. He did not want to remember. The memories disturbed him. He was not a man of passion but one of cool reason. He had been rather alarmed at the passionate self that had emerged during that particular encounter. He looked forward to returning to Mobley and then Bristol. After that, he hoped, he would never see her again. The memories would fade.

He made his bow and would have hastened away, but Mrs. Cross called to him.

"Mr. Downes," she cried. "Oh, Mr. Downes, might we impose upon you for a few minutes, I wonder? My niece is unwell."

He could see when he looked more closely at Lady Stapleton that she was leaning rather heavily on her aunt's arm and that her face and even her lips were ashen pale and her eyes half closed—and that until her aunt spoke his name, she had been quite unaware of his presence.

Her eyes jolted open and her glance locked with his.

The Povises had already left for the Continent with a group of friends and acquaintances. They intended to wander south at a leisurely pace and spend Christmas in Italy. Helena might have gone with them. Indeed, they had urged her to do so, and so had Mr. Crutchley, who had had designs on her for a number of years past, though she had never given him any encouragement. It was sure to be a gay party. She would have enjoyed herself immensely if she had gone along. She would have avoided this dreariest of dreary winters in England—and it was still only November. She could have stayed away until spring or even longer. Perhaps she could even have persuaded her aunt to go with her if she had set her mind to it.

But she had not gone.

She did not know why. She was certainly not enjoying London. There were almost daily entertainments, and she attended most of them for her aunt's sake. The company, though sparse, was congenial. She was treated with respect and even with warmth wherever she went—even on that evening when she had worn her bronze satin and Lady Francis Kneller had quite frankly and quite sincerely commended her bravery. Being in one comfortable home was certainly preferable to moving from one inn to another. And coach travel day after day could be tedious and even downright uncomfortable. She should be happy. Or since happiness was not a possible state for her, contented. She should be contented.

She felt lethargic and even ill. Her aunt had a bad cold soon after returning to town, but Helena did not catch it from her. It would have been better if she had, she thought. She would have suffered for a few days and then recovered. As it was, she felt constantly unwell without any specific symptoms that she might treat. Even getting out of bed in the mornings—her favorite time of day—had become a chore. Sometimes she lay late in bed, awake and bored and uncomfortable, but lacking the energy to get up, only to feel faintly nauseated and unable to eat any breakfast when she did make the effort.

She knew why she felt that way, of course. She was living through an obsession—and it was no new thing. If it had been, perhaps she would have been better able to deal with it. But it was not new. She had been obsessed once before and just the memory of it—long suppressed but never quite hidden below consciousness—could have her poised with her head hanging over the close stool, fighting to keep the last meal down.

Now she was obsessed again. Not in any way she could explain clearly to herself. Although she saw him almost daily, she never again felt the urge to seduce him—though the knowledge that it would not be an easy thing to do a second time was almost a temptation in itself. She just could not keep her eyes off him when he was in a room with her. Though that was not strictly accurate. She rarely looked directly at him. She would scorn to do so. He would surely notice. Other people would. She kept her eyes off him. But every other part of her being was drawn to him as if to a powerful magnet.

She was not even sure that it was just a sexual awareness. She imagined sometimes being in bed with him again, doing with him the things they had done on that one night they had spent together. But though the thoughts were undeniably arousing, she always knew that it was not that she wanted. Not just that anyway. She did not know what she wanted.

She wanted to forget him. That was what she wanted. She hated him. Those words they had spoken while waltzing would not fade from her mind.

Are we nothing, then? Nothing at all to each other?

We are nothing. We cannot be. Because there was that night.

There was a deep pit of emptiness in her stomach every time she heard the echo of those words of his—and she heard it almost constantly.

She should go away. She should have gone with the Povises. She had stayed for her aunt's sake, she had told herself. But when had she ever considered anyone's feelings except her own? When had she ever had a selfless motive for anything she had ever done—or not done? She should go away. She should go to Scotland for Christmas—horrid thought. But *he* would be going away for Christmas. He would be going to his father's estate near Bristol. She had heard Lady Francis Kneller talking about it. The Grainger girl would doubtless be going there, too. They would be betrothed—and married by the spring. Perhaps then she would know some peace.

Peace! What a ridiculous hope. Her last chance for any kind of peace had disappeared over a year ago with the marriage of another man.

She decided to accompany her aunt to the library one morning, despite the fact that she felt not only nauseous but even dizzy at breakfast, and even though her aunt urged her to go back to bed for an hour. She would feel better for a little fresh air, she replied.

She did not feel better. She sat with a newspaper while her aunt chose a book, but she did not read even the headlines. She was too busy imagining the humiliation should she vomit in such a public place. She mastered the urge as she had done on every previous occasion, even in the privacy of her own rooms.

But a wave of dizziness took her as they reached the door on their way out. It was so strong that her aunt noticed and became alarmed. She took Helena's arm and Helena unashamedly leaned on her for support. She drew a few deep breaths of the cold outside air, her eyes half closed. And then her aunt spoke.

"Mr. Downes," she called, her voice breathless with distress. "Oh, Mr. Downes, might we impose upon you for a few minutes, I wonder? My niece is unwell."

Helena's eyes snapped open. There he was, tall and broad and immaculately groomed and frowning at her as if he were quite out of humor. He of all people! There was suddenly another wave of nausea to be fought.

Chapter 7

She pushed away from her aunt's side and stood upright. "I am quite well, I thank you," she said. "Good morning, Mr. Downes."

The effect of her proud posture and brisk words was quite marred by the fact that she swayed on the spot and would perhaps have fallen if Mrs. Cross had not grasped her arm and Edgar had not lunged forward to grab her by the waist.

"I am *quite well,*" she said testily. "You may unhand me, sir."

"You are not well, Helena," her aunt insisted mildly. "Mr. Downes, *may* we impose upon you to call us a hackney cab?"

"No!" Lady Stapleton said as Edgar looked back over his shoulder toward the road. "Not a hackney cab. Not a carriage of any sort. I shall walk home. The fresh air will feel good. Thank you for your concern, Mr. Downes, but we need not detain you. My aunt's arm will be quite sufficient for my needs."

She was attempting her characteristic mocking smile, but it looked ghastly in combination with parchment white face and lips. The foolish woman was obviously trying to defy an early winter chill.

"I shall summon a hackney cab, ma'am," he said and turned away from her in order to hail one.

"I shall vomit if I have to set foot inside a carriage," she said from behind him. "There. Is that what you wanted, Mr. Downes? To hear me admit something so very ungenteel?"

"My dear Helena," her aunt said, "Mr. Downes is just being—"

"Mr. Downes is just being his usual overbearing self," Lady Stapleton said. "If you must offer your assistance, sir, give me your arm and escort me home. I can lean more heavily on yours than I could on Letty's."

"Helena, my dear." Mrs. Cross sounded shocked. "Mr. Downes probably has business elsewhere."

"Then he can be late," her niece retorted, taking Edgar's offered arm and leaning much of her weight on it. "Oh, I do wish I had gone to Italy with the Povises. How tiresome to be in England when it is so cold and sunless and cheerless."

"I have no business that cannot be delayed, ma'am," Edgar told Mrs. Cross. "I shall escort you home, Lady Stapleton, and then go to fetch a physician if you will tell me which. I suppose you have not consulted him lately." It was a statement rather than a question.

"How kind of you, sir," Mrs. Cross said.

"I do not consult a physician every time I am subjected to an overheated library and half faint from the stuffiness," Lady Stapleton said. "I shall be quite myself in a moment."

But she was very far from being herself even five minutes later. She continued to lean heavily on his arm and walked rather slowly along the street. She did not speak again, even to contradict Mrs. Cross, who proceeded to tell Edgar that her niece had not been in the best of health for some little while. By the time they came in sight of her house, her eyes were half closed and her footsteps lagged more than ever.

"Perhaps, ma'am," Edgar suggested to Mrs. Cross, "you could go ahead to knock on the door and have it open by the time Lady Stapleton arrives there." And without warning to his flagging companion, he stopped, released her arm, and scooped her up into his arms.

She spoke then while her one arm came about his neck and her head drooped to his shoulder. "Damn you, Edgar," she said, reminding him of how she had sworn at him on a previous occasion. "Damn you. I suppose you were waiting outside that library for the express purpose of humiliating me. How I hate you." But she did not struggle to be set down.

"Your effusive expressions of gratitude can wait until you are feeling more the thing," he said.

The flat-nosed pugilist was in the hall and looked to be

bracing himself to take his mistress in his own arms. Edgar swept by him with hardly a glance and carried his burden upstairs. She was certainly no light weight. He was thankful when he saw Mrs. Cross outside Lady Stapleton's bedchamber, holding open the door. Had she been ascending the stairs behind them, he might have forgotten that he was not supposed to know where the lady's bedchamber was.

He set her down on the bed and stood back while her aunt removed her bonnet and a maid, who had rushed in behind them, drew off her half boots. She was still terribly pale.

"Who is your physician?" he asked.

"I have none." She opened her eyes and looked up at him. Some of her hair had come loose with the bonnet. The richness of its chestnut waves only served to make her face look more colorless. "I have no need of physicians, Mr. Downes. I need a warm drink and a rest. I daresay I shall see you at Lady Carew's musical evening tonight."

"Oh, I think not, Helena," Mrs. Cross said. "I will send a note around. The marchioness will understand."

"You need a physician," Edgar said.

"And you may go to the devil, sir," she said sharply. "Might I expect to be granted the privacy of my own room? It is not seemly for you to be standing there looking at me here, is it?" The old mockery was back in both her face and her voice. It was the very room and the very bed, of course. . . .

"When you are feeling better, Helena," Mrs. Cross said with gentle gravity, "you will wish to apologize to Mr. Downes. He has been extraordinarily kind to us this morning, and there is no impropriety with both Marie and me here, too. We will leave you to Marie's care now. Sir, will you come to the drawing room for tea or coffee—or something stronger, perhaps?"

"Thank you, ma'am," he said, turning toward the door, "but I really do have business elsewhere. I shall call tomorrow morning, if I may, to ask how Lady Stapleton does."

Lady Stapleton, he saw when he glanced back at the bed before leaving the room, was lying with her eyes closed and a contemptuous smile curling her lip.

"I am worried about her," Mrs. Cross said after he had closed the door. "She is not herself. She has always had so much restless energy. Now she seems merely restless."

"Would *you* like me to summon a physician, ma'am?" he asked.

"Against Helena's wishes?" she said, raising her eyebrows and laughing. "You do not know my niece, Mr. Downes. She was unpardonably rude to you this morning. I do apologize for her. I am sure she will do so for herself when she feels better and remembers a few of the things she said to you."

Edgar doubted it. "I understand that Lady Stapleton prides herself on her independence, ma'am," he said. "She was embarrassed to have to accept my assistance this morning. No apology is necessary."

They were in the hall already and the manservant, looking his usual surly self, was waiting to open the door onto the street.

"You are gracious, sir," Mrs. Cross said.

He wished she would see a physician, Edgar thought as he strode along the street in an effort not to be quite impossibly late for a meeting he had arranged with a business associate. She was not the type of woman to be always having the vapors and relying upon men to support her to the nearest sofa. She had hated having to accept his help this morning. She had even damned him—and called him by his first name. Her indisposition was very real, and it had been going on for some time if her aunt was to be believed.

He was worried about her.

And then he frowned and caught the thought. *Worried* about her? About Lady Stapleton, who meant nothing to him? How had they expressed it between them during that evening when they had been waltzing? They were not adversaries or friends or lovers. They were nothing. They could be nothing, because there had been that night.

But there had been that night. He had known her body with thorough intimacy. He had known exhilarating and blazing passion with her.

Yes, he supposed she was *something*. Not anything that

could be put into words, but something. Because there had been that night.

And so he was worried about her.

She had allowed Marie to undress her and tuck her into bed. She had allowed her aunt back into her room to draw the curtains across the window and to send for a hot drink of weak tea—the thought of chocolate or coffee was just too nauseating. She had allowed them both to fuss—though she hated people fussing over her.

And now she had been left alone to sleep. She felt as far from sleep as she had ever felt. She lay staring up at the large silk rosette that formed the peak of the canopy over her bed. She could not believe how foolish she was. She was stunned by her own naivete.

Although her husband had been fifty-four when she married him and sixty-one when he died, he had been a vigorous man. He had had her almost nightly for the first year and with frequency after that, almost to the end. She had never conceived. She had come to believe that the fault was in herself. Although Christian had had only the one son, she had been told that his first wife had had an appalling number of stillbirths and miscarriages.

The possibility of conception had not occurred to her when she had lain with Edgar Downes—either before or during or after. Not even when she had begun to feel persistently unwell.

She was careless about her own cycle. Her monthly flow, that great nuisance to which all women were subjected, almost always took her by surprise. She had no idea if she was strictly regular or not. She was one of the fortunate women who were not troubled by either pain or discomfort or a heavy flow.

And so for a number of weeks she had allowed symptoms so obvious that they were like a hard fist jabbing at her chin to pass her by unnoticed. Even now, when she set her mind to it, she could not remember when her last flow had been. She was almost sure there had been none for a while—none since that night, anyway. She was almost sure enough to say that she was quite certain. Oh, yes, of course she was certain. And that had been well over a month ago.

She had been feeling lethargic and nauseated—especially in the mornings. Her breasts had been feeling tender to the touch.

As she stared upward, strong suspicion turned unwillingly to certainty—and to a mindless, clawing terror. She closed her eyes as the canopy began to swing about her—and then opened them again. Dizziness was only worsened when one closed one's eyes. She drew deep breaths, held them, and released them slowly through her mouth.

At the age of six-and-thirty she was with child.

She was pregnant.

She was going to swell up to a grotesque enormity just like a young bride. And then there was going to be a baby. A child. A person. For her to nurture.

No.

No, she could not do it. She could not face the embarrassment. Or the shame. Though she did not care the snap of two fingers for the shame. But the embarrassment! She was six-and-thirty. She had been a widow for ten years. If the *ton* suspected that she occasionally took lovers—and her carelessness of strict propriety had made that almost inevitable—then they would guess too that she was worldly-wise and knowledgeable enough to take care of herself. It was unpardonably gauche to allow oneself to be impregnated, especially when one did not have a live husband upon whose paternity to foist the love child.

She would be the laughingstock.

She did not care about that. Why should she care what people thought about her? She had not cared for a long time.

Her terror had little to do with either shame or embarrassment. It had everything to do with the fact that there was going to be a *baby.* A child who was half hers and would come from her body. A child she would be expected to nurse and to love and to teach.

She had involved someone else, drawn someone else into her own darkness. A child. An innocent.

Her mind reached frantically about. If she searched carefully for a good home, if she gave the baby up at birth, if she was careful never to see it again, never to let it know who or what its mother was, would the child have a chance?

But she could not think clearly. She had only just realized the truth, though it had been staring her in the face for some time. He had stopped a short distance from the house and taken her totally by surprise by picking her up and carrying her the rest of the way. She had felt the strength of his arms and the sturdiness of his body—and she had known in a blinding flash the nature of her obsession with him. Her body had been speaking for a few weeks but her mind had not been listening. She had this man's child growing inside her.

And so she had damned him and would have used worse language on him if she had had the energy.

Where would she go? She closed her eyes and found to her relief that the dizziness had gone. Scotland? Her cousins were respectable people. They would not appreciate the notion of entertaining a pregnant woman whose husband had died ten years ago. Italy? She could find the Povises and their party. If she told the story well enough, they would be amused by it. They were worldly enough to accept that such things happened.

She could not tell this story amusingly. There was a *child* involved. An innocent.

Where, then? Somewhere else in Europe? Somewhere here in England?

She could not think straight. She needed to sleep. She was mortally tired. If she could but sleep, she could clear her head and then think and plan rationally. If she could but sleep . . .

But she kept seeing Edgar Downes standing beside her bed, looking even more massive and forbidding than usual in his caped greatcoat, his booted feet set apart on her carpet, his face frowning down at her as he suggested fetching a physician.

And more alarmingly, she kept seeing him above her on the bed, his weight pressing her down, his hot seed gushing deep inside her. She kept feeling herself being impregnated.

She hated him. She did not blame him for anything. It had

been all her fault. She had seduced him and had taken no precautions to avoid the consequences. But she hated him anyway.

He of all people must never know the truth. She would never be able to live with that humiliation. He would probably proceed to take charge, to send her somewhere where she could bear the child in comfort and secrecy. He would probably find a home for it. He would probably support it until it was adult and he could find it suitable employment. He would see her as just a weak woman who could not possibly manage alone.

He must never find out. He was not going to organize the life of *her* child. He was not going to take her child away from her or lift from her shoulders the responsibility of caring for it. It was her child. It was inside her body. Now. And not *it*. He. Or she. A real person.

She was biting her upper lip. After a while she tasted blood. She did not sleep.

Lady Stapleton and Mrs. Cross were not at the Carews' musical evening. Mrs. Cross had sent a note making their excuses, the marchioness explained when someone noted their absence. Lady Stapleton was indisposed.

It was only surprising that most of them remained healthy in such dreary weather, someone remarked.

Fanny Grainger had mentioned seeing Lady Stapleton at the library looking quite ill, Lady Grainger reported.

She had been looking not quite herself for a few weeks, the Countess of Thornhill said. Poor lady. Some winter chills were very hard to shake.

But look at the gowns she wore, Mrs. Turner remarked—or rather did not wear, her tone implied. It was no wonder she took chills.

No one picked up that particular conversational cue.

"I must pay her a call," Cora Kneller announced in the carriage on the way home. "I wonder if she has seen a physician. At least she is fortunate to have Mrs. Cross to tend to her. Mrs.

Cross is a very amiable and sensible lady. I like her excessively."

"I shall come with you, Cora," her brother said.

"Oh good." She looked only pleased and not even mildly suspicious, as Lord Francis did. "I will not need your escort then, Francis. You may take the children to the park."

"They will probably take me, my love," he said. "But I shall allow myself to be dragged along."

And so Edgar made his promised morning call in company with his sister. He hoped that Lady Stapleton would have kept to her bed so that they might make their inquiries of Mrs. Cross and spend just a short while in conversation with her. But when they were shown up to the drawing room, it was to find both ladies there.

Lady Stapleton was looking more herself. There was little color in her cheeks, but she was looking composed and was dressed with her usual elegance. She even favored Edgar with her usual mocking smile as she greeted him. He and Cora were invited to have a seat and Mrs. Cross rang for tea.

"I was quite disturbed to hear last evening that you were indisposed," Cora said. "I can see for myself this morning that you are still not quite the thing. I do hope you have consulted a physician."

Lady Stapleton smiled at Edgar. "I have not," she said in her velvet voice. "I do not believe in physicians. But thank you for your concern, Lady Francis. And for yours, sir."

Edgar said nothing. He merely inclined his head.

"Letty tells me that I owe you an apology," she said. "She tells me I was rude to you yesterday. I cannot remember saying anything I did not mean, but perhaps I was feeling ill enough to say something to offend. I do beg your pardon."

"Yesterday?" Cora said with bright curiosity. "Did you see Lady Stapleton yesterday, Edgar, and said nothing last evening when we were discussing her absence? How provoking of you!"

"Ah, but doubtless Mr. Downes was too modest to admit to his own gallantry," Lady Stapleton said, her eyes mocking him. "I leaned heavily on his arm all the way home from the library, and he actually carried me the last few yards and all the way upstairs to my bedchamber. My aunt was with us, I hasten to add. Your brother has amazing strength, Lady Francis. I weigh a ton."

"Oh, Edgar." Cora looked at him curiously. "How thoughtful of you. And you did not say a word about it. I am not surprised that you wished to come to pay your respects today. But *you* are quite well, ma'am?" She turned her attention to Mrs. Cross.

The two of them proceeded to discuss Lady Stapleton's health almost as if the lady herself was not present. Mrs. Cross was worried because her niece had been under the weather for a week or more—yes, definitely more—but refused to seek a cure. She was ill enough each morning to be quite unable to eat any breakfast and her energy seemed to flag several times each day. She had come near to fainting on more than one occasion. And such behavior was quite unlike her.

Lady Stapleton kept her eyes on Edgar while they spoke, a look of mocking amusement in her eyes.

"I know just what it is like to be unable to eat breakfast," Cora said. "I sympathize with you, Lady Stapleton. It happened to me during the early months when I was expecting all four of my children. And yet breakfast has always been my favorite meal."

Lady Stapleton raised both eyebrows, but continued to look at Edgar. "Goodness me," she said. "We will be embarrassing Mr. Downes. I do believe he is blushing."

He was not blushing, but he was feeling remarkably uncomfortable. Only Cora would speak so indelicately in mixed company.

"Oh, Edgar will not mind," Cora said. "Will you, Edgar? But of course in my case, Lady Stapleton, it was a natural effect of my condition and passed off within a month or two. So did the dreadful tiredness. I do hate being tired during the day. But in your case such symptoms are unnatural and should be confided to a physician. It is unmannerly of me to press you on the issue, however, when I am not a relative or even a particularly close acquaintance. I am a concerned acquaintance, though."

"Thank you," Lady Stapleton said. "You are kind."

The conversation moved on to a more general discussion of health and by natural progressions through the weather and Christmas and some of the more attractive shops on Oxford Street.

Edgar did not participate. His discomfort had turned to something more extreme, though he was trying to tell himself not to be so foolish. She was his age, she had once told him. As far as he knew, she had never had children, though she had been married for a number of years and had admitted to numerous lovers since her widowhood. Was it possible for a woman to have a child at the age of six-and-thirty? Foolish question. Of course it was possible. He knew women who had borne children at an even more advanced age. But a first child? Was it possible? After years of barrenness or else years of careful guarding against such a thing?

It surely was not possible. How she would laugh at him if she knew the suspicions that were rushing their course through his brain. Just because Cora had compared the early months of her pregnancies with Lady Stapleton's illness. What an absurdity for him to take the extra step of making the direct comparison.

But then Cora did not know—and in her innocence would not even suspect—that the lady had had a lover just over a month ago. Neither would her aunt suspect it.

"And what are your plans for Christmas, Mr. Downes?" Mrs. Cross asked him suddenly.

He stared at her blankly for a moment. "I will be going down to Mobley Abbey, ma'am, to spend the holiday with my father," he said.

"There will be quite a house party there," Cora said. "Francis and I and the children will be going, of course, and several of our friends. I am looking forward to it excessively."

"And Mr. Downes's future bride will be there, Letty," Lady Stapleton said, looking at Edgar as she spoke. "Did you not know that he has come to town for the express purpose of choosing a bride from the *ton*? He is to take her to Mobley

Abbey to present her to his father for approval. A Christmas bride. Is that not romantic?" She made it sound anything but.

This time Edgar really did flush.

"Now you are the one to have embarrassed Mr. Downes, Helena," Mrs. Cross said reproachfully. "But there is nothing to be embarrassed about, sir. I wish you joy of your quest. Any young lady would be fortunate indeed to be your choice."

"Thank you, ma'am," he said and noticed with some relief that Cora was getting to her feet to take her leave. He stood up and the other two ladies did likewise. He made his bow to them and then waited while Cora thought of something else she must tell Mrs. Cross before they left. He looked closely at Lady Stapleton, who smiled back at him.

Are you with child? he wanted to blurt out. But it was a ridiculous notion. Bizarre. She was a thirty-six-year-old widow. With whom he happened to have had sexual relations—twice—just over a month before. And now she was suffering from morning sickness and unusual tiredness and fainting spells when she tried to push on with her usual daily activities. And she was unwilling to see a physician.

He felt dizzy himself for a moment.

He could not imagine a worse disaster. It could not possibly be. But what other explanation could there be? Morning sickness. Tiredness. Even he was aware of those two symptoms as very characteristic of pregnancy in its early stages.

He followed his sister downstairs with some longing for the fresh air beyond the front door—even if it was chilly, damp, windblown air. He had to think. He had to convince himself of his own foolishness. But was it more foolish to think that it might be or to imagine that it could not possibly be?

Was she pregnant?

By him?

Chapter 8

Helena had decided to stay in town over Christmas. After a few days of suppressed terror and near panic, she calmed down sufficiently to decide that she had to plan carefully, but that there was no immediate hurry. She was a little over one month pregnant. Soon the nausea and the tiredness would pass off. Her condition would not be evident for a few months yet. She need not dash off somewhere in a blind panic. There was time to think and to plan.

Soon most of her acquaintances would disperse to their various country estates for the holiday. Some would remain and others would arrive, but the people she most wanted to be rid of would be gone. Edgar Downes would be gone and so would that bold, curiously appealing sister of his and her family. They were taking a number of other people with them to Mobley Abbey—the Carews, the Bridgwaters, the Thornhills, the Greenwalds. And very probably the Graingers, too.

She felt sorry for Fanny Grainger, though it was not normally in her nature to feel sorry for people. Perhaps she pitied the girl because she was reminded of herself at that age, or a little younger. So unhappy and fatalistic. So very obedient. Like a lamb to the slaughter, to use the old cliché. Fanny would be quite suffocated by Edgar Downes.

She forced herself to attend most of the social functions to which she was invited—and she was invited everywhere—while she was careful to curtail her morning activities and to keep most of her afternoons free so that she might rest. She succeeded in feeling and looking a little better than she had with the result that her aunt, though not quite satisfied, stopped pressing her to consult a physician.

Sooner or later, Helena thought, she was going to have to see a doctor. How embarrassing that was going to be. But she would think of it when the time came—after Christmas. By then she would have decided where to go and exactly what to do with the child. Perhaps she would keep it, she thought sometimes, and live somewhere on the Continent with it, thumbing her nose at public opinion. Probably she would give it up to a carefully chosen family and disappear from its life. She was not worthy of being a mother.

She took care to think of the child as *it*. Terror could return in a hurry when she began to think of its personhood and to wonder about its gender and appearance. Would it be a boy who would look like *him*? She would shake off the speculations. She could not imagine a real live child, born of her own body, in helpless need of her arms and her breasts and her love.

She was incapable of love. She knew nothing of nurturing.

Oh, yes, she rather thought she would give up the child. *It*.

She saw Edgar Downes frequently. They became very skilled at avoiding each other, at sitting far from each other at dinner and supper tables, at joining different conversational or card-playing groups, at sitting on opposite sides of a room during concerts. They never ignored each other—that might have been as noticeable to a society hungry for something to gossip about as if they had been constantly in each other's pocket. When they did come face to face, they smiled politely and he asked about her health and she assured him that she was quite well, thank you.

They watched each other. Not with their eyes—a strange notion. They were *aware* of each other. She was sure it worked both ways. She felt that he watched her, though whenever she glanced at him to confirm the feeling, she was almost always wrong. When he asked about her health, she sensed that the question was not a mere courtesy. For days after he had carried her to her bed and then called on her with his sister, she had half expected him to return with a physician. It was just the sort of thing she would expect him to do—take charge, impose his will upon someone who had no wish to be beholden to him in any way, do what he thought was best regardless of her feelings.

And she was always aware of him. She could not rid herself of the obsession and in the end stopped trying. Soon he would be gone and she would not have daily reminders of him. Within eight months his child would be gone—from her womb and from her life. She would have her own life, her own particular hell, back again.

She thought of him constantly—not sexual thoughts. They would have been understandable and not particularly disturbing. She kept thinking of him escorting her home, his arm solid and steady beneath her own, his pace reduced to fit hers. She kept thinking of him lifting her into his arms and carrying her into the house and up two flights of stairs as if she weighed no more than a feather. She kept thinking of his near-silence when he had called with Lady Francis, of that frowning, intent look with which he had regarded her, as if he were genuinely worried about her health. She kept imagining herself leaning into his strength, abandoning all the burdens of her life to him, letting him deal with them for her. She kept thinking of herself sleeping in his arms. Just sleeping—nothing else. Total relaxation and oblivion. Safety. Peace.

She hated the feeling. She hated the weakness of her thoughts. And so she hated him even as she was obsessed by him.

By the middle of December she was impatient for his departure. He had come to choose a bride. He had chosen her long ago. Let him take her to his father, then, and begin a grand Christmas celebration. She could not understand why he delayed. She resented the delay. She wanted to be free of him.

She wanted desperately to be free. And she laughed contemptuously to herself whenever she caught herself in the thought. Had she forgotten that there would never be freedom, either in this life or the next? Had hope somehow been reborn in her even as she knew that despair was the only end of any hope? She had dulled her sensibilities to reality before that dreadful evening when desperate need had tempted her to seduce Edgar Downes. Perhaps, she sometimes thought, she would have fought the temptation harder if she had had even an inkling of the fact that he would not be easily forgotten. That he would impregnate her.

She waited with mingled patience and impatience for him to be gone.

Edgar had always thought of himself as a decisive man, both by nature and training. He had never been a procrastinator—until now.

He delayed in making his intentions clear to Miss Grainger and her parents. And he delayed in speaking with Lady Stapleton and putting his suspicions into words. As a result, with only two weeks to go until Christmas, he suddenly found himself in a dreadful coil indeed.

He was at a dance at Mrs. Parmeter's—she and her husband were newly arrived in London to take in the Christmas parties. He had just finished dancing a set of country dances with the Duchess of Bridgwater and had joined a group that included Sir Webster. The conversation, inevitably he supposed considering the date, centered about Christmas and everyone's plans for the holiday.

"Your father is to entertain quite a large house party at Mobley Abbey, I hear, Mr. Downes," Mrs. Parmeter said, smiling at him with marked condescension. As a new arrival she was not as accustomed as most of her other guests to finding herself entertaining a mere merchant.

"Yes, indeed, ma'am," he said. "He is delighted that there will be such a large number, children included. He is passionately fond of children."

Sir Webster was coughing against the back of his hand and shifting his weight from foot to foot. "I must commend you on the number of guests with whom you have filled your drawing room, ma'am," he said.

"Yes." Mrs. Parmeter smiled graciously and vaguely. "And Sir Webster was telling us that he and his lady and *Miss Grainger* are to be among the guests, Mr. Downes," she said, placing particular emphasis on the one name. She raised her eyebrows archly. "Is there to be an interesting announcement during Christmas, sir?"

"Oh, I say." Sir Webster sounded suitably mortified. "I was merely saying, ma'am—"

"I am certainly hoping that Sir Webster and Lady Grainger and their daughter will be among my father's guests," Edgar said, aghast at what he was being forced into—as a businessman he had perfected the art of avoiding being maneuvered into anything he had not pondered and decided for himself. At least he had the sense to leave the woman's final question alone.

"I am sure you are, sir," Mrs. Parmeter said. "You know, I suppose, that Lady Grainger's father is Baron Suffield?"

"Yes, indeed, ma'am," Edgar said.

She turned her conversation on other members of the group and soon enough Edgar found himself with Sir Webster, a little apart from the rest of them.

"I say—" that gentleman began. "Mrs. Parmeter totally misunderstood me, you know. I was merely saying—" But he could not seem to remember what it was he had been merely saying.

Perhaps, Edgar thought, it was as well to have his hand forced. He had only two weeks left in which to keep his promise. There was no one more suitable—or more available—than Miss Grainger. There was that young man of hers, of course—he should have found a way of dealing with that problem by now. And there was that other problem, too—but no. She appeared to have recovered from her indisposition whatever it had been, though she still seemed paler than he remembered her to have looked. He could not do better than Miss Grainger—not in the time allowed at least. And perhaps he had carried the courtship rather too far to back off now without humiliating the girl and her family. Certainly the father seemed to expect a declaration.

"But my father would be delighted to entertain you and your wife and daughter at Mobley, sir," Edgar said, releasing the man from his well-deserved embarrassment. "And my sister and I would be delighted, too, if you would join us and other of our friends there for Christmas. If you have no other plans, that is. I realize that this is rather short notice."

"No," Sir Webster said quickly, "we have no other plans, sir. We were thinking of staying in town to enjoy the festivities. That was our plan when we came here. We were undecided whether to stay too for the Season. Fanny would enjoy it and it is time to bring her out, I suppose. It is difficult to part with a daughter, Mr. Downes. Very difficult. One wants all that is the best for her. We will accept your gracious invitation, sir. Thank you. And we will decide later about the Season."

There would be no Season if he came up to scratch, Edgar understood. And probably no Season if he did not either. The Graingers were said to be too poor to afford such an expense. But he was not going to pick up the cue this time. He merely smiled and bowed and informed Sir Webster that Cora would write to their father tomorrow.

His father would read eagerly between the lines of that particular letter, he thought. Or perhaps not between the lines either. Cora would surely inform him that Miss Grainger was the one, that he might prepare to meet his future daughter-in-law within the fortnight.

Edgar felt half robbed of breath. But it was a deed that must be done. It was time to stop dragging his feet. Young Jack Sperling could not be helped. This was the real world. And the girl's age could not be helped. Young ladies were married to older men all the time. He would be kind to her and generous to her. He would treat her with affection. So would his father and Cora. She would be taken to the bosom of their family with enthusiasm, he did not doubt. She would learn to settle to a marriage that could be no worse than thousands of marriages that were contracted every year. And he would settle, too. He would enjoy having children of his own. Like his father, he was fond of children.

Children of his own. There—that thought again. That nagging suspicion. His eyes found out Lady Stapleton. She was at the other side of the room—without ever looking at each other for any length of time, they always seemed to maneuver matters so—talking and laughing with Mr. Parmeter and the Earl of Thornhill. She was wearing the scarlet gown she had worn that first night—the one with all the tiny buttons down the back. It must have taken him all of five minutes . . .

She looked healthy enough and cheerful enough. She looked pale. She did not look as if she felt nauseated. But this was the evening rather than the morning. Besides, Cora had said that the feeling passed after a couple of months. It was two months since . . . Well, it was two months. She did not look larger. But it was only two months.

It could not possibly be. Beautiful and alluring as she looked, it was a mature beauty and a mature allure. But she was only six-and-thirty. She was still in her fertile years. She had never had a child before—at least he did not believe so. Why would she conceive now? But why not?

Such conflicting thoughts had teemed in his head for the past two weeks. They had woven themselves into his dreams—when he had been able to sleep. They had kept him awake.

He caught her eye across the room, something that rarely happened. But instead of looking away from each other, both continued to look as if daring the other to be the first to lose courage. She raised one mocking eyebrow.

He despised indecisiveness. If there was one single factor that could keep a man from success in the business world, he had always found, it was just that—being indecisive, allowing misplaced caution and unformed worries to hold one back from action that one knew must be taken. He knew he must talk with her. And time was running out. He should already have left for Mobley. He must do so within the next few days.

He must talk to Lady Stapleton first. He did not want to—he would do almost anything to get out of doing so if he could. But he could not. Not if he was to know any peace of mind over Christmas. He walked across the center of the drawing room, empty now between sets, and she smiled that smile of hers to see him come. She did not turn away or even look away from him.

"Ma'am?" He bowed to her. "May I have the honor of dancing the next set with you?"

"But of course, Mr. Downes," she said. That low velvet voice of hers always jolted him, no matter how often he heard it. "It is a waltz, and I know you perform the steps well." She set her hand in his. It was quite cold.

"And how do you do, ma'am?" he asked her when they had taken their positions on the floor and waited for the music to begin.

"Very well, thank you, Mr. Downes." Her perfume brought back memories.

There was no dodging around it, he decided as the pianist began playing and he set his hand at the back of her waist and took her other in his own. And so he simply asked the question.

"Are you with child?" His voice was so low that he was not sure the sound of it would carry to her ears.

Clearly it did. She mastered her surprise almost instantly and smiled with brutal contempt. "You must think yourself one devil of a fine lover, Mr. Downes," she said. "Is it the factor by which you measure your success? Have you peopled Bristol with bastard children?"

But not quite instantly enough. For the merest fraction of a second—had he not been looking for it he would certainly have missed it—there had been something other than contempt in her eyes. There had been fright, panic.

"No," he said. "But I believe I have got you with child." Now that the words were out, now that he had seen that fleeting reaction, he felt curiously calm. Almost cold.

"Do you?" she said. "And do you realize how absurd your assumption is, sir? Do you know how old I am?"

"You told me once," he said. "I do not believe you are past your childbearing years. Are you?"

"You are impertinent, sir," she said. "You dare ask such a question of a lady, of a virtual stranger?"

"A stranger whom I bedded two months ago," he said. "One who is to bear my child seven months from now, if I am not much mistaken."

She smiled at him—a bright social smile, as much for the

benefit of the other dancers and watchers as for his, he guessed. "You, Mr. Downes," she said, "may go to hell."

"But I notice," he said, "that you have not said no, it is not true. I notice such things, ma'am. I have been and still am a lawyer. Is it that you are afraid to lie? Let me hear it. Yes or no. Are you with child?"

"But I am not on the witness stand, Mr. Downes," she said. "I do not have to answer your questions. And I scorn to react to your charge that I am afraid to answer. I will not answer. I choose not to."

"Have you seen a physician?" he asked her.

She looked into his eyes and smiled. "You are a divine waltzer, Mr. Downes," she said. "I believe it is because you are so large. One instinctively trusts your lead."

"Do you still suffer from morning sickness?" he asked.

"Of course," she said, "it is not just your size, is it? One cannot imagine enjoying a waltz with an ox. You have a superior sense of rhythm." Her smile turned wicked.

"I shall find out for myself tomorrow," he said. "You once invited me to escort you to one of the galleries. I accept. Tomorrow morning will be the time. We have arranged it this evening. You may tell Mrs. Cross that if you will. If you will not, I will tell her when I come for you that I have come to discuss your pregnancy."

"Damn you, Mr. Downes," she said sharply. "You have the manners of an ox even if not the dancing skills of one."

"Tomorrow morning," he said. "And if you have any idea of bringing your aunt with you, be warned that we will have our frank talk anyway. I assume she does not know?"

"Damn you to hell," she said.

"Since we are dancing for pleasure," he said, "we might as well concentrate on our enjoyment in silence for the rest of the set. I believe we have nothing further to say to each other until tomorrow."

"How your underlings must hate you," she said. "I am not your underling, Mr. Downes. I will not be overborne by you. And I will not be blackmailed by you."

"Will you not?" he said. "You will tell Mrs. Cross the truth, then, and have that servant of yours refuse me admittance tomorrow morning? I believe I might enjoy pitting my strength against his."

"Damn you," she said again. "Damn you. Damn you."

Neither of them spoke after that. When the music drew to an end, he escorted her to her aunt, stayed to exchange civilities with that lady for a few minutes, and then took himself off to the other side of the room.

He felt rather as if he had been tossed into the air by that ox she had spoken of and then trodden into the ground by it after landing. It was true, then. He could no longer lull himself with the conviction that his suspicions were absurd. She had not admitted the truth, but the very absence of such an admission was confirmation enough.

She was with child. By him. He felt as dizzy, as disoriented, as if the idea had only now been planted in his brain.

What the devil were they going to do?

And why the devil did he need to pose that question to himself?

She damned him to hell and back throughout a sleepless night. She broke a favorite trinket dish when she picked it up from her dressing table and hurled it against the door. She considered calling his bluff and telling her aunt the truth, though she had hoped to go away somewhere alone so that no one need know, and then instructing Hobbes to deny him entry.

But he would come tomorrow morning even if she told her aunt and even if Hobbes tried to prevent him. She had great faith in Hobbes's strength and determination, but she had a nasty feeling that neither would prevail against Edgar Downes. He would come and drag the truth from her and proceed to take charge of the situation no matter what she did.

She would not dance to his tune. Oh, she would not. She did not doubt that he would plan everything down to the smallest detail. She did not doubt that he would find her a safe and comfortable nest in which to hide during the remainder of her confinement and that he would find the child a respectable home afterward. He would do it all with professional efficiency and confidentiality. No one would ever suspect the truth. No one would ever know that the two of them had been more to each other than casual social acquaintances. And he would pay for everything. She did not doubt that either. Every bill would be sent to him.

She would not allow it to happen. She would shout the truth from the rooftops before she would allow him to protect her reputation and her safety. She would keep her child and take it with her wherever she went rather than allow him neatly to hide its very existence.

And yet, she thought, mocking herself, she did not even have the courage to tell her aunt. She would go out with him tomorrow morning, two acquaintances visiting a gallery together, a perfectly respectable thing to do, and she would allow herself to be browbeaten.

Never!

She would fight Edgar Downes to the death if necessary. The melodramatic thought had her lip curling in scorn again.

She mentioned to her aunt at the breakfast table that Mr. Downes would be calling later to escort her to the Royal Academy. He had mentioned wanting to go there while they had danced the evening before and she had commented that it was one of her favorite places. And so he had asked to escort her there this morning.

"I have promised to show him all the best paintings," she said.

Mrs. Cross looked closely at her. "Are you feeling well enough, Helena?" she asked. "I have become so accustomed to your staying at home in the mornings that I have arranged to go out myself."

"Splendid," Helena said. "You are going shopping?"

"With a few other ladies," Mrs. Cross said. "Will you mind?"

"I hardly need a chaperone at my age, Letty," Helena said. "I believe Mr. Downes is a trustworthy escort."

"Absolutely," her aunt agreed. "He is an exceedingly pleasant man. I was quite sharp with Mrs. Parmeter last evening when she remarked on his background as if she expected all of us to begin to tear him apart. Mr. Downes is more the gentleman than many born to the rank, I told her. I believe he has a soft spot for you, Helena. It is a shame that as his father's only son he feels duty bound to marry a young lady so that he may set up his nursery and get an heir for that estate near Bristol. The Grainger girl will not suit him, though she is pretty and has a sweet enough nature. She has not had the time or opportunity to develop enough character."

"And I have?" Helena smiled. "You think he would be better off with me, Letty? Poor Mr. Downes."

"You would lead him a merry dance, I daresay," Mrs. Cross said. "But I believe he would be equal to the task. However, he must choose a young lady."

"How lowering," Helena said with a laugh. "But I would not be young again for a million pounds, Letty. I shudder to remember the girl I was."

She would gain one advantage over Mr. Edgar Downes this morning at least, she thought while she began to talk about other things with her aunt. She would confront him on home ground. Her aunt was going out for the morning. That would mean that she and Mr. Downes need not leave the house. She would not have to be smilingly polite lest other people in the streets or at the gallery take note. She could shout and scream and throw things to her heart's content. She could use whatever language suited her mood.

Only one thing she seemed incapable of doing—at least she had been last night. She could not seem to lie to Edgar Downes. She could get rid of him in a moment if only she could do that. But she scorned to lie. She would withhold the truth if she could, but she would not lie.

She went upstairs after breakfast to change her dress and have her hair restyled. She wanted to look and feel her very best before it came time to cope with her visitor.

She waited for an hour in the drawing room before he came. She had instructed Hobbes to show him up when he arrived.

Chapter 9

Edgar was rather surprised to be admitted to her house without question. The manservant, his face quite impassive, led the way upstairs, knocked on the drawing room door, opened it, and announced him.

She was there alone, standing by the fireplace, looking remarkably handsome in a dark green morning gown of simple, classic design. Her chin was lifted proudly. She was unsmiling, the customary mocking expression absent from her face. She was not ready for the outdoors.

"Thank you, Hobbes," she said. "Good morning, Mr. Downes."

Her face was pale. There were shadows beneath her eyes. Perhaps, he thought, she had slept as little as he. The thought that this proud, elegant woman was pregnant with his child was still dizzying. It still threatened to rob him of breath.

"I suppose it was too much to expect," he said, "that you would not somehow twist the situation to impose some sort of command over it. We are not to view portraits and landscapes?"

"Not today or any other day, Mr. Downes," she said. "Not together at least. My aunt is from home. I would have had Hobbes deny you admittance but you would have made a scene. You are so ungenteel. If you have something to say that is more sensible than what you were saying last evening, please say it and then leave. I have other plans."

He could not help but admire her coolness even while he was irritated by it. Most women in her situation would be distraught and clinging and demanding to know his intentions.

"Thank you for offering," he said, walking farther into the room after removing his greatcoat—the servant had not offered to take it downstairs—and tossing it onto a chair. "I believe I will sit down. But do have a seat yourself, ma'am. I am gentleman enough to know that I may not sit until you do."

"You are impertinent, Mr. Downes," she said.

"But then I am also, of course," he said, gesturing toward the chair closest to her, "quite bourgeois, ma'am."

She sat and so did he. She was furious, he saw, though she would, of course, scorn to glare. She sat with her back ramrod straight and her jaw set in a hard line.

"You are with child," he said.

She said nothing.

"It is a reality that will not go away," he said. It had taken the whole of a sleepless night finally to admit that to himself. "It must be dealt with."

"Nothing in my life will be dealt with by you, Mr. Downes," she said. "I deal with my own problems, thank you very much. I believe this visit is at an end."

"I believe, ma'am," he said, "it is *our* problem."

"No!" Her nostrils flared and both her hands curled into fists in her lap. "You will not treat this as a piece of business, Mr. Downes, to be dealt with coldly and efficiently and then forgotten about. I will not have a quiet hideaway found for me or a discreet midwife. I will not have a decent, respectable home found for the child so that I may return to my usual life with no one the wiser. You may be expert at dominating your subordinates with that confident, commanding air of yours. You will not dominate me."

Good Lord!

He leaned back in his chair, set his elbows on the arms, and steepled his fingers beneath his chin. He stared at her for a long time before speaking.

"You realize, I suppose," he said at last, "what you have admitted to me." If there had been one thread of hope left in him, it was gone. On the whole, he was glad of it. He liked to have issues crystal clear in his mind.

There was a flush of color to her cheeks. But her expression did not change. She did not speak.

"You have misunderstood my character," he said. "There will be no hideaway, no decent home for the child away from his mother, no resumption of your old way of life, no sweeping of anything under the carpet. We will marry, of course."

Her head snapped back rather as if he had punched her on the chin. Her eyes widened and her eyebrows shot up. And then she laughed.

"Marry!" she said. "We will marry? You jest, sir, of course."

"I do not jest," he said. "Of course."

"Mr. Downes." All the old mockery was back in her face. No, it was more than mockery—it was open contempt. "Do you seriously imagine that *I* would marry *you*? You are presumptuous, sir. I bid you a good morning." She was on her feet.

"Sit down," he told her quietly and sat where he was, engaging in a silent battle of wills with her. He never lost such battles. This time, after a full minute of tension, he tacitly agreed to accept a compromise when she turned and crossed the room to the window. She stood with her back to him, looking out. He remained seated.

"I thank you for your gracious offer, Mr. Downes," she said, "but my answer is no. There. You have done the decent thing and I have been civil. We are even. Please leave now."

"We will marry by special license before going down to Mobley Abbey for Christmas," he said.

She laughed again. "Your Christmas bride," she said. "You are determined to have her one way or another, then? But have you not already invited Miss Grainger in that capacity? Do you have ambitions to set up a harem, Mr. Downes?"

He dared not think of that invitation to the Graingers. Not yet. Experience had taught him that only one sticky problem could be dealt with at a time. He was dealing with this one now.

"Better still," he said, "we could take the license with us and marry there. It would please my father."

"Your father would be quite ecstatic," she said, "to find that you had brought home a bride as old as yourself. He wants grandchildren, I do not doubt."

"And that is exactly what he will have, ma'am," he said.

He could see from the hunching of her shoulders that she had only just realized her mistake. Although she must have known for a lot longer than he, although she was carrying the child in her own womb, he supposed that the truth must seem as unreal to her as it did to him.

"It will be easier if you accept reality," he said. "If we both do. We had our pleasure of each other two months ago without a thought to the possible consequences. But there have been consequences. They are in the form of an innocent child who does not deserve the stigma of bastardy. We have created him or her. It is our duty to give him parents who are married to each other and to nurture him to the best of our ability. We have become rather unimportant as individuals, Lady Stapleton. There is someone else to whose whole life this issue is quite central—and yet that person is at the mercy of what is happening in this room this morning."

"Damn you," she said.

"Which would you prefer?" he asked her briskly. "To marry here or at Mobley? The choice is yours."

"How clever you are, Mr. Downes." She turned to look at him. "Giving the illusion of freedom of choice when you have me tied hand and foot and gagged, too. I will make no choice. I have not even said I will marry you. In my world, you know—it may be different with people of your class—a woman has to say that she does or that she will before her marriage can be declared valid. So I do still have some freedom, you see."

He got to his feet and walked toward her. But she held up both hands as he drew close.

"No," she said. "That is far enough. You are too tall and too large, Mr. Downes. I hate large men."

"Because you are afraid you will not have total mastery over them?" he said.

"For exactly that reason." Her voice was sharp. "I made a mistake two months ago. I rarely make mistakes. I chose the wrong man. You are too—too *big.* You suffocate me. Go away. I have been remarkably civil to you this morning. I can become ferociously uncivil when aroused. Go away." Her breathing was ragged. She was agitated.

"I am not going to hurt you," he told her. "I am not going to touch you against your will." He clasped his hands behind his back.

She laughed. "Are those the sentiments of an ardent bridegroom, Mr. Downes?" she said. "Do you speak only in the present tense or do your words have a more universal meaning? You would never touch me against my will? You would be facing an arid, celibate life, sir, unless you would take your ease with mistresses."

"I have a strong belief in marital fidelity," he said.

"How bourgeois!" She laughed again.

"Yes."

"Mr. Downes." Her arms dropped to her sides. Both the agitation and the contempt were gone from her face and she looked at him more earnestly than she had ever done before. Her face was pale again. "I cannot marry you. I cannot be a wife. I cannot be a mother."

He searched her eyes but they gave nothing away. They never did. This woman hid very effectively behind her many masks, he realized suddenly. He did not know her at all, even though he had had thorough sexual knowledge of her body.

"Why not?" he asked.

"Because." She smiled the old smile. "Because, Mr. Downes. Because."

"And yet," he said, "you are to be a mother whether you wish it or not. The deed is done and cannot be undone."

She closed her eyes and looked as if she were about to sway on her feet. But she mastered herself and opened her eyes again. "I will deal with it," she said. "I cannot keep the child. I cannot marry you. I would destroy both of you. Believe me, Mr. Downes. I speak the truth."

He frowned, trying to read her eyes again. But there were no depths to them. They were quite unreadable. "Who hurt you?" he asked her. He remembered asking her the question before.

She laughed. "No one," she said. "Absolutely no one, sir."

"I am going to be your husband," he said. "I would hope to be your companion and even your friend as well. There may be many years of life ahead for us."

"You are not going to be talked out of this, are you?" she said. "You are not going to take no for an answer. Are you?"

He shook his head.

"Well, then." Her head went back and both her eyes and her lips mocked him. "Behold your Christmas bride, Mr. Downes. It is a Christmas and a bride that you will come to regret, but we all choose our own personal hells with our eyes wide open, I have found. And it will happen at Mobley. I would see the ecstasy in your father's eyes as we tie the eternal knot." There was harsh bitterness in her voice.

He inclined his head to her. "I do not believe I could ever regret doing the right thing, ma'am," he said. "And before you can tell me how bourgeois a sentiment that is, let me forestall you. I believe we bourgeoisie have a firmer, less cynical commitment to decency and honor than some of the gentry and aristocracy. Though I daresay that like all generalizations there are almost as many exceptions as there are adherents to the rule."

"I will not allow you to dominate me," she said.

"I would not wish to dominate a wife," he told her.

"Or to touch me."

"As you wish," he said.

"I will make you burn for me, Edgar," she said. "But I will not let you touch me."

"Perhaps," he said.

Her lip curled. "I cannot make you quarrel, can I?" she said. "I would love to have a flaming row with you, Mr. Downes. It is your power over me, perhaps, that you will not allow it."

"Perhaps," he agreed.

"Do you realize how frustrating it is," she asked him, "to quarrel with someone who will not quarrel back?"

"Probably as frustrating," he said, "as it is going to be to burn for you when you refuse to burn for me."

She smiled slowly at him. "I believe," she said, "that if I did not resent and hate you so much, Mr. Downes, I might almost like you."

He did not hate her or particularly resent her. He did not like the situation in which he found himself, but in all fairness he could not foist the blame entirely on her. It took two to create a child, and neither of them had been reluctant to engage in the activity that had left her pregnant. He did not like her. She was bitter and sharp-tongued and did nothing to hide her contempt for his origins. But there was something about her that excited him. There was her sexual allure, of course. He had no doubt that his frustrations would be very real indeed if she meant what she said. But it was not just a sexual thing. There was something challenging, stimulating about her. She would not be easy to manage, but he was not sure he wanted to manage her. She would never be a comfortable companion, but then comfort in companionship could become tedious. Life with her would never be tedious.

"Have I silenced you at last?" she asked. "Are you wounded? Are you struggling not to humiliate yourself by confessing that you *love* me?"

"I do not love you," he said quietly. "But you are to be my wife and to bear my child. I will try to respect and like you, ma'am. I will try to feel an affection for you. It will not be impossible, perhaps. We are to share a child. I will certainly love our child, as will you. We will have that to bring us together."

"Why, Mr. Downes," she said, "I do believe there is a streak of the romantic in you after all."

The door opened behind them.

"Oh," Mrs. Cross said, startled. "Mr. Downes is here with you. I am so sorry, Helena. I assumed you were alone. I wondered why you were back so soon."

"You need not leave, Aunt," Lady Stapleton said, moving past Edgar to take Mrs. Cross by the arm. She was smiling when she turned back to him. "You must make your curtsy to Mr. Downes, who is now my affianced husband. We are to marry at Mobley Abbey before Christmas."

Mrs. Cross's face was the picture of astonishment. She almost gaped at Edgar. He bowed to her.

"I have offered for Lady Stapleton's hand, ma'am," he told her, "and she has done me the great honor of accepting me."

"Oh, come now, Mr. Downes." Lady Stapleton sounded amused. "This is my aunt you are talking to. The truth is, Letty, that I am two months with child. Edgar and I became too—*ardent* one night before your return from the country and having learned of the consequences of that night, he has rushed here to make amends. He is going to make an honest woman of me. Wish us joy."

Mrs. Cross appeared speechless for a few moments. "I do," she said finally. "Oh, I do indeed. Pardon me, Helena, Mr. Downes, but I do not know quite what to say. I do wish you joy."

"Of course you do," Lady Stapleton said. "You commented just this morning, did you not, that Mr. Downes had a soft spot for me." Her eyes mocked him even as her aunt flushed and looked mortified. "It appears you were right."

"Ma'am." Edgar addressed himself to Mrs. Cross, ignoring the bitter levity of his betrothed's tone. "We will be marrying by special license at Mobley Abbey, as Lady Stapleton mentioned. My father and my sister will be in attendance, as well as a number of our friends. I would be honored if you would be there, too, and would remain to spend Christmas with us. My father would be honored."

"How kind of you, sir." The lady was recovering some of her composure. "How very kind. I would, of course, like to be at Helena's wedding. And I have no other plans for the holiday."

Edgar looked at Lady Stapleton. "There will perhaps be time to invite other members of your family or other particular friends if you wish," he said. "Is there anyone?"

"No," she said. "This is no grand wedding celebration we are planning, Edgar. This is a marriage of necessity."

"Your stepson is at Brookhurst only thirty miles from Mobley, is he not?" he said. "Perhaps—"

Her face became a mask of some strong emotion—horror, terror, revulsion, he could not tell which.

"No!" she said icily. "I said no, Mr. Downes. No! I will

have my aunt with me. She will be family enough. She is the only relative I wish to acknowledge. But yes, you must come, Letty. I will not be able to do this without you. I do not wish to do it at all, but Mr. Downes has been his usual obnoxious, domineering self. I shall lead him a merry dance, as you said I would if I ever married him, but he has been warned and has remained obdurate. On his own head be it, then. But you must certainly come to Mobley with me."

"Have you offered Mr. Downes a cup of tea, Helena?" her aunt asked, looking about her at the empty tables.

"No, I have not," her niece said. "I have been trying to get rid of him since he set foot inside the door. He will not leave."

"Helena!" her aunt said, looking mortified again. "Mr. Downes, do let me send for some tea or coffee."

"Thank you, ma'am." He smiled. "But I have other business to attend to. I shall see you both in my sister's drawing room this evening? I shall have the announcement made there and put in tomorrow morning's papers. Good day to you, Mrs. Cross. And to you, Lady Stapleton." He bowed to each of them as he retrieved his greatcoat.

"I must remember," Lady Stapleton said, "to start offering you tea whenever I set eyes on you, Edgar. It seems the only sure way to be rid of you."

He smiled at her as he let himself out of the room, feeling unexpectedly amused. For a mere moment there seemed to be an answering gleam in her own eyes.

His betrothed. Soon to be his wife. The mother of his child. He shook his head as he descended the stairs in an effort to clear it of that dizziness again.

Edgar was glad to get out again during the afternoon. He had arrived home to find both Cora and Francis there, having just returned from their usual morning outing with their children.

"Edgar," Cora had said, smiling brightly, "have you concluded all your business? Are you going to be ready to leave for Mobley tomorrow after tonight's farewell party? We met Lady Grainger and Miss Grainger in the park, did we not,

Francis? They are extremely gratified to have been invited to Mobley. I have written to Papa to tell him—"

Cora's monologues could sometimes continue for a considerable length of time. Edgar had cut her off.

"Lady Stapleton and Mrs. Cross will be coming, too," he had told her and Francis. Francis's eyebrows had gone up.

"Are they?" Cora had said. "Oh. How splendid. We will be a merry house party. Papa will—"

"I will be marrying Lady Stapleton at Mobley before Christmas," Edgar had announced.

For once Cora had been speechless—and inelegantly open-mouthed. Lord Francis's eyebrows had remained elevated.

There had been no point in mincing matters. It was rather too late for that. "She is two months with child," he had said. "With my child, that is. We will be marrying."

Francis had shaken his hand and congratulated him and said all that was proper. Cora had been first speechless and then garrulous. By the time Edgar escaped the house, she had talked herself into believing that she, that he, that Francis, that everyone concerned and unconcerned must be blissfully happy with the betrothal. Lady Stapleton would be *just* the bride for Edgar, Cora had declared. Lady Stapleton would not allow herself to be swept along by the power of his character, and he would be the happier for it. Cora had never been so pleased by anything in her life, and Papa would be deliriously happy. Francis was called upon to corroborate these chuckle-headed notions.

"I believe it might well turn into a good match, my love," he had said less effusively than she, but with apparent sincerity. "I cannot imagine Edgar being satisfied with anything less. And the lady certainly has character—and beauty."

But of course Cora had issued the reminder Edgar had not needed before he made his escape.

"Oh, Edgar!" Her eyes had grown as wide as saucers and her hand had flown to her mouth and collided with it with a painful-sounding slap. "Whatever are you going to do about Fanny Grainger? You have all but *offered* for her. And she is coming to *Mobley*."

Edgar had no idea what he was going to do about Fanny

Grainger, apart from the fact that he was not going to marry her. He had not offered for her, but he had come uncomfortably close. And last evening he had even taken the all-but-final step of inviting her and her parents to spend Christmas at Mobley. Everyone of course took for granted that he had invited her there for only one reason.

He liked the girl, even though he had not wished to marry her. The last thing he wanted to do was to leave her publicly humiliated. But it seemed that that was what he was fated to do. Unless . . .

It was purely by chance—entirely, amazingly coincidental—that as he was walking along Oxford Street he caught a glimpse of the young man she had met on almost the exact same spot a few weeks ago when Edgar had come upon them. Jack Sperling was hurrying along, his head down, clearly intent on getting where he was going in as little time as possible. One could understand why. The wind cut down the street rather like a knife.

Edgar stepped to one side to impede his progress. Sperling looked up, startled. "I do beg your pardon," he said before frowning and looking distinctly unfriendly. "Oh, you," he added.

"Good afternoon." Edgar touched the brim of his beaver hat and did what it was not in his nature to do—he acted on the spur of the moment. "Mr. Sperling, is it not?"

"I am in a hurry," the young man said ungraciously.

"I wonder if I could persuade you not to be?" Edgar said.

Unfriendliness turned to open hostility. "Oh, you need not fear that your territory is going to be poached upon," he said. "She has sent me a letter this morning and has explained that it will be the last. *She* will not see me again, and *I* will not see her. We both have some sense of honor. Sir," he added, making the word sound like an insult.

"I really must persuade you not to be in a hurry," Edgar said. "I need to talk to you."

"I have nothing to say to you," Jack Sperling said. "Except this. If you once mistreat her and if I ever hear of it, then you had better learn to watch your back." His voice shook.

"It is dashed cold out here," Edgar said, shivering. "That

coffee shop is bound to be a great deal warmer. I believe they serve good coffee. Let us go and have some."

"You may drop dead, sir," the young man said.

"I do hope not," Edgar said. "Let me say this. I am going to be married within the next week or so—but not to Miss Grainger. However, she is to be a guest at my father's home and I feel a certain sense of responsibility for her happiness, since I seem to have been at least partly responsible for her unhappiness. Perhaps you and I could discuss the matter in civil fashion together?"

Jack Sperling stared at him for a few moments, deep suspicion in his face. Then he turned abruptly and strode in the direction of the coffee shop.

They emerged half an hour later and went their separate ways after bidding each other a civil good afternoon. His father was going to have far more than he bargained for this Christmas, Edgar thought, having added yet one more guest to the list.

Chapter 10

The marriage of Lady Stapleton and Edgar Downes was solemnized in the small church at the village of Mobley, two miles from the abbey, six days before Christmas. There was a respectable number of guests in attendance, all the invited house guests having already arrived for the holiday, with the exception of the Graingers and Jack Sperling. A few of Edgar's closer colleagues and some of the elder Mr. Downes's old friends had been invited to come out from Bristol.

Edgar's first intention, which was to marry quickly and quietly in London, had been set aside—partly by Lady Stapleton's choice. There was no point in undue stealth. The truth would soon be known whether they tried to stifle it or not. And neither one of them made any attempt to stifle it. She had announced the truth to her aunt; he had confessed it to his sister and brother-in-law. She had talked about it quite freely and unblushingly during the party at which the announcement of their betrothal was made—just as if there were nothing shameful in such an admission and nothing ungenteel about such a public topic of conversation.

But then Lady Stapleton had always been known for her outspoken ways—and for treading very close to the edge of respectability without ever stepping quite beyond.

Lady Stapleton and Mrs. Cross had shared a carriage to Mobley Abbey with Cora and her youngest child, Annabelle. Lord Francis had ridden with Edgar, one or other of the former's three sons as often as not up before them. The Duke and Duchess of Bridgwater with their infant son, The Earl and Countess of Thornhill, the Marquess and Marchioness of

Carew, the Earl and Countess of Greenwald, all with three children apiece, had left London in a vast cavalcade of carriages a day later.

Before any of them had arrived, wedding preparations had been in full flight at Mobley—Cora had written again to her father. And the elder Mr. Downes had greeted his future daughter-in-law with hearty good humor, regardless of either her age or her condition.

For a few days there was no chance to think about Christmas. The wedding superseded it in importance and excitement value. Edgar had brought home a Christmas bride.

Helena armed herself with scorn—for herself and her own weakness in agreeing to this marriage, for Edgar's foolish sense of honor, for the whole hypocrisy of the joyful nuptials for which everyone seemed to be preparing.

She had prepared herself to find his father coarse and vulgar. She found instead a man who was loud and hearty and who bore an almost uncanny physical resemblance to his son—but who was not vulgar. He lacked Edgar's refinement of speech and manner—he had, of course, had his son educated in the best schools—but he was no less genteel than many gentlemen of her acquaintance. She had prepared herself to find Mobley Abbey a garish and distasteful display of wealth. A great deal of wealth had quite obviously been expended on its restoration so that its ecclesiastical origins were breathtakingly apparent; at the same time as it was a cozy and comfortable private home. Every last detail gave evidence of impeccable taste.

It was disappointing, perhaps, to have little outside of herself on which to turn her scorn. But then she had never deceived herself about the main object of her bitterness and hatred. She had always been fair about that at least.

At first she decided to wear her bronze silk for her wedding. But she had an unaccustomed attack of conscience just the day before. None of these people—not even Edgar—had deserved such a show of vulgarity. She had an ensemble she had bought for a winter fête in Vienna and had worn only once—she had never found a suitable occasion on which to wear it again. She wore it for her wedding—a simple, expertly designed white wool dress with round neck, straight, long sleeves, and straight skirt slightly flaring from its high waistline; a white pelisse and bonnet, both trimmed with white fur; and a white muff and half boots.

At least there was an element of irony in the simple, elegant, eminently respectable attire, she thought, surveying herself in the mirror before leaving for the church. It was a wonderfully virginal outfit.

She did not want to marry. Not Edgar. Anyone but him. But there was no choice, of course. She would not allow the twinge of panic she felt to grow into anything larger. She smiled mockingly at her image. She was a bride—again. She wondered if she would make as much a disaster of this marriage as she had of the first. Undoubtedly she would. But he had been warned. He could never say he had not been.

She had asked the Marquess of Carew if he would be so good as to give her away, though she imagined that that foolish formality might have been dispensed with if she had talked to the vicar. The idea of a thirty-six-year-old widow having to be given away to a new husband was rather absurd. She had asked Lord Carew because he was a mild-mannered, kindly gentleman. Sometimes he reminded her of—no! He did not. He walked with a limp and had even been thoughtful enough to ask her if it would embarrass her. She had assured him it would not. It rather fascinated her to observe that the marchioness, who was many times more beautiful than he was handsome, nevertheless seemed to worship the ground he trod on. But Helena had never denied the existence of romantic and marital love—only of it as a possibility in her own life.

Her bridegroom was dressed very elegantly and fashionably in a dark blue, form-fitting tailed coat, buff pantaloons, white linen, and highly polished Hessians. She looked at him dispassionately as she walked toward him along the aisle of the small old church, oblivious to the guests, who turned their heads to watch her approach, and oblivious to either the marquess's limp or the steadying hand he had laid over her own on his arm. Edgar Downes looked solid and handsome and very much in command of his own life. He looked magnificent.

She experienced a growingly familiar feeling as she stood beside him and the marquess gave her hand into his. The feeling of being small and frail and helpless—and safe and secure. All illusions. His eyes, she saw when she looked up, were steady on hers. She did not want to gaze back, but having once looked, she had no choice. She would not lower her eyes and play the part of the demure bride. She half smiled at him, hiding her fear behind her customary mask.

Fear? Yes, she admitted, turning the mockery inward, too. Fear.

She listened to him promise her the moon and the stars in a firm voice that must have carried to the back pew of the church. She heard herself, almost as if she listened to someone else, promise him her soul. She watched the shiny gold ring, bright symbol of ownership, come to rest on her finger. She heard the vicar declaring that they were man and wife. She lifted her face to her new husband, feeling a wave of the nausea that had been disappearing over the past week.

He looked into her eyes and then at her lips, which she had drawn into a smile again. And then he took her completely by surprise. He clasped both her hands in his, bowed over them, and raised them one at a time to his lips.

She could have howled with fury. Tears sprang to her eyes and she bit hard on her upper lip. With her eyes and her lips she might have mocked his kiss on the mouth. She might have reminded him silently of his promise never to touch her without her permission. She might have put him subtly in the wrong. His kiss on her hands was startling in the illusion it gave of reverence and tenderness. She had to fight a painful ache in her throat to keep the humiliating tears from spilling over. But he must have seen them swimming in her eyes—he looked into them as soon as he raised his head. How she hated him.

He was her husband. And already he was establishing mastery.

* * *

Before suspecting her pregnancy, he had not once thought of marrying her. He had been horrified by his suspicions and even more so by their confirmation. He had felt that he was being forced into something very much against his will. He had not wanted to marry her.

And yet once it had become fact, once he had persuaded her to accept him, once he had acquired the special license, once the wedding preparations had been set in motion, he had felt a curious elation, a strange sense of—rightness. He found it hard to believe that the obvious had been staring him in the face ever since his arrival in London and he had not opened up his eyes and seen.

She was the very woman for him.

She was a woman of character and experience, someone he would find an interesting and a stimulating companion. He knew that he had a strong tendency to dominate other people, to take charge, to insist on doing things the way he knew they must be done. It was a tendency that worked to his advantage in his professional life. It was a tendency that might well be disastrous in his marriage. He would make a timid mouse out of a young, inexperienced girl—Miss Grainger, for example—within a month of wedding her. He did not want a timid mouse. He wanted a companion.

Even one who had sworn that she would never allow him to touch her. Even one who had promised to lead him a merry dance. Even one who rarely looked at him without that mockery in her eyes and on her lips.

He had always intended to make a marriage with whomever he ended up wedding. He intended to make a marriage with Helena Stapleton. A real marriage. The challenge of overcoming such hostility was strangely exhilarating. And he would overcome it.

The woman herself was exciting, of course. She was extremely beautiful, the sort of woman who was probably lovelier now in her maturity than she had been as a young girl. Or perhaps it was just that he was a mature man who saw more beauty in a woman of his own age than in someone who was little more than a child.

By the time his wedding day arrived, Edgar had admitted to himself that he was in love with his bride. He would not go as far as believing that he loved her. He was not even sure he liked her. He did not know her well enough to know if the unpleasant side of her nature she delighted in showing to him was the product of a basically unpleasant disposition or if it was merely the outer symptom of a troubled, wounded soul. He rather suspected the latter, though she denied having ever been deeply hurt. He faced the challenge of getting to know her. He might well not like her when he did. And even if he did, he might never grow to love her as he had always dreamed of loving a wife.

But he was certainly *in* love with her. It was a secret which he intended to guard very carefully indeed, for a lifetime if necessary. The woman did not need any more weapons than she already possessed.

His wedding was like a dream to him. And as with many dreams, he determinedly imprinted every detail on his memory so that he would be able to relive it in the future. There was his father, hearty and proud—and afraid for the son whom he loved with unabashed tenderness. There was Cora, armed with half a dozen of Francis's large handkerchiefs because she always cried at weddings, she had explained, but was sure to cry *oceans* at her only brother's. And there was Francis beside her, looking faintly amused and also solicitous of the wife he adored. There were all the other guests, an illustrious gathering for the wedding of a man who could not even claim the title of gentleman for himself.

And then there was his bride—and once she appeared, nothing and no one else mattered until they were out on the church steps some time later. She usually wore vivid colors and dramatically daring styles and looked vibrantly beautiful. This morning, all in pure white from head to toe, she looked almost ethereal. It was an incongruous word to use of her of all people. Her beauty robbed him of breath and of coherent thought. He felt, he thought in some alarm as she came closer to the altar rail, almost like weeping. He did not do so.

He spoke his commitment to her and to their marriage in the

guise of the words of the nuptial service. He ignored the slight tone of mockery with which she made her promises to him. She would live those promises and mean them eventually. She was going to be a challenge, but he had never yet failed in any of the challenges he had set himself. And success had never been as important to him as it was with this one.

She was his wife. He heard the vicar announce the fact and felt the shock of the reality of the words. She was his wife. It was the moment at which he was invited to kiss her, though the vicar did not say so in words. He felt the expectation in the gathered guests. She lifted her face to his—and he saw the mockery there and remembered the promise he had made her. This was ritual, of course, and hardly subject to that promise. But he would give her no weapon wittingly.

He kissed the backs of her hands instead of her lips and for that public moment made no secret of his feelings for his new wife. He felt a moment of exultation when he raised his head and saw the brightness of tears in her eyes. But he did not doubt she would make him pay for that moment of weakness.

Oh, he did not doubt it. He counted on it!

He led his bride from the dark unreality of the church interior into the reality of a cold, bright December outdoors.

"You look remarkably beautiful this morning, Helena," he told her in the brief moment of privacy before their guests came spilling out after them.

"Oh, and so do you, Edgar," she said carelessly. "Remarkably beautiful."

Touché!

Helena was feeling irritable by the time she was finally alone in her own bedchamber for the night. The combination of a wedding and an imminent Christmas was enough, it seemed, to transport everyone to great heights of delirious joy. What she had done by coming here with Edgar and marrying him was land herself in the middle of glorious domesticity.

It was the last thing she wanted.

Domesticity terrified her more than anything else in life.

The elder Mr. Downes—her father-in-law, who had actually invited her today to call him *Papa*—seemed endlessly genial. The noise and activity by which he had been surrounded all day—by which they had *all* been surrounded—had been appalling to say the least. The adults had been in high spirits. There was no word to describe in what the children had been—and there had been hordes of children, none of whom had been confined to the nursery. Helena had understood—she hoped fervently that she had misunderstood—that they would not be this side of Christmas.

She had found it impossible to sort them all out, to work out which children belonged to which adults, which names belonged to which children. The smallest infant belonged to the Bridgwaters, and she *thought* she knew which four belonged to Cora and Francis. Gracious heaven, they were her niece and nephews. But the others were unidentified and unidentifiable. And yet her father-in-law knew them all by name and they all knew him by name. He was Grandpapa to every last one of them—except to the one who could not yet talk and even he had bounced on the grandparental knee, gurgling and chuckling with glee.

She would go mad if every day between now and Christmas was like today, Helena thought. Unalloyed exuberance and merriment. Families. Happy couples—were there no *un*happy couples in this family or among their friends? Except for Edgar and herself, of course. And children. Children made her decidedly nervous. She did not like being around them. She did not like them being around her. And yet she was to have one of her own.

She was poking at the fire, trying to coax the coals into a position in which they would burn for a long time, when the door opened abruptly behind her and Edgar walked in, wearing a dressing gown. She stood up and glared, the poker clutched in one hand.

"And what do you think you are doing here?" she asked him, preparing for battle, almost glad that there was to be someone on whom to vent her irritation. It might be their wedding night, but there were going to be no exceptions to the rule. If he wanted to know how loudly and how embarrassingly she could squawk, let him take one step farther into the room.

He took it. And then another.

"Going to bed here," he said. "Sleeping here. It is my room, Helena. Ours. I slept elsewhere until tonight for form's sake."

"Oh, no, it is not ours," she said. "It is yours or it is mine. If it is yours, I shall go somewhere else. You will not break your promise as easily as that, Edgar."

"I have no intention of breaking my promise." His voice and his whole demeanor were maddeningly cool. "The bed is wide enough to accommodate both of us without touching, and I have enough control over my instincts and emotions to keep my hands off you. We will both sleep here. In my family—in my world, I believe—husbands and wives sleep in the same bed. All night, every night."

"And you have not the courage to fight family tradition," she said, throwing into her voice all the contempt she could muster.

"I have not the inclination," he said, removing his dressing gown and tossing it over the back of a chair. She was relieved to see that he wore a decent nightshirt beneath. "You are quite safe from me, Helena. And you need to sleep. I would guess that you have not been doing enough of it lately."

"I am looking haggard, I suppose," she said testily.

"Pale and interesting." He smiled. "Come to bed. Even with that fire, the room is chilly."

There was no point in arguing with Edgar when he was cool and reasonable, she was finding. And he was always cool and reasonable. But one day she was going to goad him into a loud, undignified brawl, and then he would find that he had met his match.

She lay on her back, staring up at the canopy, her eyes gradually accustoming themselves to the darkness. He lay on his side facing away from her. He said nothing. He made no move to break his promise. She fumed. How could he expect her to *sleep*?

Was he sleeping? She listened for the sound of his breathing. She would surely hear it if he slept. Yet he was apparently relaxed. He was probably in the process, she thought, of having a good night's rest just as if he slept alone or with a bundle of rags beside him. How could he *sleep*? How could he humiliate her so?

"Damn you, Edgar," she said. One of these times she would think of something original to say, but at the moment she was not in the business of originality.

He turned over to face her and propped himself on one elbow. He rested the side of his head on his hand. "My only hope," he said, "is that you will not be standing beside St. Peter when I appear at the pearly gates."

"I am not in the mood for silly jokes," she said. "This is ridiculous. I am nothing better than a puppet, forced to move whenever you jerk on a string. I do not like the feeling."

"If you feel strings connecting you and me," he said, "they are of your own devising, Helena. I will not touch you—even with a string."

"Damn your damnable control," she told him. "I will have none of it. Make love to me. It is what we both wish to do. Let us do it, then." She surged onto her side and put herself against him. She was immediately engulfed by heat and hard muscles and masculinity—and a soaring desire. She rubbed her breasts against his chest and reached for his mouth with her own.

He kissed her back softly and without passion. She drew back her head, breathing hard.

"It is for mutual comfort, Helena," he said quietly, "and for the procreation of children. Sometimes it is for love. It is not for anger or punishment. We will not punish each other with angry passion. You need to sleep." He slipped an arm beneath her head and drew her more snugly against him. "Relax and let yourself sleep, then."

She thought she would want to die of humiliation if it had not been for one thing. He was fully aroused. She could feel the hardness of his erection against her abdomen. It was not that she had failed to make him want her, then. It was just that he wanted a submissive wife, who would give him comfort rather than passion. Never! She had only passion to give.

"Go to sleep," he murmured against her ear.

"I thought you were ruthless, Edgar," she said into his shoulder. "I expected an overbearing tyrant. I expected that you would take advantage of the smallest opportunity to get past that promise and master me. I should have known the truth when you would not quarrel with me. You think to master me in this way, do you not?"

"Go to sleep, Helena," he said, his voice sounding weary. "We are not engaged in battle but in a marriage. Go to sleep." He kissed her temple.

She closed her eyes and was quiet for a while. If he knew her as she really was, he would not wish to share a bed with her, she thought. Once he got to know her, he would leave her alone fast enough. She would be alone again. She was alone now. But he was seducing her senses with this holding and cuddling and these murmured words. He was giving her the illusion of comfort.

"Comfort," she said. "It is for comfort, you say. Do you think I do not need comfort, Edgar? Do you think it? Do you? Do you think I am made of iron?"

He sighed and dipped his head to take her mouth. His was open this time and warm and responsive. "No," he said. "I do not think that."

"Make love to me, then," she said. "Let us do it for comfort, Edgar." She was being abject. She was almost crying and her voice revealed the fact. But she would think of that later. She would despise herself—and hate him—later. At this moment she was desperate for comfort and she would not remember that there was no comfort. That there could not be any. Ever.

He lifted her nightgown and his nightshirt before turning her onto her back, coming on top of her with the whole of his weight, and pushing her legs wide apart with his knees. She would have expected to hate being immobilized by his weight. But it was deliriously arousing. There was no foreplay. She would have expected to wish for it, to need it. But she wanted only to be penetrated, to be stretched, to be filled, to be ridden hard and deep.

He was a man of such control, her husband. He was hot and damp with need. He was rigid with desire. But he worked her slowly, withdrawing almost completely before thrusting firmly and deeply inward again. If there had been foreplay, she would have been in a frenzy of passion by the time he entered her, clamping about him with inner muscles to draw him to climax and to reach desperately for her own fleeting moment of happiness.

But there had been no foreplay. Incredibly, she felt herself gradually relaxing, lying still and open beneath him, taking exquisite enjoyment from the rhythmic strokes with which he loved her. She had no idea how many minutes passed—but it seemed like a long, long time—before she heard herself moaning and realized that enjoyment had turned to a pleasurable ache and that he was going to take her over the edge to peace and happiness without any active participation on her part. For a moment she considered fighting such passivity, but the ache, the certainty that he was going to take her through it and past it to the other side was too seductive to be denied.

She sighed and shivered beneath him as he made it happen and then with dreamy lethargy observed while he completed his own journey toward comfort. It was a moment of happiness blissfully extended into several moments—a gift she accepted with quiet gratitude. The moments would pass, but for now they were hers to hold in her body and her soul. They were like the peace that was supposed to come with Christmas. And for these moments—they would pass—she loved him utterly. She adored him.

He moved off her and drew her against him again. They were both warm and sweaty. She breathed in the smell of him.

"Comforted?" he asked softly.

"Mmm," she said.

"Sleep now, then," he told her.

"Mmm." Had she been just a little wider awake, perhaps she would have fought him since the suggestion had been issued as a command. But she slid into instant obedience.

Chapter 11

Although it was the week before Christmas and life could not be said to be following any normal pattern, nevertheless Helena began to have some inkling of how her life had changed. Permanently changed.

No longer would she travel almost constantly. The realization did not upset her enormously. Traveling could be far more uncomfortable and tedious than those who only longed to do it could ever realize. More disturbing was the understanding of why she had traveled and why she had never arrived at any ultimate destination. She had traveled for escape. It was true that she had derived great pleasure from her experiences, but never as much as she had hoped for. She knew finally, as she supposed she had known all along, that she could never in this life—and perhaps beyond this life, too—leave behind the thing she most wished to escape. She could never escape from herself. Wherever she went, she took herself with her. Yes, she had known it before. She had known that she lived in her own particular hell.

She would live at Mobley Abbey much of the time from now on. Edgar explained to her that his ties with his father had always been close ones and would undoubtedly remain so. For the rest of the time she would live in Bristol, in a home she had not yet seen. It was a large home, Edgar had told her. From the sketchy descriptions he had given of it in answer to her questions, she guessed that it was also an elegant home.

She was Mrs. Downes. Her title had never meant a great deal to her. She would have shed it if she could after her first husband's death. It was a reminder of a part of her life she would forget if she could. But there had been a certain dash to being Lady Stapleton, wealthy, independent widow. She had carefully cultivated that image of herself. There was something very solidly respectable about being Mrs. Edgar Downes.

She was part of a family. Not just some cousins in Scotland and an aunt whom she treated as much as a friend as a relative, but a real family, who prided themselves on their familial closeness.

Cora had hugged her hard immediately after the wedding and cried over her and insisted that they be on a first-name basis now that they were sisters. And so must her husband and Helena, she had commanded. They really had been given no choice in the matter. Lord Francis had laughed and Helena had thought how attractive laugh lines in the corners of a man's eyes could be.

"Shall we bow to tyranny?" he had asked her, bowing over her hand. "I say we should. I must be plain Francis to you from this moment on, if you please."

What choice had Helena had but to reply graciously in kind?

Her father-in-law, that genial older version of Edgar—genial, yes, but Helena had the strange feeling that she would not wish to be the person to cross his will in any matter of importance—was all that was paternal. One would almost have sworn that he was delighted by his son's choice of a bride. He rose from the table when she entered the breakfast parlor the morning after her wedding, mortifyingly late, and reached out both hands for hers. He had kept a chair empty beside him.

"Good morning, Daughter," he said, taking both her hands in his, wringing them painfully hard, and drawing her close enough to plant a hearty kiss on her cheek.

Again, what choice did she have? She could not reply to such a greeting with a mere curt good morning. She could not call him Mr. Downes.

"Good morning, Papa," she said and took the chair beside him. The combination of calling him that and of realizing that this was the morning after her wedding night and the eyes of all the family and house guests and of Edgar himself, seated farther down the table, were on her caused her to disgrace herself utterly. She blushed. Everyone in the room knew why she and Edgar had married—and yet on the morning after her wedding night she *blushed.* How terribly gauche!

She felt trapped. Trapped into something she could not escape simply by packing her bags and planning her itinerary to wherever her fancy led her. This was to be her life, perhaps forever. And last night she had given up the one illusion of freedom and power she had still possessed. She had lacked his control, and so she had given up the greater good for—for what? Not for passion. There had been surprisingly little of that. Not even for pleasure. There had been pleasure—quite intense pleasure, in fact—but it was not for that she had begged. She had begged for comfort. And he had comforted her.

The memory frightened her. It suggested that she had needed him. Worse, it suggested that he could satisfy her need. She had been so satisfied that she had slept the night through without once waking, even when he had left the bed. But she needed no one! She refused to need anyone. Least of all Edgar. She would be swallowed up whole by him. And then, because she did not enjoy the sensation of being swallowed whole, she would find ways to fight back, to fight free. And she would destroy him. He did not deserve the misery of a shrewish wife.

She conversed brightly at the breakfast table, telling her father-in-law and her aunt, who sat at his other side, about Christmases she had spent in Vienna and Paris and Rome. Soon her audience consisted of most of the people at the table.

"And this year," Mr. Downes said, patting her hand on the table, "you will enjoy a good old-fashioned English Christmas, Daughter. There is nothing to compare to it, I daresay, though I have never been to those other places to judge for myself. I have never had a hankering for foreign parts."

"There will be the greenery to gather for the house decorations," Cora said, "and the decorating itself. And the children's party on Christmas Day and the adult ball in the evening. There will be baskets to deliver and skating parties down at the lake—the ice will be firm enough in a day or two if the weather stays cold. There will be—oh, so much. I am so *glad* that Christmas is here this year. And Helena, *you* shall help with all the plans since you are more senior in this family now than I am. You are Edgar's wife." She looked quite unabashed at having been supplanted in the role of hostess.

"It would not surprise me if there were even snow for Christmas," Mrs. Cross said, looking toward the window and drawing general attention that way. The outdoor world did indeed look gray and chilly.

"Of course there will be snow, ma'am," Mr. Downes said. "I have decreed that this is to be a perfect Christmas."

"The children will be ecstatic," the Earl of Thornhill said.

"The children of *all* ages," his wife said with a smile. "No one is more exuberant on a sleigh than Gabriel."

"And no one makes more angelic snow angels than Jane," the Earl of Greenwald said.

"I may have to challenge you on that issue," the Marquess of Carew said with a grin, "and put forward the claims of my own wife. Samantha's snow angels come with haloes."

"I notice," Cora said, "that you are conspicuously silent, Francis."

"It is against my religion, my love," he said, "to fight duels at Christmastime. Now any other time . . ." He raised his eyebrows and winked at her.

"I believe, Corey," Edgar said, "there are in the hierarchy of heavenly beings warrior angels as well as cherubic ones."

Francis laughed. So did everyone else at the table, Cora loudest of all.

"What an abomination brothers are," she said. "You are welcome to him, Helena. Perhaps you can teach him some manners."

Helena smiled and met Edgar's eyes along the table—he looked despicably handsome and at ease—but she could not join in the lively banter. It was too—cozy. Too alluring. Too tempting. It continued without her participation.

Edgar must be put in his place this morning, she decided, before he could get any ideas about last night's having begun an era of domestic bliss. And so at the end of the meal, when he waited at the door to escort her from the room, she ignored his offered arm.

"Oh, you need not worry about me, Edgar" she said carelessly. "I have things to do. You may amuse yourself to your heart's content with the other gentlemen or with whatever it is you do when you are at Mobley."

"You will need boots and a warm cloak and bonnet," he told her. "Everyone has been so caught up in the events surrounding our wedding during the past few days that my father is feeling that he has been derelict in his duties as host. He is taking everyone on an exploratory walk about the park. Most of his guests, like you, are here for the first time, you see."

"Oh," she said. And so once again she had no choice. She had not been asked if she would like to trek about the park on a gray, cold day, in company with a number of other couples. She was half of a couple now and it was assumed that she would do what Edgar decided they should do. Besides, he was the heir to all this. Of course she must go. It would be ill-mannered to refuse. And she was finding it very hard here at Mobley to be bad mannered.

"Take my arm," he said. "I will come up with you."

Staying aloof would have to be a mental thing, then, she decided. And perhaps something of a physical thing, too. Tonight she would reestablish the rules. He would learn that though she had allowed him to touch her once, she had not issued a general invitation to conjugal relations at his pleasure.

"You are feeling well enough to walk?" he asked her as they entered their bedchamber.

It was the excuse she might have thought of for herself downstairs. It was the easy solution. But she would not use her condition as an excuse for anything. She would not hide behind female frailty.

"I am quite well, thank you," she said, slipping her arm from his and making her way to her dressing room. "Why would I not be? I am expecting a baby, Edgar. Thousands of women are doing it every day."

"But only one of them is my wife," he said. "And only one of them is expecting *my* baby."

She did not even try to interpret the tone of his voice. If he was trying to establish ownership, he might save his breath. He had done that quite effectively yesterday. She belonged to him body and soul. But she would not curl into the safety and comfort that fact offered her.

"I hope, Edgar," she called from inside her dressing room, making sure that there would be no mistaking the tone of her voice at least, "you are not going to start fussing over me. How tiresome that would be."

The bedchamber was empty when she came back into it. He had gone into his own dressing room. She was not sure whether he had heard her or not.

The walk was going to be far worse of an ordeal than she had anticipated, she saw immediately on their return downstairs. The hall was teeming with not only adult humans but also hordes of infant humans, too. Every child had spilled from the nursery in order to enjoy the walk. The noise was well above comfort level. Helena grimaced and would have returned to her room if she decently could.

She, it soon became apparent, was to be favored by the personal escort of her father-in-law. He took her arm and directed Edgar to escort her aunt.

And so by association she became the focal point of all the frolicking children as they walked. Mr. Downes had four grandchildren of his own among the group and clearly he was one of their favorite humans. But there were ten other children—Helena finally counted them all—who had fully adopted him during the few days of their acquaintance with him. And so every discovery along their route, from a misshapen, cracked chestnut to a gray, bedraggled bird feather was excuse enough to dash up to "Grandpapa" so that he might scrutinize the treasure and exclaim on its uniqueness. And Helena was called upon to exclaim enthusiastically about everything, too.

The Bridgwater baby was too heavy for his mama and papa to carry by turns, Mr. Downes decided after they had walked through a landscaped grotto and about the base of a grassy hill, which the older children had to run over, whooshing down the far side with extended arms and loud shrieks like a flock of demented birds. And so he enticed the babe into his own arms and made it bounce and laugh as he tickled it and talked nonsense to it. And then he decided that he would pass along the privilege and the pleasure to his new daughter-in-law.

Helena found herself carrying the rosy-cheeked little boy, who gazed at her in the hope that this new playmate would prove as entertaining as the last. The innocence of babyhood shone out at her from his eyes and the total trust of a child who had not yet learned the treachery of the world or of those he most loved.

She was terrified. And fascinated. And very close to tears. She smiled and kissed him and made a play out of stealing the apples from his cheeks. He chuckled and bounced and invited a repetition of the game. He was soft and warm and surprisingly light. He had tiny white baby teeth.

Helena drew in a deep breath. She had a surprising memory of wanting children of her own during the early years of her first marriage, of her disappointment each month when she had discovered that she had not conceived. She had been so relieved later and ever since to be childless that she had forgotten that once upon a time she had craved the experience of motherhood. There was a child in her womb—now. This time next year, if all went well, she could be holding her own baby like this, though hers would be somewhat younger.

A surge of yearning hit her low in her womb, almost like a pain. And then an equivalent dose of panic made her want to drop the Bridgwater child and run as far and as fast as she could go. She was being seduced by domesticity.

"Let me take him from you, ma'am." The Duke of Bridgwater was a coldly handsome man, whom she would have considered austere if she had not occasionally glimpsed the warmth of his relations with his wife and son. "He entertains the erroneous belief that the arms of adults were made to be bounced in. Come along, rascal."

The child was perfectly happy to be back with his papa. He proceeded to bounce and gurgle.

"Ah, the memories, Daughter," Mr. Downes said. "Having my children small was the happiest time of my life. I would have had more if my dear Mrs. Downes had not died giving birth to Cora. After that, I did not have the heart to remarry and have children with another wife."

If Christian had lived, Helena thought, he would be older than her father-in-law was now. He would have been seventy-one. It was a fascinating thought. "Children like you," she said.

"It is because I like them," he said with a chuckle. "There is no child so naughty that I do not like him. And now I have grandchildren. I see Cora's children as often as I can. I will see yours more frequently. I will lure you from Bristol on every slight pretext. Be warned."

"I believe it will always be a pleasure to be at Mobley, sir," she said.

He looked at her with raised eyebrows.

"Papa," she added.

"I believe," he said as he turned onto a different path, leading the group downhill in the direction of what appeared to be extensive woods, "you will do very well for my son. He has waited perhaps overlong to choose a bride. His character has become set over the years and has grown in strength, in proportion to his successes in life. I was successful, Daughter, as witness Mobley Abbey, which I purchased rather than inherited. My son is many more times successful than I. It will take a strong woman to give him the sort of marriage he needs."

"You think I am a strong woman?" Helena asked.

"You were a widow for many years," he said, "when you have the beauty and the rank and wealth to have made an advantageous match at any time. You have traveled and been independent. Edgar reported to me that he had the devil's own time persuading you to marry him, despite the fact that you are with child. Yes, I believe you are a strong woman."

How looks could deceive, she thought.

A lake had come into view through the trees. A lake that was iced over.

"This will be the scene of some of our Christmas frolics," her father-in-law said. "There will be skating, I do believe. And the greenery will be gathered among these trees. We will make a great ritual of that, Daughter. Christmas is important in this family. Love and giving and peace and the birth of a child. It is a good time to have a houseful of children and other guests."

"Yes," she said.

"And a good time to have a new marriage," he said. "There are worse things to be than a Christmas bride."

The children were whooping and heading either for the lake or for the nearest climbable trees.

It seemed that he was fated to have a very prickly wife, Edgar thought the morning after his wedding. He had had hopes after their wedding night that, if they could not exactly expect to find themselves embarking on a happily-ever-after, at least they would be able to enjoy a new rapport, a starting ground for the growth of understanding and affection. But as soon as she entered the breakfast parlor he had known that she had retreated once more behind her mask. She had looked beautiful and proud and aloof—and slightly mocking. He had known that she had no intention of allowing last night to soften their relations. Her rebuff as they left the breakfast room had not taken him at all by surprise.

He watched with interest as they walked outside and he made conversation with Mrs. Cross. He watched both his father and his wife. His father, he knew, though he had said nothing to his son, was deeply disturbed by his marriage and the manner in which it had been brought about. Yet he talked jovially with Helena and involved her with the children who kept running up to him for attention and approval.

Helena disliked children, a fact that Edgar had come to realize with cold dread. And yet he learned during the course of the walk that it was not strictly the truth. When his father first deposited the Duke of Bridgwater's young son in her arms, she looked alarmed as if she did not know quite what to do with him. What she proceeded to do was amuse the child—and herself. Edgar watched, fascinated, as all the aloof mask came away and left simply a lovely woman playing with a child.

The mask came back on as soon as Bridgwater took the baby away from her.

And then they were at the lake and everyone dispersed on various courses—the children to find the likeliest playgrounds, the adults to supervise and keep them from breaking something essential, like a neck. Cora was testing the ice with a stout stick, his father with the toe of his boot. Francis was bellowing at his youngest son to get off the ice—*now*! One group of children proceeded to play hide-and-seek among the tree trunks. The more adventurous took to the branches. Helena stood alone, looking as if she would sneak off back home if she could. Mrs. Cross had first bent to listen to something Thornhill's daughter was saying to her and had then allowed herself to be led away.

Edgar was about to close the distance between himself and his wife, though she looked quite unapproachable. Why could she not simply relax like everyone else and enjoy the outing? Was she so determined *not* to enjoy it? He felt a certain annoyance. But then Cora's youngest son, who had escaped both the ice and his father's wrath, tugged on his greatcoat and demanded that Uncle Edgar do up a button that had come undone at his neck. Edgar removed his gloves, went down on his haunches, and wrestled with the stubborn buttonhole.

When he stood up again, he could not immediately see Helena. But then he did. She was helping one of the Earl of Greenwald's young sons climb a tree. Edgar had noticed the lad standing forlornly watching some larger, bolder children, but lacking the courage to climb himself. Helena had gone to help him. She did so for all of ten minutes, patiently helping him find his footing on the bark and then slide out along one of the lower branches, encouraging him, congratulating him, laughing at his pleasure, catching him when he jumped, coaxing him when he lost his courage, starting all over again when he scampered back to the starting point.

She was that woman unmasked again—the one who forgot to be the dignified, cynical Lady Stapleton, the one who had forgotten her surroundings, the one who clearly loved children with a patient, compassionate warmth.

Edgar stood with his shoulder against a tree, watching, fascinated.

And then the child jumped with a bold lunge and bowled her right off her feet in his descent so that they both went down on the ground, the child squealing first with fright and then with delight when he realized he was not hurt, Helena laughing with sheer amusement.

She turned her head and caught herself being watched.

She lifted the child to his feet, dusted him off with one hand, directed him to his father, and sent him scampering away. She dusted herself off, her face like marble, and turned to walk away into the trees, in a direction no one else had taken. She did not look at Edgar or anyone else.

He sighed and stood where he was for a moment. Should he go after her? Or should he leave her alone to sulk? But sulk about what? That he had watched her? There was nothing secret in what she had been doing. She had been amongst the crowd, playing with one of the children. But her awareness that he was watching her had made her self-conscious or angry for some reason. It was impossible to know what was wrong.

He knew his wife as little today, Edgar thought, as he had known her that first evening, when he had looked up from his conversation with the Graingers and had seen her standing in the doorway, dressed in scarlet. She was a mystery to him—a prickly mystery. Sometimes he wondered if the mystery was worth probing.

But she was his wife.

And he was in love with her, even if he did not love or even particularly like her.

He pushed his shoulder away from the tree and went after her.

Chapter 12

She had not wandered far. But she was half hidden behind the tree trunk against which she leaned. She was staring straight ahead and did not shift her gaze when Edgar came in sight. But he cut into it when he went to stand before her. He set one hand against the trunk beside her head and waited for her eyes to focus on his.

"Tired?" he asked.

"No."

"It has been a long walk for you," he said, "with the added strain of having to converse with a new father-in-law."

"Would you make a wilting violet of me, Edgar?" she asked, one corner of her mouth tilting upward. "It cannot be done. You should have married one of the young virgins."

"You are good with children," he said.

"Nonsense!" Her answer was surprisingly sharp. "I dislike them intensely."

"Greenwald's little boy had been abandoned by the older tree climbers," he said. "He would have been left in his loneliness if you had not noticed. You made him happy."

"Oh, how easy it is to make a child happy," she said impatiently, "and how tedious for the adult."

"You looked happy," he said.

"Edgar." She looked fully into his eyes. "You would possess me body and soul, would you not? It is in your nature to want total control over what is in your power. You possess my body and I suppose I will continue to allow you to do so, though I did resolve this morning to remind you of your promise and to force you on your honor to keep it. But there is that damnable detail of a shared bed, and I never could resist an available man. You will *not* possess my soul. You may prod and probe as much as you will, but you will not succeed. Be thankful that I will not allow you to do so."

He was hurt. Partly by her careless dismissal of him as merely an available man—but then such carelessness was characteristic of her. Mainly he was hurt to know that she was quite determined to keep him out of her life. He might possess her body but nothing else. More than ever she seemed like a stranger to him—a stranger who was not easy to like, but one he craved to know and longed to love.

"Is the reality of your soul so ugly, then?" he asked.

She smiled at him and lifted her gloved hands to rest on his chest. "You have no idea how appealing you look in this greatcoat with all its capes," she said, "and with that frown on your face. You look as if you could hold the world on your shoulders, Edgar, and solve all its problems while you did so."

"Perhaps," he said, "I could help solve your problems if you would share them with me, Helena."

She laughed. "Very well, then," she said. "Help me solve this one. How do I persuade a massive, masterly, frowning man to kiss me?"

He searched her eyes, frustrated and irritated.

She pulled a face and then favored him with her most mocking smile. "You like only more difficult problems, Edgar?" she asked him. "Or is it that you have no wish to kiss me? How dreadfully lowering."

He kissed her—hard and open-mouthed. Her hands came to his shoulders, her body came against his, and for a few moments hot passion flared between them. Then he set his hands at her waist, moved her back against the tree, and set some space between them. Irritation had turned to anger.

"I do not like to be played with like a toy, Helena," he said, "to be used for your pleasure at your pleasure, to be seduced as a convenient way of changing the subject. I do not like to be mocked."

"You are very foolish, Edgar," she said. "You have just handed me a marvelous weapon. Do you not like to be *mocked,* my dear? I am an expert at mockery. I cannot be expected to resist the challenge you have just set me."

"Do you hate me so much, then?" he asked her.

She smiled. "I lust after you, Edgar," she said. "Even with your child in my womb, I still lust after you. Is it not enough?"

"What have I done to make you hate me?" he asked. "Must I take sole blame for your condition?"

"What have you done?" She raised her eyebrows. "You have married me, Edgar. You have made me respectable and safe and secure and rich. You *are* very wealthy, are you not? Wealthier than your father even before you inherit what is his? You have made me part of an eminently respectable family. You have brought me to this—to Mobley Abbey at Christmastime and surrounded me with respectable families and children. *Children* wherever I turn. It is to be what your father calls a good old-fashioned Christmas. I do not doubt it, if today is any indication—yet today Christmas has not even started. And if all this is not bad enough, you have tried to take my soul into yourself. You have suffocated me. I cannot breathe. This is what you have done to me."

"My God." His hand was back on the tree trunk beside her head. He had moved closer to her though he did not touch her. "My God, Helena, who was he? What did he do to you? Who was it who hurt you so badly?"

"You are a fool, Edgar," she said coldly. "No one has hurt me. No one ever has. It is I who have done all the hurting. It is in my nature. I am an evil creation. You do not want to know me. Be content with my body. It is yours. You do not want to know *me.*"

He did not believe her. Oh, yes, she hurt people. He did not doubt that he was not the first man she had used and scorned. But he did not believe it was in her very nature to behave thus. There would not be the bitterness in her smile and behind her eyes if she were simply amoral. Nor that something more than bitterness that he sometimes almost glimpsed, almost grasped. What was that other something? Despair? Something or someone had started it all. Probably someone. Some man. She had been very badly hurt at some time in her past. So badly that she had been unable to function as her real self ever since.

But how was he to find out, to help her when she had shut herself off so entirely from help?

There was a glimmering of hope, perhaps. The things that suffocated her must also frighten her—her marriage to him, his family, his father's guests and their children, Christmas. Why would she fear such benevolent things? Because they threatened her bitterness, her masks? The masks had come off briefly already this morning—first with the Bridgwater baby and then with the Greenwald child. And perhaps even last night when she had allowed herself to be comforted.

"You were right about one thing," she said. "I *am* tired. Take me home, Edgar. Fuss over your pregnant wife."

He took her arm in his and led her back to the others so that he could signal to his father that he was taking Helena back to the house. His father smiled and nodded and then bent down to give his attention to Jonathan, the Thornhills' youngest son. Greenwald's little boy briefly danced up to Helena and told her that he was going skating as soon as the ice was thick enough.

"I am going to skate like the wind," he told her.

"Oh, goodness," she said, touching a hand lightly to his woolly cap. "That *is* fast. Perhaps all we will see is a streak of light and it will be Stephen skating by."

He chuckled happily and danced away.

Her voice had been warm and tender. She might believe that she disliked children, but in reality she loved them altogether too well.

They walked in silence through the woods and up the slope to the wider path. She leaned on him rather heavily. He should not, he thought, have allowed her to make such a lengthy walk when only a week or so ago she had still been suffering from nausea and fatigue.

"Tell me about your first marriage," he said.

She laughed. "You will find nothing there," she said. "It lasted for seven years. He was older than your father. He treated me well. He adored me. That is not surprising, is it? I am reputed to have some beauty even now, but I was a pretty girl, Edgar. I turned heads wherever I went. I was his prize, his pet."

"You were never—with child?" he asked.

"No." She laughed again. "Never once, though not for lack of trying on his part. You can imagine my astonishment when you impregnated me, Edgar. Seven years of marriage and a million lovers since then had convinced me that I was safely barren."

Did she realize, he wondered, how her open and careless mention of those lovers cut into him? But he had no cause for complaint. He had never been deceived about her promiscuous past, of which he had been a part. She had never even tried to keep it a secret.

"His poor first wife suffered annual stillbirths and miscarriages for years and years," she said. "Was not I fortunate to be barren?"

"There was only one survivor?" he asked.

"Only Gerald, yes," she said. "Though why he survived when none of the others did was a mystery—or so Christian always said. He was neither tall nor robust nor handsome; he was shy and timid; he was not overly intelligent. He excelled at nothing he was supposed to excel at. He had only one talent—a girlish talent, according to his father. He played the pianoforte. I believe Christian would have been just as happy if none of his offspring had survived."

Her first husband did not sound to have been a pleasant man. Edgar could not imagine his own father being impatient with either him or Cora if they had been less than he had dreamed of their being. His father, for all his firm character and formidable abilities in his career, gave unconditional love to those nearest and dearest to him—and to their spouses, too. Had Sir Christian Stapleton treated Helena, as he appeared to have treated his only son, with such contempt that she had forever after treated herself that way? Could that account for her bitterness? Her despair?

"Your child will have his father's love," he told her. "Or hers. I do not care what its gender is or its looks or abilities or nature or talents or lack thereof. I do not care even if there are real handicaps. The child will be mine and will be deeply loved."

If he had thought to soften her, he was much mistaken.

"You think that now, Edgar," she said contemptuously. "But if it is a son and he has not your splendid physique or can look at two numbers and find himself unable to add them together or sneaks away to play the pianoforte when you are trying to train him to take over your business, then you will compare him to yourself and to his grandfather and you will find him wanting. And he will know himself despised and become a weak, fragile creature. But he may not come to me for comfort. I shall not give it. I shall turn my back on him. I will not have this pregnancy romanticized. I will not think in hazy terms of a cuddly baby and doting motherhood and strong, protective fatherhood. The stable at Bethlehem must have been drafty and uncomfortable and smelly and downright humiliating. How dare we make beatific images of it! It was nasty. That was the whole point. It was meant to be nasty just as the other end of that baby's life was. *This* is what I am prepared to do for you, that stable was meant to tell us. But instead of accepting reality and coping with it, we soften and sentimentalize everything. What did you *do* to inspire this impassioned and ridiculous monologue?"

"I dared to think of my child with love," he said, "though she or he is still in your womb."

"Oh, Edgar," she said wearily, "I did not realize you were such a decent man. One's first impression of you is of a large, masterful, ruthless man. Our first encounter merely confirmed me in that belief. I wish you were not so decent. I am terrified of decency."

"And I, ma'am," he admitted, "am totally baffled by you. You would have me believe that you are anything but decent. And yet you will help a lonely child climb a tree and touch his head with tenderness. And you will passionately defend a woman and child whose courage and suffering have been softened to nothing by the sweet sentiments that surround the Christmas story. And you keep me at arm's length so that I will not be drawn into your own unhappiness. That *is* the reason, is it not?"

She set the side of her head against his shoulder and sighed. "The walk out did not seem nearly this long," she said. "I am very weary, Edgar. Weary of being prodded and poked and invaded by your questions. Have done now. Come upstairs with me when we reach the house. Lie down with me. Hold me as you did last night. You did, did you not? All night? Your arm must have gone to sleep. Hold me again, then. And draw me farther into this terror of a marriage. Perhaps I will sleep and when I awake will have more energy with which to fight you. I will fight, you know. I hate you, you see."

Surprisingly he smiled and then actually chuckled aloud. She had spoken the words almost with tenderness.

Oh, yes, he would draw her farther into the terror—of their marriage, of her new family, of her proximity to children, of Christmas. She was right about one thing. He could be a ruthless man when his mind was set upon something. His mind was set upon something now. More than his mind—his heart was set upon it. He wanted a marriage with this woman.

A real marriage.

He had spotted her weakness now—she had handed him the knowledge on a platter. He was an expert—a ruthless expert—at finding out weaknesses and probing and worrying them until he had gained just what he wanted. He would have to say that Helena, Mrs. Edgar Downes, did not stand one chance in a million.

Except that she was quite irritatingly stubborn. A worthy opponent. He could not stand an opponent who cowered into submission at the first indication of the formidable nature of his foe. There was no challenge in such a fight. Helena was not such an opponent. She could still tell him she hated him, even while conceding a physical need for his arms to hold her.

"Shall I carry you the rest of the way?" he asked her, feeling her weariness.

"If you try it, Edgar," she said, "I shall bar the door of your bedchamber against you from this day forward and screech out most unladylike answers to anything you care to call through it. I shall shame you in front of your father and your sister and all these other nauseatingly respectable people. I am not a sack of potatoes to be lugged about merely because I have the despicable misfortune to be in a delicate condition and to be your property."

"A simple no, thank you would have sufficed," he said.

"I wish you were not so large," she said. "I wish you were small and puny. I *hate* your largeness."

"I believe," he said as they stepped inside the house, "I have understood your message. Come. I'll take you up and hold you while you sleep."

"Oh, go away," she said, dropping his arm, "and play billiards or drink port or do whatever it is you do to make another million pounds before Christmas. I have no need of you or of sleep either. I shall write some letters."

"After you have rested," he said firmly, taking her arm and drawing it through his again. "And if it is a real quarrel you are hankering for, Helena, I am almost in the mood to oblige you." He led her toward the stairs.

"Damn you," she said. "I am not. I am too weary."

He chuckled again.

Jack Sperling arrived at Mobley Abbey early in the afternoon, the Graingers just before teatime.

Jack was shown into the library on his arrival, and Edgar joined him there with his father.

"Sperling," he said, inclining his head to the young man, who bowed to him. "I am pleased to see that you had a safe journey. This is the young gentleman I spoke of, Father."

"Mr. Sperling." The elder Mr. Downes frowned and looked him over from head to toe. "You are a very young gentleman."

"I am two-and-twenty, sir," the young man said, flushing.

"And I daresay that like most young gentlemen you like to spend money as fast as you can get your hands on it," Mr. Downes said. "Or faster."

The flush deepened. Jack squared his shoulders. "I have worked for my living for the past year, sir," he said. "Everything I earn, everything I can spare from feeding myself and setting a roof over my head is used to pay off debts that I did not incur."

"Yes, yes," Mr. Downes said, his frown suggestive of irritation. "You are foolish enough to beggar yourself for the sake of an extravagant father, I daresay. For the sake of that ridiculous notion of a gentleman's honor."

The young man's nostrils flared. "Sir," he said, "with all due respect I will not hear my father insulted. And a gentleman's honor is his most precious possession."

Mr. Downes waved a dismissive hand. "If you work for my son and me, young man," he said, "you may grow rich. But if you intend to spend your hard-earned pounds on paying a father's debts, you are not the man for us. You will need more expensive and more fashionable clothes than those you are wearing and more than a decent roof over your head. You will need a wife who can do you credit in the business world. I believe you have a lady in mind. You will need to think of yourself, not of creditors to whom you owe nothing if you but forget about a gentleman's honor. The opportunity is there. My son has already offered it and I am prepared to agree with him. But only if you are prepared to make yourself into a singleminded businessman. Are you?"

Jack had turned pale. He could work for these two powerful men, who knew how to be successful, how to grow rich. As a gentleman with a gentleman's education and experience as his father's steward and more lately as a London clerk, he could be trained by them, groomed by them for rapid promotion until he was in a position to make his own independent fortune. It was the chance of a lifetime, a dream situation. He would be able to offer for Fanny Grainger. All he had to do was swallow a few principles and say yes.

Edgar watched his face. This was not an approach he would have taken himself. His father had grown up in a harsher world.

"No, sir." Jack Sperling's face was parchment white. The words were almost whispered. But they were quite unmistakable. "No, thank you, sir. I shall return to town by stage. I thank you for your time. And for yours, sir." His eyes turned on Edgar.

"Why not?" Mr. Downes barked. "Because you are a *gentleman,* I suppose. Foolish puppy."

"Yes, sir," Jack said, very much on his dignity. "Because I am a gentleman and proud of it. I would rather starve as a gentleman, sir, than live as a rich man as a— As a—" He bowed abruptly. "Good day to you."

"Sit down, Mr. Sperling," Mr. Downes said, indicating a chair behind the young man. "My son judged you rightly, it seems. I might have known as much. We have business to discuss. Men who go into trade for the sole purpose of getting rich, even if it means turning their backs upon all their responsibilities and obligations and even if it means riding roughshod over the persons and livelihoods and feelings of everyone else—such men often do prosper. But they are not men I care to know or do business with. You are not such a man, it seems."

Jack looked from him to Edgar.

"It was a test," Edgar said, shrugging. "You have passed it."

"I would have appreciated your trust, sir," the young man said stiffly, "without the test. I am a gentleman."

"And I am not, Mr. Sperling," Mr. Downes said. "I am a businessman. Sit down. You are a fortunate young man. You know, I suppose, what gave my son the idea of taking you on as a bright prospect for our business."

"Mr. Downes was obliged to marry Lady Stapleton," Jack Sperling said, "and wished to reduce the humiliation to Miss Grainger, who expected his offer. Yes, I understand, sir."

"It is in our interest to make you an acceptable groom for the lady," Mr. Downes said, "who will be arriving here with her mama and papa before the day is out, I daresay." Jack Sperling flushed again. "But make no mistake, young man. There is no question of your being paid off. We demand work of our employees."

"I would not accept a single farthing that I had not earned, sir," Jack said. "Or accept a bride who had been bought for me."

"And about your father's property," Mr. Downes said. "Your *late* father?"

The young man inclined his head. "He died more than a year ago," he said.

"And the property?" Mr. Downes was drumming the fingers of one hand on the arm of his chair. "It has been sold?"

"Not yet," Jack said. "It is in a state of some dilapidation."

"I am willing to buy it," Mr. Downes said. "As an investment. As a business venture. When the time is right I will sell it again for a profit—or my son will if it is after my time. To you, Mr. Sperling. When you can afford to buy it. It will not come cheaply."

Edgar noted the whiteness of the young man's knuckles as his hands gripped the chair arms. "I would not expect it to, sir," he said. "Thank you, sir."

"We are good to our employees, Mr. Sperling," Mr. Downes said. "We also expect a great deal of them."

"Yes, sir."

"For the next week, we will expect you to enjoy Christmas at Mobley and to court that young lady with great care. Her father does not know you are to be here unless you have informed the lady and she has informed him. He will not take kindly to a suitor who is to be a clerk in my son's business until he has earned his first promotion—not when he expected my son himself."

"No, sir."

"He will perhaps be reconciled when he understands that you are a favored employee," Mr. Downes continued. "One who is expected to rise rapidly in the business world and eventually rival us in wealth and influence. Being a gentleman himself, he will doubtless be even further reconciled when he knows that our business is to invest in buying and improving your father's property with a view to preparing it as your country residence when you achieve stature in the company."

The young man's eyes closed tightly. "Yes, sir."

Mr. Downes looked at his son. "I believe we have said everything that needs to be said." He raised his eyebrows. "Have we forgotten anything?"

Edgar smiled. "I believe not," he said. "Except to thank Mr. Sperling for his willingness to help me out of a tight spot."

"You will go to Bristol when my son returns there after Christmas, then," Mr. Downes said. "He will put you to work. For a trial period, it is to be understood. Pull the bell rope, will you please, Edgar? My butler will show you to your room, Mr. Sperling, and explain to you how to find the drawing room. We will be pleased to see you there for tea at four o'clock."

"Thank you, sir." Jack got to his feet and bowed. He inclined his head to Edgar. He followed the butler from the room.

"I have never regretted my retirement," Mr. Downes said after the door had closed behind them. He chuckled. "But it feels damned good to come out of it once in a while. I believe you judged his character well, Edgar. I thought for one moment that he was going to challenge me to a duel."

"You were formidable." Edgar laughed, too. "Poor young man. One almost forgot that he is the one doing me a favor."

"One cannot afford to have weak employees merely as a favor, Edgar," his father said. "That young man will do very nicely indeed if I am any judge of character. You do not regret the young lady?"

"I am married to Helena," Edgar said rather stiffly.

"The answer you would give, of course," his father said. "Damn it, Edgar, we did not go around bedding respectable women before marrying them in my day. I am disappointed in you. But you have done the right thing and one can only hope all will turn out for the best. She is a handsome woman and a woman of character. Though one wonders what she was about, allowing herself to be bedded and her a lady."

"That is her concern, Father," Edgar said firmly, "and mine."

"The right answer again." Mr. Downes rose to his feet. "I have promised to show Mrs. Cross the conservatory. A very ladylike person, Edgar. She reminds me of your mother, or the way your mother would have been." He sighed. "Sometimes I let a few days go by without thinking about her. I must be getting old."

"You must be forgiving yourself at last," Edgar said quietly.

"Hmm." His father led the way from the room.

Chapter 13

The Graingers arrived at Mobley Abbey in time to join the family and the other guests in the drawing room for tea. Helena had at first been rather surprised to find that they still planned to come for Christmas, even after learning of Edgar's betrothal and imminent marriage to her. But it was not so very surprising after she had had time to think about it a little more.

The Graingers were not wealthy. It was very close to Christmas. If they admitted to their disappointment and returned to their own home, they would be compelled to go to the expense of celebrating the holiday there with all their expectations at an end. General opinion had it that Sir Webster would not be able to afford to take his daughter back to town for a Season. She would sink into spinsterhood and he would have the expense of her keep for the rest of his life.

They had lost the very wealthy Edgar Downes as a matrimonial prospect, but spending Christmas at Mobley Abbey would at least give them the chance of continuing in the company of several of the *ton*'s elite, of enjoying the hospitality of wealthy hosts, and of keeping their hopes alive for a little longer. In such a social setting, who knew what might turn up?

And so it was not so surprising after all that they had come, Helena thought, greeting them as they appeared in the drawing room. They were gracious in their congratulations to her. Miss Grainger was quite warm in hers.

"Mrs. Downes," she said. "I am very pleased for you. I am sure you will be happy. I like Mr. Downes," she added and blushed.

Helena guessed that the girl was sincere. She would have

married Edgar without a murmur of protest, but she would have been overwhelmed by him.

"Thank you," she said and saw the girl almost at the same moment suddenly stare off to her right as if her eyes would pop from their sockets. She visibly paled.

"Oh," she murmured almost inaudibly.

Edgar had come up and was greeting the Graingers. Helena linked her arm through Fanny's. "Come and meet my father-in-law," she said. He was speaking with Helena's aunt and the young man who had arrived earlier. Helena had been introduced to him but had not had a chance to converse with him.

"Papa," she said, "this is Miss Grainger, just lately arrived from London with her mama and papa."

Fanny curtsied and focused the whole of her attention on Mr. Downes. It seemed to Helena that she was close to fainting.

"Ah," Mr. Downes said heartily. "As pretty as a picture. Welcome to my home, Miss Grainger. And—Sir Webster and Lady Grainger?" Edgar had brought them across the room. "Welcome. You met Mrs. Cross in London, I daresay. Allow me to present Mr. Sperling, a young gentleman my son recently discovered in London as a particularly bright prospect for our business. We need gentlemen of education and breeding and enterprise to fill the more challenging positions and to rise to heights of responsibility and authority and wealth. I daresay that in five or ten years Mr. Sperling may make me look like a pauper." He rubbed his hands together and laughed merrily.

Mr. Sperling bowed. Fanny curtsied deeply without once looking at him. Sir Webster cleared his throat.

"We are acquainted with Mr. Sperling," he said. "We are—or were—neighbors. How d'ye do, Sperling?" He had pokered up quite noticeably.

"Acquainted? Neighbors?" Mr. Downes was all astonishment. "Well now. Who says that coincidences never happen these days? Amazing, is it not, Edgar?"

"Astonishing," Edgar agreed. "You and Lady Grainger—and Miss Grainger, too—will be able to help us make Mr. Sperling feel more at home over Christmas then, sir."

"Yes, certainly. My dear Mrs. Cross," Mr. Downes was saying, beaming with hearty good humor, "please do pour the tea, if you would be so good."

Helena caught him alone after he had escorted her aunt to the tea tray. The Carews, she noticed, those kindest of kind people, were taking a clearly uncomfortable Mr. Sperling and Fanny Grainger under their wing while Edgar had taken the Graingers to join Cora and Francis.

"Sit here, Daughter," Mr. Downes said, indicating a large wing chair beside the fire. "We have to be careful to look after you properly. It was thoughtless of me to take you so far from the house this morning."

"Nonsense," she said briskly. "What are you up to, Papa?"

"Up to?" He looked at her in astonishment. "I am protecting my daughter-in-law and my future grandchild. Both are important to me."

"Thank you." She smiled. "Who is Mr. Sperling? No." She held up a staying hand. "Not the story about Edgar's having discovered a prodigy quite by chance. The real story."

His eyes were shrewd and searching. "Edgar has not told you?" he asked.

"Let me guess." She perched on the edge of the chair he had indicated and looked up at him. "It does not take a great deal of ingenuity, you know. Mr. Sperling is a young and rather good-looking gentleman. He is a neighbor of the Graingers. Fanny Grainger, when she set eyes on him a few minutes ago, came very near to fainting—a little excessive for purely neighborly sentiment. His own face, when we came closer, turned parchment pale. Can he by any chance be the ineligible suitor? The man she is not allowed to marry?"

"I suppose," her father-in-law conceded, "since we have just established that coincidences do happen, it might be possible, Daughter."

"And Edgar, feeling guilty that the necessity of marrying me forced him to let down the Graingers, whose hopes he had raised," Helena said, "devised this scheme of making Mr. Sperling more eligible and bringing the lovers together. And you are aiding and abetting him, Papa. A more unlikely pair of matchmakers it would be difficult to find."

"But make no mistake," Mr. Downes said. "Business interests always come first with Edgar as with me. He would not have brought that young man to Mobley or offered him the sort of employment that will involve a great deal of trust on his part if he had not been convinced that Mr. Sperling was the man for the job. There is no sentiment in this, Daughter, but only business."

"Poppycock!" she said, startling him again. "Perhaps the two of you believe the myth that has grown up around you that you are ruthless, hard-nosed, heartless businessmen to whom the making of money is the be-all and end-all of existence. Like most myths, it has hardly a grain of truth to it. You are soft to the core of your foolish hearts. You, sir, are an impostor."

His eyes twinkled at her. "It is Christmas, Daughter," he said. "Even men like my son and me dream of happy endings at Christmas, especially those involving love and romance. Leave us to our dreams."

Edgar, Helena noticed, was laughing with the rest of his group and setting an arm loosely about Cora's shoulders in an unconscious gesture of brotherly affection. He looked relaxed and carefree. But dreams—they were the one thing she must never cultivate. When one dreamed, one began to hope. One began to have images of happiness and of peace. Peace on earth and goodwill to all men. How she hated Christmas.

Her father-in-law patted her shoulder even as her aunt brought them their tea. "Let me dream, Daughter," he said. And she knew somehow that he was no longer talking about Fanny Grainger and Mr. Sperling.

The next day saw the return of some of the wedding guests who had come out from Bristol for that occasion and now came to Mobley Abbey to spend Christmas. Some of Edgar's personal friends were among them and some of his father's. Almost without exception, they had sons and daughters of marriageable age.

He had invited them, Mr. Downes explained to his son, when it had become obvious to him that his home was to be filled with aristocratic guests. He had welcomed the connections—he had wanted both his son and his daughter to marry into their class, after all—but he would not turn his back on his own. He was a man who aimed always to expand the horizons of his life, not one who allowed the old horizons to fade behind him as he aggressively pursued the new.

"But more than that, Edgar," he explained, "I realized the great gap there would be between the older, married guests and the children, with only Miss Grainger between. This was when it appeared that you would be celebrating your betrothal to her over Christmas. It seemed important that she have company of her own age. Under the changed circumstances, it seems even more important. And I like young people. They liven up a man's old age."

"The old man being you, I suppose," Edgar said with a grin. "You have more energy than any two of the rest of us put together, Papa."

His father chuckled.

But Edgar was pleased with the addition of more young people and of his own friends. He was more relaxed. He was able to see Fanny Grainger and Jack Sperling relax more.

The house guests had all arrived safely—and only just in time. The following night, the night before the planned excursion to gather greenery for decorating the house, brought a huge fall of snow, one that blanketed the ground and cut them off at least for a day or two from anywhere that could not be reached by foot.

"Look," Edgar said, leaning against the window sill of his bedchamber just after he had got out of bed. He turned his head to glance at Helena, who was still lying there, awake. "Come and look."

It is too cold," she complained.

"Nonsense," he said. "the fire has already been lit." But he went to fetch her a warm dressing gown and set it about her as she got out of bed, grumbling. "Come and look."

He kept an arm about her shoulders as she looked out at the

snow and the lowering clouds which threatened more. Indeed more was already sifting down in soft, dancing flakes. She said nothing, but he saw wonder in her eyes for a moment—the eternal wonder that children from one to ninety always feel at the first fall of snow.

"Snow for Christmas," she said at last, her voice cool. "How very timely. Everyone will be delighted."

"My first snowball will be targeted for the back of your neck," he said. "I will treat you to that delicious feeling of snow melting in slow trickles down your back."

"How childish you are, Edgar," she said. "But why the back of the neck? My first one will splatter right in your face."

"Is this a declaration of war?" he asked.

"It is merely the natural reaction to a threat," she said. "Will the gathering of greenery have to be canceled? That snow must be several inches deep."

"Canceled?" he said. "Quite the contrary. What could be better designed to arouse the spirit of Christmas than the gathering of greenery in the snow? There will be so many distractions that the task will take at least twice as long as usual. But distractions can be enormous fun."

"Yes," she said with a sigh.

It struck him suddenly that he was happy. He was at Mobley Abbey with his family and friends, and Christmas was just a few days away. There was enough snow outside that it could not possibly all melt before Christmas. And he was standing in the window of his almost warm bedchamber with his arm about his pregnant wife. It was strange how happiness could creep up on a man and reveal itself in such unspectacular details.

He dipped his head and kissed her. She did not resist. They had made love each night of their marriage and though there had been little passion in the encounters, there had been the warmth of enjoyment—for both of them. He turned her against him, opened her mouth with his own, and reached his tongue inside. One of her arms came about his neck and her fingers twined themselves in his hair.

He would enjoy making love with her in the morning, he thought, with the snow outside and all the excitement of that fact and the Christmas preparations awaiting them. There could surely be no better way to start a day. It felt good to be a married man.

She drew back her head. "Don't, Edgar," she said.

He released her immediately. How foolish to have forgotten that it was Helena with all her prickliness to whom he was married. "I beg your pardon," he said. "I thought I had been given permission to have conjugal relations with you."

"Don't be deceived by snow and Christmas," she said. "Don't imagine tenderness where there is none, Edgar—either in yourself or in me. We married because I seduced you and we enjoyed a night of lust and conceived a child. It can be a workable marriage. I like your father and your sister and your friends. And I am reconciled to living in one place—even Bristol, heaven help me—and doing all the domestic things like running your home and being your hostess. I am even resigned to being a mother and will search out the best nurse for the child. But we must not begin to imagine that there is tenderness. There is none."

If he had fully believed her, he would have been chilled to the bone. As it was, he felt as if someone had thrown a pail of snow through the window and doused him with it.

"There must at least be an attempt at affection," he said.

"I cannot feel affection," she said. "Don't try to tempt me into it, Edgar. You are a handsome man and I am strongly attracted to you. I will not try to deny that what we do together on that bed is intensely pleasurable to me. But it is a thing of the body, not of the emotions. I respect you as a man. I do believe sometimes I even like you. Do the same for me if you must. But do not waste emotion on me."

"You are my *wife,*" he said.

"I hurt badly what I am fond of," she said. "I hurt badly and forever. I do not *want* to be fond of you, Edgar. And I am not trying to be cruel. You are a decent man—I do wish you were not, but you are. Don't make me fond of you."

Did she realize what she was saying? She was *fond* of him and desperately fighting the feeling. But what had she done? He had been very deaf, he realized. She had insisted every time he had asked that no one had ever hurt her, that she had done the hurting. He had not listened. Someone must have hurt her, he had thought, and he had asked his questions accordingly. He had asked the wrong questions. Whom had she hurt? *I hurt badly and forever.* The words might have sounded theatrical coming from anyone else. But Helena meant them. And he had felt the bitterness in her, the despair, the refusal to be drawn free of her masks, the refusal to love or be loved.

"Very well, then," he said and smiled at her. "We will enjoy a relationship of respect and perhaps even liking and of unbridled lust. It sounds good to me, especially the last part."

He drew one of her rare amused smiles from her. "Damn you," she said without any conviction at all.

"We had better dress and go downstairs," he said, "before all the snow melts."

"I would hate that snowball to miss its destiny and never collide with your face," she said.

They were back down by the lake, spread along one of its banks, searching for holly and mistletoe and well-shaped evergreen boughs of the right size. The lake itself was like a vast flat empty field of snow on which some of the children—and three or four of the young people, too—had made long slides while whooping with delight. The snow would have to be swept off before anyone could skate, though the ice had been pronounced by the head gardener to be thick enough to bear any human weight. But the skating would have to wait until tomorrow, they had all been told. Today was strictly for the gathering of greenery and the decorating of the house.

Of course it had turned out not to be strictly for any such thing, just as Edgar had predicted. There had been a great deal of horseplay and noise ever since the first one of them had set foot outside the house. A vicious snowball fight had been waged and won and lost before any of them had succeeded in getting even twenty yards from the house. Edgar's first snowball had been safely deflected by Helena's shoulder—she had seen it coming. Her own had landed squarely in the middle of his laughing face.

"If you think to win any war against me, Edgar," she had told him while he shook his head like a wet dog and wiped his face with his snowy gloves, "let that be a warning to you."

"You win," he had said, smiling ruefully and setting a hand at the back of her neck. When he had picked up a palmful of snow she did not know. But every drop of it, she would swear, had found its way down inside her cloak and dress.

Samantha, Marchioness of Carew, and Jane, Countess of Greenwald, had shown all the little girls and some of the older ones too how to make snow angels and soon there was a heavenly host of them spread out on what was usually a lawn.

By slow degrees they had all made their way to the lake and the woods and been divided into work parties. Both her father-in-law and her husband had tried to persuade Helena to return to the house instead of going all the way. She wished they had not. She might have gone back if she had been left to herself. But once challenged, she had had no choice but to go. Not that she felt too weak or fatigued. She just did not want any more merriment.

In the event she soon became involved in it. It really was irresistible. There were children to be helped and children to be played with and young people and people of her own generation to be laughed with. She had forgotten how warm and wonderful family life could be. She had forgotten how exhilarating a good old-fashioned English Christmas could be. She had forgotten how sheerly pleasurable it was to relax and interact with other people of all ages, talking and teasing and being teased and laughing.

It was so easy to be seduced by Christmas. The thought was conscious in her mind more than once, but she could not seem to fight against it. Stephen, the little Greenwald boy, appeared to have adopted her as a favored aunt and had persuaded a few of the other children of similar age to do likewise. When she should have been directing them in the carrying of a largish pile of holly to the central cache close to the lake, she found herself instead dancing in a ring with the children, chanting "Ring around the rosy" and actually tossing herself into the snow with them when everyone's favorite line had been chanted—"We all fall down." And laughing as merrily as any of them as she staggered back to her feet and dusted herself off.

She had known it would happen. She had fought weakly against it and allowed Christmas and the snow to win—for now. Perhaps even in the afterlife, she thought, there were brief vacations from hell. Perhaps only so that it would appear even worse afterward. She tried not to watch Edgar climbing trees for mistletoe, lifting nephews and a niece and other children on his broad shoulders by turns so that they could reach the desired holly branches—why did the best ones always seem to be above the reach of an outstretched arm? Why were the best of all things just beyond one's grasp?

A surprise awaited everyone when the greenery was finally gathered and piled neatly in one place ready to be hauled back to the house. A group of warmly clad gardeners and house servants had built a large bonfire and were busy warming chocolate and roasting chestnuts over it.

They all suddenly realized how cold they were and how tired and thirsty—and hungry. There was a great deal of foot stamping and glove slapping and talking and laughing. And someone—Helena thought it was probably one of the Bristol guests—started singing, a bold gamble when he might have ended up singing an embarrassed solo. But of course he did not. Soon they were all singing one carol after another and being very merry and very sentimental and only marginally musical. Helena shivered and found a log on which to sit, her gloved hands warming about her chocolate cup.

"I suppose," Edgar said, seating himself beside her, "I will have my head bitten off when I ask if you are over tired?"

"Yes," she said, "I suppose you will."

He had been offering affection this morning. It was something Edgar would do, of course. A perfectionist in all things, he would not be satisfied with a forced marriage to a woman whose behavior in London must have disgusted as well as excited him. He would try to create a marriage of affection out of what they had. And she had rebuffed him.

Would it be possible? she wondered and was frightened by the question which expressed itself quite verbally in her mind. The answer was very clear to her. Of course it would be possible. One could not respect a man and like him and admire him and find him attractive and enjoy intimacies with him without there being the possibility of affection for him. Indeed, if she let down all her inner guard, she might even admit to herself . . . No!

Dared she allow the element of affection to creep into their relationship? Perhaps after all there was an end to punishment and self-loathing. Perhaps Edgar was strong enough . . . Certainly he was stronger than . . . No!

Her cup was empty and had lost its comforting warmth. She set it down on the ground at her feet. When Edgar took her hand in his, she curled her fingers about it. He was singing with everyone else. He had a good tenor voice. She had not heard him sing before. He was her husband. Their lives were linked together for all time. It was his child she carried. They were to be parents together—perhaps more than once. That was a new thought. Perhaps they would have more than one child. There would be other occasions like this down the years.

Did she dare to let go and simply enjoy? When someone else, because of her, would suffer for the rest of a lifetime?

She turned her head to look at her husband. Decent, strong, honorable Edgar. Who deserved far better. But who would never have it unless she dared give more in her marriage than she had been prepared to give. And who might forever be sorry if she did.

He looked back at her and stopped singing. He smiled and lowered his head to kiss her briefly on the lips. A small token of—affection. Was he going to pay her warning no heed then?

"Such a bleak look, Helena," he said. "Yet you have been looking so happy."

"Let us not start this again," she said.

But his next words had her jumping to her feet in terror and panic.

"Tell me about your stepson," he said. "Tell me about Sir Gerald Stapleton."

She turned and stumbled off in the direction of the house.

She tried to shake off his arm when he caught up to her and took her in his grasp.

"I was right, then," he said. "I picked on the right person. Steady, Helena. You cannot run all the way home. We will walk. You cannot run from yourself either. Have you not realized that yet? And you will not run from me. But we will take it slowly—both the walk and the other. Slow your steps."

A chaplain praying over a condemned man must speak in just that quiet, soothing voice, she thought.

"Damn you, Edgar!" she cried. "Damn you, damn you, damn you!"

"Calm yourself," he said. "Walk slowly. There is no hurry."

"I hate you," she said. "Oh, how I hate you. You are loathsome and I hate you. Damn you," she added for good measure.

Chapter 14

Incredibly, nothing more was said on the subject of Helena's stepson. They walked home in silence and Edgar took her straight to their bedchamber, where she slumped wearily onto the bed, taking the time only to remove her boots and outdoor garments before she did so. He went to stand at the window until he looked over his shoulder and noticed that she had not covered herself, though the room was rather chilly. He wrapped the top quilt carefully about her to the chin. She was already asleep.

She slept deeply for two hours while Edgar first watched her, then returned to his place at the window, and finally went downstairs when he saw that everyone else was coming back to the house, loaded with greenery. He helped to carry armfuls inside while their original bearers stamped snow-packed boots on the steps and slapped at snowy clothing. He took the Bridgwater baby from the duke's arms and had unwound him from his many layers of warm clothing before a few of the nurses came hurrying downstairs to whisk him and most of the other children back up to the nursery with them. They were to be tidied and warmed and fed and put down for an obligatory rest before the excitement was to resume with the decoration of the house.

Edgar told several people who asked that his wife had merely felt herself tiring and was now having a sleep.

"I warned her that it would be too much for her," Mr. Downes said. "You should have taken a firmer hand with her yourself, Edgar. You must not allow her to risk her health."

"I believe Helena is not one to take orders meekly, Papa," Edgar said.

"Oh, dear, no," Mrs. Cross agreed. "There was never anyone more stubborn than Helena, Mr. Downes. But she was exceedingly happy this morning. She still has a way with children, just as she always used to have. Children warm quickly to her, perhaps because she warms quickly to them. Yes, thank you, sir. You are most kind." Mr. Downes was taking her cloak and bonnet from her and looking around in vain for a footman who might be standing about doing nothing.

"Let me take you to the drawing room, ma'am," Edgar said, offering his arm, "where there will be a warm fire and probably some warm drinks too before nuncheon."

"Thank you," she said. "I must admit to feeling chilly. But I do not know when I have enjoyed myself as much as I have this morning, Mr. Downes. You cannot know what it means to me to be part of such a happy family Christmas."

"You always will be from now on, ma'am," he said, "if my wife and I have anything to say in the matter. Did you ever visit Helena during her first marriage?"

"Oh, yes, indeed," she said, "two or three times. She had a gift for happiness in those days. I suppose the marriage was not entirely to her liking—Sir Christian Stapleton was so much older than she, you know. But she made the best of it. She had that vibrancy and those smiles." She smiled herself. "Perhaps they will come back now. I am confident they will. This is a far better match for her."

"Thank you," he said. "I hope you are right. Did you know Sir Christian's son?"

"Poor boy," she said. "He was very lonely and timid and not much loved by his father, I believe. But Helena was good to him. She set herself to mothering him and shielding him from his father's impatience—she could always wheedle him with her sunny ways. They both worshiped her. But you do not want to be hearing this, Mr. Downes. That was a long time ago. I am very glad Helena has a chance at last to have a child of her own—and a husband of her own age. I was shocked at first and was perhaps not as kind to you as I ought to have been. I do apologize for that. You are a fine young man, I believe."

"You were all that was gracious, ma'am," he said. "Take this chair while I fetch you a drink. You should be warm again in a moment."

By the time Helena woke up nuncheon was over—Edgar had a tray sent up to her—and the drawing room, the dining room, the ballroom, and the hall were being cleared, ready for the decorating. The older children had already come downstairs and the younger ones were being brought just as she came down herself. There was much to do and many people to do it. It was certainly not the time for a serious talk.

Edgar had been appointed to direct most of the men and some of the bigger children in the decoration of the ballroom. It involved much climbing of ladders and leaning out precariously into space. Cora shrieked when she saw her eldest son, ten rungs up one of the ladders, intent on handing his father a hammer. She showed every intention of climbing up herself to rescue him, though she was terrified of heights, and was banished to the drawing room.

Stephanie, Duchess of Bridgwater, and Fanny Grainger, self-proclaimed experts in the making of kissing boughs, were constructing the main one for the drawing room with the help of some of the other ladies. Helena, self-proclaimed nonexpert, was making another with the help of far too many children for any degree of efficiency. She had thrown herself into the task, Edgar noticed, with bright-faced enthusiasm. Of course the sleep had done her good, she had assured his father and a few other people who had thought to ask. All her energy was restored and redoubled. She smiled dazzlingly. She ignored her husband as if he did not exist.

She could not continue to do so indefinitely, of course. Finally all was done and they were summoned to the drawing room for hot punch—hot lemonade for the children—and for the first annual ceremony of the raising of the kissing bough, Mr. Downes announced when they were all assembled. Adults chuckled and children squealed with laughter.

It was finally in place at the very center of the room below the chandelier. They all gazed at it admiringly. The Marquess of Carew began a round of applause and Fanny blushed while the duchess laughed.

"It would seem appropriate to me," Mr. Downes said, "for the bough to be put to the test by the new bride and groom. We have to be sure that it works."

There was renewed applause. There were renewed shrieks from the children. The Earl of Thornhill whistled.

"Pucker up, Edgar, old chap," Lord Francis said.

Well, Edgar thought, stepping forward and reaching for his wife's hand, he had not kissed her at their wedding. He supposed he owed everyone this.

"Now, let me see." He played to the audience, setting his hands on Helena's shoulders and looking upward with a frown of concentration. "Ah, yes, there. Dead center. That should work." He grinned at her. She gazed back, the afternoon's bright gaiety still in her face. "Happy Christmas, Mrs. Downes."

They lingered over the kiss, entirely for the benefit of their cheering audience. It was not exactly his idea of an erotic experience, Edgar thought, to indulge in public kissing. But he was surprised by the tide of warmth that flooded over him. Not physical warmth—or at least not *sexual* warmth. Just the warmth of love, he and his wife literally surrounded by family and friends at Christmas.

He smiled down at her when they were finished. "It works exceedingly well," he said. "But we do not expect anyone to believe it merely because we have said so. Do we, my love? You are all welcome to try for yourselves."

Rosamond, young daughter of the Carews, pulled the marquess out beneath the bough, and he bent over her, smiling, and kissed her to the accompaniment of much laughter. No one, it seemed, was prepared to take Edgar at his word or that of anyone who came after him and confirmed his opinion. Hardly anyone went unkissed, and those who did—those children of middle years who were both too old and too young to kiss and pulled gargoyle faces at the very thought—did so entirely from choice.

Jack Sperling and Fanny Grainger were almost the last. Edgar had watched them grow progressively more self-conscious and uncomfortable until finally Jack got up his courage, strode toward her, and led her onto the recently vacated space beneath the bough with all the firm determination any self-respecting man of business could possibly want in an employee. Their lips clung together with very obvious yearning—for perhaps the duration of one whole second. And then she scurried away, scarlet to the tips of her ears, her eyes avoiding those of her suitor—and those of her barely smiling parents.

The elder Mr. Downes was last.

"Well, Mrs. Cross," he said heartily, "I am not sure I believe all these young folk. There is something sorry seeming about that bough, pretty as it is and loaded down with mistletoe as it is. I believe you and I should see what all the fuss is about."

Mrs. Cross did not argue or even blush, Edgar was interested to note. She stepped quietly under the bough and lifted her face."I believe we should, sir," she said.

It felt strange watching his father kissing a woman, even if it was just a public Christmas kiss beneath mistletoe. One tended not to think of one's own father in such terms. It was not the sort of smacking kiss his father often bestowed on Cora and his grandchildren. Brief and decorous though it was, it was definitely the sort of kiss a man exchanges with a woman.

"Well, what do you say, ma'am?" His father was frowning ferociously and acting to the audience of shrieking, bouncing children, who had lost some interest in the proceedings until Grandpapa had decided to take a turn.

"I think I would have to say it really is a kissing bough, sir," Mrs. Cross said calmly and seriously. "I would have to say it works very nicely indeed."

"My sentiments entirely," he said. "Now I am not so sure about that monstrous concoction of ribbons and bows that is hanging in the hall. The children's creation with the help of my daughter-in-law, I believe. *That* is no kissing bough." He still had his hands on Mrs. Cross's waist, Edgar noticed, while grimacing from the noise of children screeching in indignation.

"*What?*" his father said, looking about him in some amazement. "It *is*?"

The children responded like a Greek chorus.

And so nothing would do but Mr. Downes had to tuck Mrs. Cross's arm beneath his and lead them all in an unruly procession down the stairs to the hall, where Helena's grotesque and ragged creation hung in all its tasteless glory. He kissed Mrs. Cross again, with a resounding smack of the lips this time, and pronounced the children's kissing bough even more effective than the one in the drawing room.

The children burst into mass hysteria.

It had been a thoroughly enjoyable afternoon for all. But parents were only human, after all. The children were gradually herded in the direction of the nursery, where it fell to the lot of their poor nurses to calm their high spirits. Something resembling quiet descended on the house. The conservatory would be the quietest place of all, Edgar thought. He would take his wife there. They could not suspend indefinitely the talk that this morning's revelation had made inevitable.

He had to find out about Gerald Stapleton.

But Cora had other ideas. She reached Helena's side before he did. "The children's party on Christmas Day needs to be planned, Helena," she said, "as well as the ball in the evening. Papa has had all the invitations sent out, of course, and the cook has all the food plans well in hand. But there is much else to be organized. Shall we spend an hour on it now?"

"Of course," Helena said. "Just you and I, Cora?"

"Stephanie was a governess before she was a duchess," Cora said. "Did you know that? She is wonderful with children."

"Then we will ask her if she wishes to help us plan games," Helena said.

They went away to some destination unknown, taking the duchess with them as well as the wife and daughter of one of Edgar's Bristol friends. After they returned, it was time to change for dinner. And dinner, with so many guests, and with so many Christmas decorations to be exclaimed over and so many Christmas plans to be divulged and discussed, lasted a great long while. So did coffee in the drawing room afterward, with several of the young people entertaining the company informally with pianoforte recitals and singing.

But it could not be postponed until bedtime, Edgar decided. And certainly not until tomorrow. He had started this. He had thought methodically through all he knew of Helena and all she had told him and not told him and had concluded that her first husband was not the key figure in her present unhappiness and bitterness. It was far more likely to have been the son. Her reaction to his question this morning had left him in no doubt whatsoever. She had been so shocked and so distressed that she had not even tried to deceive him with impassivity.

They must talk. She must tell him everything. Both for her own sake and for the sake of their marriage. Perhaps forcing her to confront her past in his hearing was entirely the wrong thing to do. The bitterness that was always at the back of her eyes and just behind her smiles might burst through and destroy the fragile control she had imposed on her own life. The baring of her soul, which she had repeatedly told him she would never do, might well destroy their marriage almost before it had begun. She might loathe him with a very real intensity for the rest of their lives.

But their marriage stood no real chance if she kept her secrets. They might live together as man and wife in some amity and harmony for many years. But they would be amicable strangers who just happened to share a name, a home, a bed, and a child or two. He wanted more than that. He could not be satisfied with so little. He was willing to risk—he *had* to risk—the little they had in the hope that he would get everything in return and with the very real risk that he would lose everything.

But then his life was constantly lived on a series of carefully calculated risks. Of course, as an experienced and successful businessman, he never risked all or even nearly all on one venture. No single failure had ever ruined him, just as no single success had ever made him. This time it was different. This time he risked everything—everything he had, everything he was.

He had realized in the course of the day that he was not only in love with her. He loved her.

He might well be headed toward self-destruction. But he had no choice.

She was conversing with a group of his friends. She was being her most vibrant, fascinating self, and they were all charmed by her, he could see. He touched her on the arm, smiled, and joined in the conversation for a few minutes before addressing himself just to her.

"It is a wonderfully clear night," he said. "The sky will look lovely from the conservatory. Come and see it there with me?"

She smiled and he caught a brief glimpse of desperation behind her eyes.

"That is the most blatantly contrived invitation a man ever offered his new bride, Edgar," one of his friends said. "We have all done it in our time. 'Come and see the stars, my love.' "

The laughter that greeted his words was entirely good-natured.

"Take no notice, Edgar," one of the wives told him. "Horace is merely envious because he did not think of it first."

"I will come and see the stars," Helena said in her lowest, most velvet voice, leaving with their friends the impression that she expected not to see a single one of them.

Which was, in a sense, true.

He stood at one of the wide windows of the conservatory, his hands clasped at his back, his feet slightly apart. He was looking outward, upward at the stars. He looked comfortable, relaxed. She knew it was a false impression.

She liked the conservatory, though she had not had the chance to spend much time here. There were numerous plants and the warmth of a summer garden. Yet the outdoors was fully visible through the many windows. The contrast with the snowy outdoors this evening was quite marked. The sky was indeed clear.

"The stars are bright," she said. "But you must not expect to see the Bethlehem star yet, Edgar. It is two nights too early."

"Yes," he said.

She had not approached the windows herself. She had seated herself on a wrought-iron seat beneath a giant palm. She felt curiously calm, resigned. She supposed that from the moment she had set eyes on Edgar Downes and had felt that overpowering need to do more than merely flirt with him this moment had become inevitable. She had become a firm believer in fate. Why had she returned to London at very much an off-season for polite society? Why had he chosen such an inopportune time to go to London to choose a bride?

It was because they had been fated to meet. Because *this* had been fated.

"He was fourteen when I married his father," she said. "He was just a child. When you are nineteen, Edgar, a fourteen-year-old seems like a child. He was small and thin and timid and unappealing. He did not have much promise." Because she had been unhappy herself and a little bewildered, she had felt instant sympathy for the boy, more than if he had been handsome and robust and confident.

"But you liked him," Edgar said.

"He had had a sad life," she said. "His mother abandoned him when he was eight years old to go and live with her two sisters. He had adored her and had felt adored in return. Christian tried to soften the blow by telling him that she was dead. But when she really did die five years later, Gerald suddenly found himself thrust into mourning for her and knew that she had loved him so little. Or so it seemed. One cannot really know the truth about that woman, I suppose. Everything about him irritated Christian. Poor Gerald! He could do nothing right."

"And so you became a new mother to him?" he asked.

"More like an elder sister perhaps," she said. "I talked to him and listened to him. I helped him with his lessons, especially with arithmetic, which made no sense at all to him. When Christian was from home I listened to him play the pianoforte and sometimes sang to his accompaniment. He had real talent, Edgar, but he was ashamed of it because his father saw it as unmanly. I helped him get over his terrible conviction that he was unlovable and worthless and stupid. He was none of the three. He was sweet. It is a weak word to use of a boy, but it is the right word to use of Gerald. There was such sweetness in him." He had filled such a void in her life.

"I suppose," Edgar said, breaking the silence she had been unaware of, "he fell in love with you."

"No," she said. "He grew up. At eighteen he was pleasing to look at and very sweet natured. He was—he was youthful."

Edgar had braced his arms wide on the windowsill and hung his head. "You seduced him," he said. He was breathing heavily. "Your husband's son."

She set her head back against the palm and closed her eyes. "I loved him," she said. "As a *person* I loved him. He was sweet and trusting and far more intelligent and talented than he realized. And he was vulnerable. His sense of his own worth was so very fragile. I knew it and feared for him. And I—I wanted him. I was horrified. I hated myself—*hated* myself. You could not know how much. No one could hate me as I hated myself. I tried to fight but I was very weak. I was sitting one day on a bridge, one of the most picturesque spots in the park at Brookhurst, and he was coming toward me looking bright and eager about something—I can no longer remember what. I took his hands and— Well. I frightened him and he ran away. Of all the shame I have felt since, I do not believe I have ever known any of greater intensity than I felt after he had gone. And yet it happened twice more before he persuaded Christian to send him away to university."

She had thought of killing herself, she remembered. She had even wondered how she might best do it. She had not had enough courage even for that.

"Now tell me that you are glad I have told you, Edgar," she said after a while. "Tell me you are proud to have such a wife."

There was another lengthy silence. "You were young," he said, "and found yourself in an arranged marriage with a much older man. There were only five years between you and your stepson. You were lonely."

"Is it for me you try to make excuses, Edgar?" she asked. "Or for yourself? Are you trying to convince yourself that you have not made such a disastrous marriage after all? There are no excuses. What I did was unforgivable."

"Did you beg his pardon later?" he asked. "Did he refuse to grant it?"

"I saw him only once after he left for university," she said. "It was at his father's funeral three years later. We did not speak. There are certain things for which one cannot ask for pardon, Edgar, because there is no pardon."

He turned to look at her at last. "You have been too hard on yourself," he said. "It was an ugly thing, what you did, but nothing is beyond pardon. And it was a long time ago. You have changed."

"I seduced you a little over two months ago," she said.

"I am your equal in age and experience, Helena," he said, "as I suppose all your lovers have been. You have had to convince yourself that you are promiscuous, have you not? You have had to punish yourself, to convince yourself that you are evil. It is time you put the past behind you."

"The past is always with me, Edgar," she said. "The past had consequences. I destroyed him."

"That is doubtless an exaggeration," he said. "He would not dally with his father's wife and went away. Good for him. He showed some strength of character. Perhaps in some way the experience was even the making of him. You have been too hard on yourself."

"It is what I hoped would happen," she said. "I went to Scotland after Christian's death and waited and waited for word that Gerald was somehow settled in life. Then I went traveling and waited again. I finally heard news of him last year in the late summer. Doubtless you would have too, Edgar, if you moved in *tonnish* circles. Doubtless Cora and Francis heard. He married."

"Well, then." He had come to stand in front of her. He was frowning down at her. "He has married. He has found peace and contentment. He has doubtless forgotten what has so obsessed you."

"Fool!" she said. "I finally confirmed him in what all the

experiences of his life had pointed to—that he was unlovable and worthless. He married a whore, Edgar."

"A whore?" he said. "Those are strong words."

"From a woman who has admitted to having had many lovers?" she said. "Perhaps. But she worked in a brothel. Half the male population of London paid for her services, I daresay. I suppose that is where Gerald met her. He took her and made her his mistress and then married her. Is that the action of a man with any sense of self-worth?"

"I do not know," he said. "I do not know the two people or the circumstances."

She laughed without any humor whatsoever. "I do know Gerald," she said. "It is just what he would do and just the sort of thing that for years I dreaded to hear. He thought himself worthy of nothing better in a wife than a whore."

"How old was he last year?" Edgar asked. "Twenty-nine? Thirty?"

"No," she said, "you will not use that argument with me, Edgar. I will not allow you to talk me out of my belief in my own responsibility for what has become of him. I will not let you forgive me. You do not have the power. No one does."

He went down on his haunches and reached out his hands to her.

"Touch me now," she said, "and I will never forgive you. A hug will not solve it, Edgar. I am not the one who needs the hug. And you cannot comfort me. There is no comfort. There is no forgiveness. And do not pretend you do not feel disgust—for what I did, for what I trapped you into, for the fact that I am bearing your child."

He drew breath and sighed audibly. "How long ago did this happen, Helena?" he asked. "Ten years? Twelve?"

"Thirteen," she said.

"Thirteen." He gazed at her. "You have lived in a self-made hell for thirteen years. My dear, it will not do. It just will not do."

"I am tired." She got to her feet, careful not to touch him. "I am going to bed. I am sorry you have to share it with me, Edgar. If you wish to make other arrangements—"

He grabbed her then and drew her against him and she felt the full force of his strength. Although she fought him, she could not free herself. After a few moments she did not even try. She sagged against him, soaking up his warmth and his strength, breathing in the smell of him. Feeling the lure of a nonexistent peace.

"Hate me if you will," he said, "but I will touch you and hold you. When we go to bed I will make love to you. You are my wife. And if you are so unworthy to be forgiven and to be loved, Helena, why is it that I can forgive you? Why is it that I love you?"

She breathed in slowly and deeply. "I am so tired, Edgar," she said. So tired. Always tired. Not just from her pregnancy, surely. She was soul-weary. "Please. I am so tired." Was that abject voice hers?

"We will go to bed, then," he said. "But I want you to see something first." He led her to the window, one arm firmly about her waist. "You see?" He pointed upward to one star that was brighter than all the others. "It is there, Helena. Not only on the night of Christmas Eve. Always if we just look for it. There is always hope."

"Dreamer," she said, her voice shaky. "Sentimentalist. Edgar, you are supposed to be a man of reason and cold good sense."

"I am also a man who loves," he said. "I always have from childhood on. And I am what you are stuck with. For life, I am afraid. I'll never let you forget that that star is always there."

There was such a mingling of despair and hope in her that her chest felt tight and her throat sore. She buried her face against his shoulder and said nothing. After a few minutes of silence he took her up to bed.

Chapter 15

Edgar was up before dawn the next morning, a little earlier than usual. The fire had not yet been made up. He shivered as he stretched his arms above his head and looked out through the window. As last night's clear sky had suggested, there had been no more snow.

He was tired. Nevertheless he was glad to be up. He had slept only in fits and starts through the night, and he had felt Helena's sleeplessness, though they had not spoken and had lain turned away from each other for most of the night after he had made love to her.

Her story had been ugly enough. What she had done had been truly shameful. She had been a married woman, however little say she had had in the choice of her husband. She had known and understood the boy's vulnerability—and he had been her husband's son. She had been old enough to know better, and of course she *had* known better. The attraction, the desire had been understandable—the son had been far closer to her own age than the father. That she had given in to temptation was blameworthy. She had been morally weak.

Her conscience had not been correspondingly weak. She had punished herself ever since. She had refused either to ask forgiveness or to forgive herself simply because she thought her sin unforgivable. She had never allowed herself to be happy or to love—or be loved. He guessed that her extensive travels had been her way of trying to escape from herself. It might be said that true repentance should have made her celibate. But Edgar believed he had been right in what he had said to her the night before. She had punished herself with promiscuity, with the conviction that she was truly depraved.

Their marriage stood not one chance in a million of bringing either of them contentment. Unless . . .

It would be an enormous risk. He had known that all through the night. She was quite convinced that she had destroyed her stepson, that her betrayal had been the final straw in an unhappy life of abuse. And she had been quite certain of her facts when describing the man's marriage. He had married a prostitute taken from a London brothel.

It seemed very probable that she was right. And if she was, there would never be any peace for her. He might argue until kingdom come that Sir Gerald Stapleton had been abused by both his father and mother, far more important people in his life than she had ever been, and that he had not used his individual freedom when he was old enough to fight back against his image of himself as a victim. Helena would forever blame herself.

And so he must do today the only thing he could do. It was the only hope left, however slim it might be. He must remember what he had told his wife last night about the star. It was always there, the Christmas star perhaps, constant symbol of hope. There must always be hope. The only thing left when there was no hope was despair. Helena had lived too long with despair.

Her stillness and quietness did not deceive him. She was awake, as she had been most of the night. He crossed to the bed and set a hand on her shoulder.

"I am going to Bristol," he said. "There is some business that must be taken care of before the holiday. I will stay at the house tonight and return tomorrow."

He expected questions. What business could possibly have arisen so suddenly two days before Christmas when there had not even been any post yesterday?

"Yes," she said. "All right."

He squeezed her shoulder. "Get some rest," he said.

"Yes."

The dusk of dawn had still not given place to the full light of day when Edgar led his horse from the stables, set it to a cautious pace to allow it to become accustomed to the snowy roads, and set his course for Brookhurst, thirty miles away.

It was an enormous relief to have Edgar gone for the day. It would have been difficult to face him in the morning after the night before. Helena was annoyed with herself for giving in to his constant needling and pestering. She should never have told him the truth. She had done so as a self-indulgence. It had felt surprisingly cathartic sitting there in the quiet, darkened conservatory, reliving those memories for someone else's ears. She almost envied papists their confessionals.

But it had not just been self-indulgence. She had owed him the truth. He was her husband. And therein lay the true problem. She was unaccustomed to thinking sympathetically about another person, caring about his feelings. It was something she had not done in years. And something she ought not to do now. What good could ever come of her sympathy, of her compassion?

She cared about him. He was a decent man, and he had been good to her. But she must not care *for* him or allow herself to be comforted by his care. She remembered what he had said the night before—*why is it that I love you?* She shook her head to rid her mind of the sound of his voice saying those words.

She was glad he had gone. There was no business in Bristol, of course. His friends had looked surprised and his father astonished when she had given that as an explanation for his absence. He had gone there so that he could be away from her for a day, so that he could think and plan. There would be a greater distance between them by the time he returned, once he had had the chance to digest fully what she had told him. And a greater distance on her part, too—she must return to the aloofness, the air of mockery that had become second nature to her for a number of years but that had been deserting her since their marriage. She was glad she had not told him the one, final truth.

She was glad he had gone.

She spent a busy day. She walked into the village during the morning with Cora and Jane, Countess of Greenwald, to purchase some prizes for the children's games at the Christmas party. The children, the young people, and most of the men had gone out to the hill to ride the sleds down its snowy slopes. After nuncheon she was banished to her room by her father-in-law for a rest and was surprised to find that she slept soundly for a whole hour. And then she went outside when it became obvious that the duke and duchess, who were going to build a snowman for their little boy, had acquired a sizable train of other small children determined to go along to see and to help.

"You are remarkably good with children, Mrs. Downes," the Duke of Bridgwater told her when three snowmen of varying sizes and artistic merit were standing in a row. "So is Stephanie. I might have stayed inside the house and toasted my toes at the fire."

It was surprising in a way that he had not done so. Helena had been acquainted with him for several years and had always known him as an austere, correct, rather toplofty aristocrat. He still gave that impression when one did not see him in company with his wife or his son. Their company was obviously preferable to toasted toes this afternoon, despite his words.

For a moment Helena felt a pang of emptiness. She favored the duke with her mocking smile."It must be incipient maternity that is causing me to behave so much out of character, your grace," she said. "I have never before been accused of anything as shudderingly awful as being good with children."

"I do beg your pardon, ma'am," he said with a gleam in his eye. "I experienced much the same horror less than a month ago when my butler observed me to be galloping—*galloping*, ma'am—along an upper corridor of my home with my son on my shoulders. Why I confess to this next detail I do not know—I was *whinnying*." He grimaced.

Helena laughed.

The evening was spent in the drawing room. Family and guests passed the time with music and cards and conversation and a vigorous game of charades, suggested by the young son and daughter of one of Mr. Downes's friends and participated in with great enthusiasm by all the young people and a few of the older ones, too.

A definite romance was developing between Fanny Grainger and Mr. Sperling, Helena noticed. They were being very careful and very discreet and were watched almost every moment by Sir Webster and Lady Grainger, who dared not appear too disapproving, but who were far from being enthusiastic. But matters had been helped along by her father-in-law's apparently careless remark at tea that Edgar's business was to buy and renovate Mr. Sperling's country estate as a future home for the young man when he should have risen high enough in the company's ranks to need it as a sign of status.

Edgar either felt very guilty about Miss Grainger, Helena concluded, or he had a great soft heart, inherited with far tougher attributes from his father. She strongly favored the soft heart theory.

It felt good to be alone again, Helena thought, to be free of him for one day at least. She wondered if he had got safely to Bristol. She wondered if he had dressed warmly enough for the journey or if he had caught a chill. She wondered what he was doing this evening. Was he sitting at home, brooding? Or enjoying his solitude? Was he out visiting friends or otherwise amusing himself? She wondered if he kept mistresses. She supposed he must have over the years. He was six-and-thirty after all and had never before been married. Besides, he was an experienced and skilled lover. But she could not somehow imagine the very respectable, very bourgeois Edgar Downes keeping a mistress now that he had a wife. Not that she would mind. But she had a sudden image of Edgar doing with another woman what he did with her in their bed upstairs and felt decidedly irritable—and even murderous.

She did not care what he was doing tonight in Bristol. She was just happy to be able to converse and laugh and even join in the charades without feeling his eyes on her.

Was he thinking about her?

She hoped he was not wasting time and energy doing any such thing since she was certainly not thinking about him.

* * *

Sir Gerald Stapleton's butler would see if he was at home, he told Edgar with a stiff bow when the latter presented himself and his card at the main doors of Brookhurst late in the afternoon. He showed Edgar into a salon leading off the hall.

At least, Edgar thought, the long journey had not been quite in vain. Stapleton might refuse to see him, but clearly he had not gone away for Christmas. The butler would have known very well then that he was not at home. He stood at the window. There was as much snow here as at Mobley. It was an elegant house. The park was large and attractive, even with its snow cover.

He turned when the door opened again. The man who stepped inside did not surprise him, except perhaps in one detail. He was not particularly tall or broad or handsome. He was well dressed though with no extravagance of taste. There was something quite ordinary and unremarkable about his appearance. Except for his pleasant, open countenance—that was the surprise. Though a man might look that way merely out of politeness when he had a visitor, of course.

"Mr. Downes?" he said, looking at the card in his hand.

Edgar inclined his head. "From Bristol, as you see on the card," he said. "My father owns Mobley Abbey thirty miles from here."

"Ah, yes," Sir Gerald Stapleton said. "That is why the name seemed familiar to me. The snow must make for slow travel. You are on your way to Mobley for Christmas? I am glad you found Brookhurst on your way and decided to break your journey here. I will send for refreshments."

"I came from Mobley Abbey today," Edgar said, "specifically to see and to speak with you. I am recently married. My wife was Lady Stapleton, your father's widow."

Sir Gerald's expression became instantly more guarded. "I see," he said. "My felicitations to you."

"Thank you," Edgar said. It was very difficult to know how to proceed. "And to my wife?" he asked.

Sir Gerald looked down at the card and placed it absently into a pocket. He was clearly considering his reply. "I mean you no offense, sir," he said at last. "I have no kind feelings for Mrs. Downes."

Ah. It was not simply a case then of something Helena had blown quite out of proportion with reality. Sir Gerald Stapleton had neither forgotten nor forgiven.

"Then you mean me offense," Edgar said quietly.

Sir Gerald half smiled. "I would offer you the hospitality of my home," he said, "but we would both be more comfortable, I believe, if you stayed at the village inn. It is a posting inn and quite respectable. I thank you for informing me."

"She believes she destroyed you," Edgar said.

Sir Gerald pursed his lips for a moment. "She did not do that," he said. "You may inform her so, if you wish."

"She believes she betrayed your trust at a time in your life when you were particularly vulnerable," Edgar said. "She believes you have never recovered from her selfish cruelty. And so she has never forgiven herself or stopped punishing herself."

"Helena?" Sir Gerald said, walking toward the fireplace and staring down at the fire burning there. "She was so much in command of herself. So confident. So without conscience. I remember her at my father's funeral, cold and proud—and newly wealthy. I beg your pardon, sir. I speak of your wife and do not expect you to remain quiet while you hear her maligned. You may assure her that she has had no lasting effect on my life. You may even say, if you will, that I wish her well in her new marriage. That is all I have to say on the subject. If we can find some other topic of mutual interest, I will order hot refreshments to warm you before you return to the cold. I would like to hear about Mobley Abbey. I hear that it has been restored to some of its earlier splendor."

There was no avoiding it. "My wife believes that your marriage was an outcome of your lasting unhappiness," Edgar said, wondering if he was going to find himself fighting a duel before the day was out—or at dawn the next day.

"My marriage." Sir Gerald's face had lost all traces of good humor. "Have a care what you say about my marriage, sir. It is not open for discussion. I believe it would be best for both of us if we bade each other a civil good afternoon while we still may."

"Sir Gerald," Edgar said, "I love my wife."

Sir Gerald closed his eyes and drew breath audibly. "You can love such a woman," he said, "and yet you believe that I cannot? You believe that I must have married out of contempt for my wife and contempt for myself?"

"It is what my wife believes," Edgar said.

Sir Gerald stood with his back to the fire for a long while in silence. Finally he strode toward the door and Edgar prepared to see him leave and to know that he must return to Mobley with nothing more comforting for Helena than an assurance from her stepson that she had had no permanent effect on his life. But Sir Gerald stood in the doorway, calling instructions to his butler.

"Ask Lady Stapleton if she would be so good as to step down here," he said.

He returned to his position before the fire without looking at Edgar or exchanging another word with him. A few minutes passed before the door opened again.

She was a complete surprise. She was small, slender, dark-haired, decently dressed, and very pretty in an entirely wholesome way. She had a bright, intelligent face. She glanced at Edgar and then looked at her husband in inquiry.

"Priss?" Sir Gerald held out one arm to her, his expression softened to what was unmistakably a deep affection. "Come here, my love. This is Mr. Edgar Downes of Bristol. He has recently married Helena. My wife, Lady Stapleton, sir."

She looked first into her husband's face with obvious concern and deep fondness as she moved toward him until he could circle her waist with his arm and draw her protectively to his side. Then she turned to Edgar. Her eyes were calm and candid. "Mr. Downes," she said, "I wish you happy."

"You sent Peter back to the nursery?" Sir Gerald asked her.

"Yes." She smiled at him and then turned back to Edgar. "Has my husband offered you refreshments, Mr. Downes? It is a chilly day."

She spoke with refined accents and with a graciousness that appeared to come naturally to her.

"Priss." Sir Gerald took one of her hands in both of his. "Mr. Downes says that Helena has never forgotten what happened and has never forgiven herself."

"I told you she probably had not, Gerald," she said.

"She believes she destroyed me," he said.

She tipped her head to one side and looked at him with such tenderness that Edgar found himself almost holding his breath. "She was very nearly right," she said.

Sir Gerald closed his eyes briefly. "She considers our marriage as evidence that she succeeded," he said.

"It is understandable that she should think that," she said gently.

"She wants my forgiveness." He looked up. "I suppose that *is* why you came, Mr. Downes? I cannot give it. But you may describe my wife to her, if you wish, and tell her that Lady Stapleton is the woman I honor above all other women and love more than my own life. Will it suffice? If it will not, I have nothing more to offer, I am afraid."

Edgar found himself locking eyes with Lady Stapleton and feeling shock at the sympathy that passed between them.

"If Mrs. Downes has not forgotten the pain of that time in her life, sir," she said, "neither has my husband. It is a wound very easily rubbed raw. I have tried to convince Gerald that in reality there are very few people who are monsters without conscience. I have told him that Helena has probably always regretted what happened. She is very unhappy?"

"Very, ma'am," he said.

"And you are fond of her." It was a statement, not a question. Her intelligent eyes searched his face.

"Yes, ma'am."

"Gerald." She turned to him and looked earnestly at him. "Here is your chance for final peace. If you forgive her, you may finally forget."

Edgar tried to picture her performing her tricks at a London brothel. It was impossible.

"You are soft-hearted and sweet-natured, Priss," her husband said. "I cannot forgive her. You know I cannot."

"And yet," she said softly, flushing, "you forgave me."

"There was nothing to forgive," he said hotly. "Good God, Priss, there was *nothing to forgive.*"

"Only because you knew me from the inside," she said. "Only because you knew of my suffering and my yearning to rise above my suffering. There are few deeds in this life beyond forgiveness, Gerald. For our own sakes we must forgive as much as for the sake of the person we forgive. I find it hard to forgive Helena. She made you so desperately unsure of yourself. But without her, dear, I would never have met you. I would still be where you found me. And so I can forgive her. She is unhappy and has been for all these years, I daresay."

Sir Gerald stood with bowed head and closed eyes. "You are too good, my love," he said after a while.

"Suffering teaches one compassion, Gerald," she said. "You know that. You can feel compassion for everyone except Helena, I believe. Mr. Downes, there is a bigger and warmer fire burning in the drawing room. Will you come up there? You still have had no refreshments. And it is dusk outside already. Will you stay here for tonight? You cannot possibly drive all the way home, and inns are dreary places at which to put up. Stay with us?"

Edgar looked at Sir Gerald, who had raised his head.

"Please accept our hospitality," he said. "Ride back to Mobley Abbey tomorrow and inform Mrs. Downes that she has my full and free forgiveness." His voice was stiff, his face set and pale. But the words were spoken quite firmly.

"Thank you," Edgar said. "I will stay."

Lady Stapleton smiled. "Come upstairs, then," she said. "I hope you like children, Mr. Downes. Our son Peter was very cross to be taken back to the nursery so early. I will have him brought back down if I may. He is a little over a year old and terrorizes his mama and papa." She crossed the room and linked her arm through Edgar's.

"I like children," he said. "My wife and I are expecting one of our own next summer."

"Oh?" she said. "Oh, splendid. And Gerald and I, too, Mr. Downes."

The drawing room was cozy and looked lived-in. Its surfaces were strewn with books and needlework, but not with breakables. The reason was evident as soon as Peter Stapleton arrived in the room. He toddled about, exploring everything with energetic curiosity, before climbing onto his father's lap and playing with his watch chain and fob.

The room was decorated for Christmas. A warm fire burned in the hearth. Sir Gerald sat in his chair by the fire, looking at ease with his child on his lap. Lady Stapleton bent her head over her embroidery after pouring the tea and handing around the cups and a plate of cakes.

It was a warm family circle, into which Edgar had been drawn by the courtesy of his hostess, who soon had him talking about his life in Bristol and about Mobley Abbey.

But it was Christmas and there was no sign of other guests and no sign that they were preparing to go elsewhere for the holiday. They were to spend it alone? He asked the question.

"Yes." Lady Stapleton smiled. "The Earl of Severn, Gerald's friend, invited us to Severn Park, but his mother and all his family are to be there and we would not intrude on a family party."

Sir Gerald's eyes watched his wife gravely.

"We are happy here together," he said.

They were not. Contented, perhaps. They were a couple who very clearly shared an unusually deep love for each other. But perhaps circumstances had deepened it. Lady Stapleton had been a whore. She would now be a pariah in society.

"I wish," Edgar said, taking himself as much by surprise as he took them, "you would return to Mobley Abbey with me tomorrow and spend Christmas there."

They both looked at him, quite startled. "To Mobley?" Lady Stapleton said.

"Impossible!" her husband said at the same moment.

"I would like you and my wife to meet each other again," Edgar said to Sir Gerald. "To see each other as people again.

To recapture, perhaps, some of the sympathy and friendship you once shared. Christmas would seem the ideal time."

"You push too hard, sir," Sir Gerald said stiffly.

"There is a large house party there," Edgar said, turning to Lady Stapleton. "My father and I have friends and their families there, all members of the merchant class. My sister—she is Lady Francis Kneller—has several of her friends there with their families. They are aristocrats and include the Duke and Duchess of Bridgwater and the Marquess and Marchioness of Carew. It would be pleasant to add three more people to our number."

She was a woman of dignity and courage, he saw. She did not look away from him as she spoke. "I believe you are fully aware, sir," she said, "of what I once was and always will be in the eyes of respectable society. I am not ashamed of my past, Mr. Downes, because it was a means of survival and I survived, but I am well aware of the restrictions it imposes upon the rest of my life. I have accepted them. So has Gerald. I thank you for your invitation, but we must decline."

"I believe," he said, not at all sure he was right, "that you might well find your fears ill-founded, ma'am. I went into polite society myself a few months ago when I was in London. I am what is contemptuously called a cit, yet I was treated with unfailing courtesy wherever I went. I know our situations are not comparable, but I know too that my father and my sister will receive with courtesy and warmth anyone I introduce to them as my friend. Lord Francis Kneller and his friends are people of true gentility. And my wife needs absolution," he added.

"Mr. Downes." She had tears in her large, intelligent eyes. "It is impossible, sir."

"I will not take my wife into a situation that might pain her," Sir Gerald said. "I will not have her treated with contempt or worse by people who are by far her inferior."

Edgar's eyes focused on the little boy, who had wriggled off his father's lap and was into his mother's silk threads, undetected.

"There are children of all ages at Mobley," he said. "I

counted fourteen, but there may well be three or four more than that. Children have an annoying tendency not to stand and be counted. Your child would have other children to play with for Christmas, ma'am."

She bit her lower lip and he saw her eyes before she turned them on her husband. They were filled with yearning. Her child was her weakness, then. And she expected another. How she must fear for their future, isolated from other children of their class.

"Gerald—" she said.

"Priss." There were both pain and tenderness in Sir Gerald's voice.

If he had calculated wrongly, Edgar thought, he had several people headed in the direction of disaster. He felt a moment's panic. But it was the sort of exhilarated panic with which he was familiar in his business life. It was a calculated risk he took. Forgiveness was not enough. Helena needed to know that she had not permanently blighted the life of her stepson. Contented as the Stapletons clearly were together, they were equally clearly not living entirely happy lives. And those lives would grow progressively less happy as the years went on and their children began to grow up.

"Please come," he said. "I will promise you the happiest Christmas you have ever known."

Lady Stapleton smiled at him, her moment of weakness already being pushed aside in favor of her usual serenity. "You can do no such thing, Mr. Downes," she said. "We would not put such responsibility on your shoulders. It is just as likely to be the most uncomfortable Christmas of our lives. But I think we should go. Gerald, I think we should."

"Priss." He frowned. "I could not bear it. . . ."

"And I cannot bear to hide here for the rest of my life," she said. "I cannot bear to keep you hiding here. And Peter adores other children. You can see that at church each week. Besides, I want to meet Helena. I want you to see her again. I want—oh, Gerald, I want freedom even if it must come at the expense of some contentment. I want freedom—for both of us and for Peter and the new baby."

"Then we will go," he said. "Mr. Downes, I hope you know what you are doing. But that is unfair. As my wife says, you cannot be held fully responsible for what we decide to do. Let us bring everything into the open, then. I will see Helena, and Priss will be taken into society. And Peter will be given other children with whom to play. We will leave in the morning? Christmas Eve? You are quite sure, Priss?"

"Quite sure, dear." She smiled at him with a calm she could not possibly be feeling.

But then Edgar, too, sat outwardly calm while inwardly he quaked at the enormity of what he had just set in motion.

Sir Gerald and his wife pounced simultaneously in the direction of their son, who was absorbed in making an impossible tangle of bright threads.

Chapter 16

Christmas Eve. It had been a relatively quiet day for Helena. Although several of the adults had made visits to the village for last-minute purchases, and the young people had gone outside for a walk and come back again with enough snow on their persons to suggest that they had also engaged in a snowball fight, and several individual couples had taken their children outside for various forms of exercise—despite these things, there had been a general air of laziness and waiting about the day. Everyone conserved energy for Christmas itself, which would start in the evening.

Dinner was to be an hour earlier than usual. The carolers would come during the evening, and Mr. Downes and all his guests would greet them in the hall and ply them with hot wassail and mince pies after they had sung their carols. Then there would be church in the village, which it seemed everyone except the younger children was planning to attend. And afterward a gathering in the drawing room to provide warm beverages after the chilly walk and to usher in the new day.

Christmas Day itself, of course, would be frantically busy, what with the usual feasting and gift-giving with which the day was always associated and the children's party in the afternoon and the ball in the evening.

Her father-in-law had not insisted today that Helena rest after nuncheon, though he did ask her if she felt quite well. He and everyone else, of course, wondered why Edgar had gone to Bristol just two days before Christmas and why he was still not back on the afternoon of Christmas Eve. She could feel the worry and strain behind Mr. Downes's smile and Cora's. She decided of her own accord an hour before tea to retire to her room for a rest.

She did not sleep. She was not really tired. That first phase of pregnancy was over, she realized. She had come for escape more than rest. There was such an air of eager anticipation in the house and of domestic contentment. One would have thought that in such a sizable house party there would be some quarreling and bickering, some jealousies or simple dislikes. There were virtually none, apart from a few minor squabbles among the children.

It was just too good to be true. It was cloying.

She felt lonely. As she had always felt—almost all her life. It seemed to her that she had always been on the outside looking in. Yet when she had tried to get in, to be a participant in a warm love relationship, she had done a terrible thing, trying to add a dimension to that love that just did not belong to it. And so she had destroyed everything—everything! If she had only remained patient and true to Christian, she realized now—and it would not have been very difficult as he had always been good to her—she might have mourned his death for a year and still been young enough to find someone else with whom to be happy.

But then she would never have met Edgar, or if she had, she would have been married to someone else. Would that have made a difference? If she had been married this autumn and had met him in the Greenwalds' drawing room, would she have recognized him in that single long glance across the room as that one person who could make her life complete? As the one love of her life?

She lay on her bed, gazing upward, swallowing several times in an attempt to rid herself of the gurgle in her throat.

Would she? Would she have fallen as headlong, as irrevocably in love with him no matter what the circumstances of her life? Had they been made for each other? It was a ridiculous question to ask herself. She did not believe in such sentimental rot. Made for each other!

But had they been?

She wished they had not met at all.

If they had not met, she would be in Italy now. She would be celebrating the sort of Christmas she was accustomed to. There would be no warm domestic bliss within a mile of her. She would not have been happy, of course. She could never be happy. But she would have been on familiar ground, in familiar company. She would have been in control of her life and her destiny. She would have kept her heart safely cocooned in ice.

Would he come home today? she wondered. Would he come for Christmas at all? But surely he would. He would come for his father's sake. Surely he would.

What if he did not? What if he never came?

She had never been so awash in self-pity, she thought. She hated feeling so abject. She hated him. Yes, she did. She hated him.

And then the door of her bedchamber opened and she turned her head to look. He stood in the open doorway for a few moments. looking back at her, before stepping inside and closing the door behind him.

She closed her eyes.

All day Edgar had been almost sick with worry. He was taking an enormous risk with several people's lives. If things went awry, he might have made life immeasurably worse for both Sir Gerald and Lady Stapleton as well as for Helena. He might have destroyed his marriage. He might have exposed his father to censure for behavior unbecoming a man with pretensions to gentility.

But events had been set in motion and all he could do now was try to direct them and control them as best he could.

The Stapletons had not changed their minds overnight. And so they set off early for Mobley Abbey on Christmas Eve on roads that were still covered with snow and still had to be traveled with care. Sir Gerald, Edgar noticed, was very tense. His wife was calm and outwardly serene. Each of them, Edgar had learned during his short acquaintance with them, felt a deep and protective love for the other. Without a doubt they had found comfort and peace and harmony together. Equally without a doubt, they were two wounded people whose wounds had filmed over quite nicely during a little more than a year of marriage—their marriage, he guessed, must have coincided almost exactly with the birth of their son. But were the wounds healed? If they were not, this journey to Mobley might rip them open again and make them harder than ever to heal.

They arrived at Mobley Abbey in the middle of the afternoon, having made good time. Edgar, who had ridden, set down the steps of the carriage himself, though it was Sir Gerald who handed his wife and sleeping child out onto the terrace. The child's nurse came hurrying from the accompanying carriage and took the baby, and Edgar directed a footman to escort them to the nursery and summon the housekeeper. He took Sir Gerald and Lady Stapleton to the library, which he was thankful to find empty, ordered refreshments brought for them, and excused himself.

He went first to the drawing room. Helena was not there. His father was, together with a number of his guests.

"Edgar!" Cora came hurrying toward him and took his arm. "You wretch! How dare you absent yourself for almost two full days so close to Christmas? Helena has been quite disconsolate and I have scarce removed my eyes from the sky for fear lest another snow storm prevent your coming back. It is to be hoped that you went to Bristol to purchase a suitably extravagant Christmas present for your wife. Some *almost* priceless jewel, perhaps?"

"Edgar," his father said, rising from the sofa on which he had been sitting and conversing with Mrs. Cross, "it is good to see you home before dark. Whatever did take you to Bristol?"

"I did not go to Bristol," Edgar said. "I told Helena I was going there because I wished to keep my real destination a secret. We are all surrounded by family and friends while Helena has only one aunt here." He bowed in Mrs. Cross's direction. "I went to see her stepson, Sir Gerald Stapleton, at Brookhurst and persuade him to come back with me to spend Christmas."

"Splendid!" Mr. Downes rubbed his hands together. "The more the merrier. My daughter-in-law's stepson, you say, Edgar?"

"What a very kind thought, Mr. Downes," Mrs. Cross said.

"Sir Gerald Stapleton?" Cora's voice had risen almost to a squeak. "And he has come, Edgar? *Alone?*"

Cora had always been as transparent as newly polished crystal. The questions she had asked only very thinly veiled the one she had not asked. Edgar looked steadily at her and at his brother-in-law beyond her.

"It is Christmas," he said. "I have brought Lady Stapleton, too, of course, and their son. If you will excuse me, Papa. I must find Helena and take her to meet them in the library. Do you know where she is?"

"She is upstairs resting," Mr. Downes said. "This will do her the world of good, Edgar. She has been somewhat low in spirits, I fancy. But then your absence would account for that." The statement seemed more like a question. But Edgar did not stay to pursue it. He left the room and, almost sick with apprehension, went up to his bedchamber.

She was lying on the bed, though she was not asleep. Their eyes met and held for a few moments and he knew with dreadful clarity that the future of her life and his, the future of their marriage, rested upon the events of the next hour. He stepped inside the room and shut the door. She closed her eyes, calmly shutting him out. She looked quite unmoved by the sight of him. Perhaps she had not missed him at all. Perhaps she had hoped he would not return for Christmas.

He sat down on the edge of the bed and touched the backs of his fingers to her cheek. She still did not open her eyes. He leaned down and kissed her softly on the lips. He felt a strong urge to avoid the moment, to keep the Stapletons waiting indefinitely in the library.

"Your father will be happy you have returned, Edgar," she said without opening her eyes. "So will Cora. Go and have tea with them. As you will observe, I am trying to rest."

"I have brought other guests," he said. "They are in the library. I want you to meet them."

She opened her eyes then. "More friends?" she said. "How pleasant for you. I will meet them later."

She was in one of her prickly moods. It did not bode well.

"Now," he said. "I wish you to meet them now."

"Oh, well, Edgar," she said, "when you play lord and master, you know, you are quite irresistible. If you would care to stop looming so menacingly over me, I will get up and jump to your command."

Very prickly. He went to stand at the window while she got up and straightened her dress and made sure at the mirror that her hair was tidy.

"I am ready," she said. "Give me your arm and lead me to the library. I shall be the gracious hostess, Edgar, never fear. You need not glower so."

He had not been glowering. He was merely terrified. Was he going about this the right way? Should he warn her? But if he did that, the chances were good that she would flatly refuse to accompany him to the library. And then what would he do?

He nodded to a footman when they reached the hall, and the man opened the library doors. Edgar drew a slow, deep breath.

"Sir Gerald and Lady Stapleton." Cora whirled around and looked at her husband, her eyes wide with dismay.

"My new daughter's stepson," Mr. Downes said, beaming at Mrs. Cross and resuming his seat beside her. "And his wife and son. More family. When was there ever such a happy Christmas, ma'am?"

"I am sure I have never known a happier, sir," Mrs. Cross said placidly.

"Tell me what you know of Sir Gerald Stapleton," Mr. Downes directed her. "I daresay Edgar will bring them to tea soon."

"Yes, my love," Lord Francis said, going to Cora's side.

"Oh, dear," Cora said. "Whatever can Edgar have been thinking of? Perhaps he does not even know." She looked suddenly belligerent and glared beyond her husband to the group of their friends, who were regarding her in silence. She lifted her chin. "Well, *I* will be civil to her. She is Helena's relative by marriage, even if it is only a *step* relationship. And she is Edgar's and Papa's guest. No one need expect me to be uncivil."

"I would be vastly disappointed in you if you were, Cora," her husband said mildly.

"And why would anyone even think of treating a lady, the wife of a baronet, a fellow guest in this home, with incivility?" the Earl of Thornhill asked, eyebrows raised.

"You do not remember who she is, Gabriel?" his wife asked. "Though I do hope you will repeat your words, even when you do."

"The lady did something indiscreet, Jennifer?" he asked, though it was obvious to all his listeners that he knew the answer very well and had done so from the start. "Everyone has done something indiscreet. I remember a time when you and I were seen kissing by a whole ballroomful of dancers—while you were betrothed to another man."

"Oh, bravo, Gabe," Lord Francis said as the countess blushed rosily. "The rest of us have been tactfully forgetting that incident ever since. Though something very similar happened to Cora and me. Not that we were kissing. We were laughing and holding each other up. But it looked for all the world as if we were engaged in a deep embrace—and it caused a delicious scandal."

"The *ton* is so foolish," Cora said.

"Sir Gerald and Lady Stapleton are guests in this home," the Duke of Bridgwater said. "As are Stephanie and I, Cora. I shall not peruse them through my quizzing glass or along the length of my nose. You may set your mind at ease."

"Of course," the duchess said, "Alistair does both those things to perfection, but he reserves them for pretentious people. I can remember a time when I was reduced to near-destitution, Cora. I can remember the fear. I was fortunate. Alistair came along to rescue me."

"There are all too many ladies who are not so fortunate," the Marquess of Carew said gently. "The instinct to survive is a strong one. I honor those who, reduced to desperation, contrive a way of surviving that does not involve robbery or murder or harm to anyone else except the person herself. Lady Stapleton is, I believe, a lady who has survived."

"Oh, Hartley," his wife said, patting his hand, "you would find goodness in a murderer about to be hanged, I do declare."

"I would certainly try, love," he said, smiling at her.

"I know the Countess of Severn," Jane, Countess of Greenwald said. "She and the earl have befriended the Stapletons. They would not have done so if Lady Stapleton was impossibly vulgar, would they?"

"There, my love," Lord Francis said, setting an arm about Cora's waist. "You might have had more faith in your friends and in me."

"Yes," she said. "Thank you. Now I wonder how poor Helena will be feeling about all this. Edgar and his surprises! One is reminded of the saying about bulls charging at gates."

"I believe both Edgar and Helena may be trusted," Lord Francis said. "I do believe those two, by hook or by crook, are going to end up quite devoted to each other."

"I hope you are right," Cora said with a loud sigh.

"What was that, Francis?" Mr. Downes called across the room. "Edgar and my daughter-in-law? Of course they are devoted to each other. He went off to bring her this secret present and she has been moping at his absence. I have great hopes. Not even hopes. Certainties. What say you, ma'am?" He turned to Mrs. Cross.

"I will say this, sir," she said. "If any man can tame my niece, Mr. Edgar Downes is that man. And if any man deserves Helena's devotion, he is Mr. Edgar Downes."

"Precisely, ma'am." He patted her hand. "Precisely. Now where is that son of mine with our new guests? It is almost teatime."

Helena looked first at the woman, who was standing to one side of the fireplace. A very genteel-looking young lady, she thought, slim and pretty, with intelligent eyes. She smiled and turned her eyes on the man. Pleasant looking, not very comfortable. Decidedly uncomfortable, in fact.

And then she recognized him.

Panic was like a hard ball inside her, fast swelling to explosion. She turned blindly, intent on getting out of the room as fast as she could. She found herself clawing at a very broad, very solid chest.

"Helena." His voice was impossibly steady. "Calm yourself."

She looked up wildly, recognized him, and was past that first moment and on to the next nightmare one. "I'll never forgive you for this," she whispered fiercely. "Let me past. I'll never forgive you."

"We have guests, my dear." His voice—and his face—was as hard as flint. "Turn and greet them."

Fury welled up in wake of the panic. She gazed into his face, her nostrils flaring, and then turned. "And *you,* Gerald," she said, looking directly at him. "What do *you* want here?"

"Hello, Helena," he said.

He looked as quiet, as gentle, as peaceful as he had always appeared. She could not believe that she had looked at him for a whole second without recognizing him. He had scarcely changed. Probably not at all. That outward appearance had always hidden his sense of rejection, insecurity, self-doubt.

"I have the honor of presenting my wife to you," he said. "Priscilla, Lady Stapleton. Helena, Mrs. Edgar Downes, my dear."

Helena's eyes stayed on him. "I have nothing to say to you, Gerald," she said, "and you can have nothing to say to me. I have no right to ask you to leave. You are my husband's guest. Excuse me, please."

She turned to find herself confronted by that same broad, solid chest.

"How foolish you are, Edgar," she said bitterly. "You think it is enough to bring us together in the same room? You think we will kiss and make up and proceed to live happily ever after? We certainly will not *kiss.* You foolish, interfering man. Let me past."

"Helena," he said, his voice arctic, "someone has been presented to you and you have not acknowledged the introduction. Is that the behavior of a lady?"

She gazed at him in utter incredulity. He dared instruct her on ladylike behavior? And to reprove her in the hearing of other people? She turned and looked at the woman. And walked toward her.

"Lady Stapleton. Priscilla," she said quietly, bitter mockery in her face, "I do beg your pardon. How pleased I am to make your acquaintance."

"I understand," the woman said, looking quite calmly into Helena's eyes. Her voice was as refined as her appearance. "I had as little wish for your acquaintance when it was first suggested to me, Helena, as you have for mine. I have had little enough reason to think kindly of you."

How dared she!

"Then I must think it remarkably kind in you to have overcome your scruples," Helena said sharply.

"I have done so for Gerald's sake," Lady Stapleton said. "And for the sake of Mr. Downes, who is a true gentleman, and who cares for you."

The woman spoke with *dignity.* There was neither arrogance nor subservience in her and certainly no vulgarity—only dignity.

"I could live quite happily without his care," Helena said.

"Helena." It was Gerald this time. She turned to look at him and saw the boy she had loved so dearly grown into a man. "I never wanted to see you again. I never wanted to hear your name. I certainly never wanted to forgive you. Your husband is a persuasive man."

She closed her eyes. She could not imagine a worse nightmare than this if she had the devising of it. "I cannot blame you, Gerald," she said, feeling all the fight draining out of her. "I would have begged your pardon, perhaps, before your father died, at his funeral, during any of the years since, if I had felt the offense pardonable. But I did not feel it was. And so I have not begged pardon and will not do so now. I will take the offense to the grave with me. I have done enough permanent damage to your life without seeking shallow comfort for myself."

"I must correct you in one misapprehension," he said, his voice shaking and breathless. "I can see that you misapprehend. Forgive me, Priss? I met my wife under circumstances I am sure you are aware of, Helena. She had been forced into those circumstances, but even in the midst of them she remained cheerful and modest and kind and dignified. She has always been far my superior. If anyone is to be pitied in this marriage, it is she."

"Gerald—" Lady Stapleton began, but he held up a staying hand.

"She is not to be pitied," he said. "Neither am I. Priss is the love of my heart and I am by now confident in the conviction that I am the love of hers. I am not in the habit of airing such very private feelings in public, but I have seen from your manner and have heard from your husband that you have bitterly blamed yourself for what happened between us and have steadfastly refused to forgive yourself or allow yourself any sort of happiness. I thought I was still bitter. I thought I would never forgive you. But I have found during the past day that those are outmoded, petty feelings. You were young and unhappy—heaven knows *I* was never happy with my father, either. And while youth and unhappiness do not excuse bad behavior, they do explain it. To hold a grudge for thirteen years and even beyond is in itself unpardonable. If it is my forgiveness you want, then, Helena, you have it—freely and sincerely given."

No. It could not possibly be as easy as that. The burden of years could not be lifted with a single short speech spoken in that gentle, well-remembered voice.

"No," she said stiffly. "It is not what I want, Gerald. It is not in your power."

"You will send him away still burdened, then?" Priscilla asked. "It is hard to offer forgiveness and be rejected. It makes one feel strangely guilty."

"It is Christmas." Edgar stepped forward. He had been a silent spectator of the proceedings until now. Helena deeply resented him. "We are all going to spend it here at Mobley Abbey. Together. And it is teatime. Time to go up to the drawing room. I wish to introduce you to my father and our other guests, Stapleton, Lady Stapleton."

They had not been introduced? *Lady Stapleton* had not yet been introduced to the Duke and Duchess of Bridgwater, the

Marquess and Marchioness of Carew, the Earl and Countess of Thornhill, and everyone else? She would be *cut.* And she must know it. She must have known it before she came. Why had she come, then? For Gerald's sake? Did she love him so much? Would she risk such humiliation for his sake? So that he too might find a measure of peace? But Gerald had done nothing to regret. Except that she had refused to accept his forgiveness.

"Take my arm, Priss." Gerald's voice was tense with protective fear.

"No." Helena stepped forward and took the woman's arm herself. Gerald's wife was smaller than she, daintier. "We will go up together, Priscilla. I will present you to my father-in-law and my sister-in-law and my aunt. And to all our friends."

"Thank you, Helena," Priscilla said quietly. If she was afraid, she did not show it.

"I must show everyone what a delightful gift my husband has brought me on Christmas Eve," Helena said. "He has brought my stepson and his wife to spend Christmas with me. And a step-grandchild, I believe. Is it a son or daughter?"

"A son," Priscilla said. "Peter. Thank you, Helena. Gerald has told me what a warm and charming woman you were. I can see that he was right. And you will see in the next day or two what a secure, contented man he is and you will forgive yourself and allow him to forgive you. I have seen enough suffering in my time to know all about the masks behind which it hides itself. It is time we all stopped suffering."

And this just before they stepped inside the drawing room to what was probably one of the worst ordeals of Priscilla's life?

"I can certainly admire courage," Helena said. "I will take you to my father-in-law first. You will like him and he will certainly like you."

"Thank you." Priscilla smiled. But her face was very pale for all that.

Chapter 17

Edgar gazed upward through the window of his bedchamber. By some miracle the sky was clear again. But then it was Christmas. One somehow believed in miracles at Christmas.

"Come here," he said without turning. He knew she was still sitting on the side of the bed brushing her hair, though her maid had already brushed it smooth and shining.

"I suppose," she said, "the Christmas star is shining as it was when we walked home from church a couple of hours ago. I suppose you want me to gaze on it with you and believe in the whole myth of Christmas."

"Yes," he said.

"Edgar." He heard her sigh. "You are such a romantic, such a sentimentalist. I would not have thought it of you."

"Come." He turned and stretched out one arm to her. She shrugged her shoulders and came. "There." He pointed upward unnecessarily. "Wait a moment." He left her side in order to blow out the candles and then joined her at the window again and set one arm about her waist. "There. Now there is nothing to compete with it. Tell me if you can that you do not believe in Christmas, even down to the last detail of that sordid stable."

She nestled her head on his shoulder and sighed. "I should be in Italy now," she said, "cocooned by cynicism. Why did I go to London this autumn, Edgar? Why did you? Why did we both go to the Greenwalds' drawing room that evening? Why did we look at each other and not look away again? Why did I conceive the very first time I lay with you when I have never done so before?"

"Perhaps we have our answer in Christmas," he said.

"Miracles?" The old mockery was back in her voice.

"Or something that was meant to be," he said. "I used not to believe in such things. I used to believe that I, like everyone else, was master of my own fate. But as one gets older, one can look back and realize that there has been a pattern to one's life—a pattern one did not devise or control."

"A series of coincidences?" she said.

"Yes," he said. "Something like that."

"The pattern of each of our lives merged during the autumn, then?" she said. "Poor Edgar. You have not deserved me. You are such a very decent man. I could have killed you this afternoon. Literally."

"Yes," he said, "I know."

She turned her head on his shoulder and closed her eyes. "She is very courageous," she said. "I could never do what she did today. She did it for him, Edgar. For Gerald."

"Yes," he said, "and for their son and their unborn child. And for herself. For them. You were wonderful. I was very proud of you."

She had taken Priscilla Stapleton about in the drawing room at teatime, introducing her to everyone as her stepson's wife, her own manner confident, charming, even regal. She had scarcely left the woman's side for the rest of the day. They had walked to and from church with Sir Gerald and his wife and shared a pew with them.

"But I did nothing," she said. "Everyone greeted her with courtesy and even warmth. It was as if they did not know, though I have no doubt whatsoever that they all did. She—Edgar, there is nothing vulgar in her at all."

"She is a lady," he said.

"Gerald is happy with her." Her eyes, he saw, had clenched more tightly shut. "He *is* happy. Is he, Edgar? Is he?" She looked up at him then, searching his eyes.

"I believe," he said, "the pattern of his life merged with the pattern of hers in a most unlikely place, Helena. Of course they are happy. I will not say they are in love, though I am sure they are. They *love* deeply. Yes, he is happy."

"And whole and at peace," she said. "I did not destroy him permanently."

"No, love," he said. "Not permanently."

She shivered.

"Cold?" he asked.

"But I might have," she said, "if he had not met Priscilla."

"And if she had not met him," he said. "They were both in the process of surviving, Helena. We do not know how well they would have done if they had not met each other. Perhaps they were both strong people who would have found their peace somehow alone. We do not know. Neither do they. I do believe, though, that they could not be so happy together if they merely used each other as emotional props. But they did meet, and so they are as we see them today."

She withdrew from him and rested her palms on the windowsill as she looked out. "I will not use you as an emotional prop either, Edgar," she said. "It would be easy to do. You organize and fix things, do you not? It comes naturally to you. You have seen that my life is all in pieces and you have sought to mend it, to put the pieces back together again, to make all right for me. You took a terrible risk today and won—as you almost always do, I suspect. It would be easy to lean into you as I was just doing, to allow you to manage my life. You can do it so much better than I, it seems. But it is my life. I must live it myself."

He felt chilled. But he had said it himself of her stepson and his wife—they could not be happy together if they depended too much upon each other. And he had spoken the truth. He could not be happy as the totally dominant partner in a marriage—even though by his nature he would always try to dominate, thinking he was merely protecting and cherishing his wife.

"Then you will do so," he said, "without my further interference. I am not sorry for what I did yesterday and today. I would do it again given the choice—because you are my wife and because I love you. But you must proceed from here, Helena—or not proceed. The choice is yours. I am going to bed. It is late and I am cold."

But she turned from the window to look at him, the old mocking smile on her lips—though he had the feeling that it was turned inward on herself rather than outward on him.

"I was not quarreling with you, Edgar," she said. "You do not need to pout like a boy. I want to make love. But not as we have done it since our marriage. I have allowed you your will because it has been so very enjoyable to do so. You are a superlative lover, unadventurous as are your methods."

He raised his eyebrows. Unadventurous?

"I want to be on top," she said. "I want to lead the way. I want you to lie still as I usually do and let me set the pace and choose the key moments. I want to make love to you."

He had never done it like that. It sounded vaguely wrong, vaguely sinful. He felt his breath quicken and his groin tighten. She was still smiling at him—and though she was dressed in a pale dressing gown with her hair in long waves down her back, she looked again in the faint light of the moon and stars like the scarlet lady of the Greenwalds' drawing room.

"Then what are we waiting for?" he asked.

He stripped off his nightshirt and lay on his back on the bed. He was thankful that a fire still burned in the grate, though the air felt chill enough—for the space of perhaps one minute. She kneeled, naked, beside him and began to make love to him with delicate, skilled hands and warm seeking mouth. The minx—of course she was skilled. He did not wish to discover where she had acquired those skills—though he really did not care. He had acquired his own with other women, but they no longer mattered. Just as the other men would no longer matter to her. He would see to it that they did not.

It was difficult to keep his hands resting on the bed, to submit to the sweet torture of a lovemaking that proceeded altogether too slowly for his comfort. It was hard to be passive, to allow himself to be led and controlled, to give up all his own initiative.

She came astride him when he thought the pain must surely soon get beyond him, positioned herself carefully, her knees wide, and slid firmly down onto him. His hands came to her hips with some urgency, but he remembered in time and gentled them, letting them rest idly there.

"Ah," she said, "you feel so good. So deep. You have not done this before, have you?"

"No."

"I will show you how good it feels to be mastered," she said, leaning over him and kissing him open-mouthed. "It does feel good, Edgar, provided it is only play. And this is play—intimate, wonderful play, which we all need in our lives. I do not wish to master you outside of this play—or you to master me. Only here. Now."

He gritted his teeth when she began to move, riding him with a leisurely rocking of her hips while she braced her hands on his shoulders and tipped back her head, her eyes closed. Fortunately the contracting of inner muscles told him that she was at an advanced stage of arousal herself. It was not long before she spoke again.

"Yes," she whispered fiercely. "Yes. Now, Edgar. *Now!*"

His hands tightened on her hips and he drove into her over and over again until they reached climax together.

"Ah, my love," she said in that throaty, velvet voice that most belonged here, in their bed. "Ah, my love." Her head was still tipped back, her eyes still closed.

He would perhaps not have heard the words if they had not sounded so strange and so new to his ears. He doubted that she heard them herself.

She did not lift herself away. She lowered herself onto him and straightened her legs so that they lay on either side of his. She snuggled her head into the hollow between his shoulder and neck and sighed.

"Do I weigh a ton?" she asked as he contrived somehow to pull the covers up over them.

"Only half," he told her.

"You are no gentleman, sir," she said. "You were supposed to reply that I feel like a mere feather."

"Two feathers," he said.

"Good night, Edgar. I did enjoy that."

"Good night, love." He kissed the side of her face. "And I enjoyed being mastered."

She laughed that throaty laugh of hers and was almost instantly asleep.

They were still coupled.

It was going to be an interesting marriage, he thought. It would never be a comfortable one. It might never be a particularly happy one. But strangely, he felt more inclined to favor an interesting marriage over a comfortable one. And as for happiness—well, at this particular moment he felt thoroughly happy. And life was made up of moments. It was a shame that this one must be cut short by sleep, but there would be other moments—tomorrow or the next day or the next.

He slept.

Christmas Day was one of those magical days that Helena had studiously avoided for ten years. It was everything that she had always most dreaded—a day lived on emotion rather than on any sane rationality. And the emotions, of course, were gaiety and love and happiness. The Downes family, she concluded—her father-in-law, her husband, her sister-in-law—used love and generosity and kindness and openness as the guiding principles of their own family lives, and they passed on those feelings to everyone around them. It seemed almost impossible that anyone *not* have a perfectly happy Christmas in their home.

And it seemed that everyone did.

The morning was spent in gift-giving within each family group. For Helena there was a great deal more to do than that. There were the servants to entertain for an hour while Mr. Downes gave them generous gifts, and there were baskets to be delivered to some of the poorer families in their country cottages and in the village. Cora and Francis delivered half of them, while Helena and Edgar delivered the others.

It felt so very good—Helena was beginning to accept the feeling, to open herself to it—to be a part of a family. To recognize love around her, to accept that much of it was directed her way—not for anything she had ever done or not done, but simply because she was a member of the family. To realize that she was beginning to love again, cautiously, fearfully, but without resistance.

She had decided to enjoy Christmas—this good old-fashioned English Christmas of her father-in-law's description. Tomorrow she would think things through, decide if she could allow her life to take a new course. But today she would not think. Today she would feel.

The young people had contrived to find time during the morning to walk out to the lake to skate. They were arriving back, rosy cheeked, high spirited, as Helena and Edgar were returning from their errands. Fanny Grainger and Jack Sperling were together, something they had been careful to avoid during the past few days.

Fanny smiled her sweet, shy smile. Jack inclined his head to them and spoke to Edgar.

"Might I have a word with you, sir?" he asked.

"Certainly," Edgar said, indicating the library. "Is it too private for my wife's ears?"

"No." Jack smiled at Helena and she adjusted her opinion of his looks. He was more than just mildly good looking. He was almost handsome. He offered his arm to Fanny and led her toward the library.

"Well." Edgar looked from one to the other of them when they were all inside the room. "The hot cider I asked for should be here soon. What shall we toast?"

"Nothing and everything." Jack laughed, but Helena noticed that his arm had crept about Fanny's waist and she was looking up at him with bright, eager eyes.

"It sounds like a reasonably good toast to me." Edgar smiled at Helena and indicated two chairs close to the fire. "Do sit down, Miss Grainger, and warm yourself. Now, of what does this nothing and this everything consist?"

"I have been granted permission by Sir Webster Grainger," Jack said, "to court Miss Grainger. There is to be no formal betrothal until I can prove that I am able to support her in the manner of life to which she is accustomed and no marriage until I am in a fair way to offering her a home worthy of a baronet's daughter. That may be years in the future. But F—Miss Grainger is young and I am but two-and-twenty. Waiting seems heaven when just a few weeks ago we thought even that an impossibility."

Helena hugged Fanny. She was not in the habit of hugging people—had not been for a long while. But she was genuinely happy for the girl and her young man. And she was happy for Edgar, who must have felt guilty about the expectations he had raised in the Graingers.

"Well." Edgar was smiling. "The long wait can perhaps be eased a little. Since you have become a close friend of my family, Miss Grainger, and you are to be a favored employee, Sperling—provided you prove yourself worthy of such a position, of course—I daresay the two of you might meet here or at my home in Bristol with fair frequency."

Fanny bit her lip, her eyes shining with tears.

"I thank you, sir," Jack Sperling said. "For everything. We both do, don't we, Fan?"

She nodded and turned her eyes on Helena. There was such happiness in them that Helena was dazzled. The girl had a long wait for her marriage—perhaps years. But happiness lay in hope. Perhaps in hope more than in any other single factor. The moment might be happy, but unless one could feel confident in the hope that there would be other such moments the happiness was not worth little.

"I will be new to Bristol," Helena said. "And though I will have Edgar and have already met here some of his friends, I will still feel lonely for a while. Perhaps we can arrange for you to stay with me for a month or two in the spring, Fanny. I believe you have an aunt in Bristol? I would be pleased to make her acquaintance."

Two of the tears spilled over onto Fanny's cheeks. "Thank you," she murmured.

The hot cider had arrived. They were all still chilled from the outdoors. They toasted one another's happiness and Christmas itself and sipped on the welcome warmth of their drinks.

Edgar did not plan to attend the children's party in the ballroom during the afternoon. They could be dizzyingly noisy and active, even the fourteen who were house guests—fifteen now that the young and very exuberant Peter Stapleton had been added to their number. With several neighborhood children added, the resulting noise was deafening. He intended only to poke his head inside the door to make sure that the ballroom was not being taken to pieces a bit at a time.

In the event he stayed. Cora's four descended upon him just as if he had a giant child magnet pinned to his chest. Then Cora herself called to him and asked if he would head one of the four race teams with Gabriel, Hartley, and Francis. Then he spotted Priscilla Stapleton and his wife playing a game in a circle with the younger children. And finally he noticed that the person seated at the pianoforte ready to play the music for the game was Sir Gerald Stapleton.

It was his wife who kept him lingering in the ballroom even after he had served his sentence as race-team leader. Children always seemed the key to breaking through all her masks to the warm, vibrant, fun-loving woman she so obviously was. Perhaps she did not know it yet and perhaps she would resist it even when she did—but she was going to be a perfectly wonderful mother. Her resistance was understandable, of course. She had convinced herself that her stepson was a child when she had tried to corrupt him. And so she feared her effect on children. But her effect was quite benevolent. The Greenwalds' Stephen adored her—she came third in his affections, behind only his mama and papa.

Edgar had decided to enjoy Christmas, to relax and let go of all his worries. He had decided not to try to control events or people any longer—not in his personal life, anyway. He had married Helena and he loved her. He had discovered her darkest secrets and had made an effort to give her the chance to put right what had happened in the past. She had not entirely spurned his efforts—she had been remarkably kind to Priscilla and to the child. She had been civil to Gerald. But she had not reacted quite as Edgar had hoped she would.

He could do no more. Or rather, he *would* do no more. The rest was up to her. If she chose to live in the hell of her own making she had inhabited for thirteen years, then so be it. He must allow it. He must allow her the freedom she craved and the freedom he knew was necessary in any relationship in which he engaged.

He was going to enjoy Christmas. It was certainly not difficult to do. Apart from the basic joyfulness of the day and its activities, there had been the happy—or potentially happy—outcome of his scheme to bring Fanny Grainger and Jack Sperling together. And there was more. His father had made several appearances at the children's party and had been mobbed each time. On his final appearance, just as the party was coming to an end, he invited Edgar and Helena, Cora and Francis to his private sitting room.

"After all," he said as they made their way there, "a man is entitled to snatch a half hour of Christmas Day to spend just with his very nearest and dearest."

But there was someone else in the sitting room when they arrived there. Edgar suppressed a smile. They would have to have been blind and foolish during the past week not to have guessed that some such thing was in the works.

Mrs. Cross smiled at them, but she looked a little less placid than her usual self. She looked very slightly anxious.

Mr. Downes cleared his throat after tea had been poured and they had all made bright, self-conscious conversation for a few minutes. "Edgar, Cora," he began, "you are my children and of course will inherit my fortune after my time. Edgar will inherit Mobley, but I have seen to it that Cora will receive almost as much since it seems unfair to me that my daughter should be treated with less favor than my son. You are wealthy in your own right, Edgar, as you are in yours, Francis. It would seem to me, therefore, that perhaps neither of my children would be too upset to find that they will receive a little less than they have always expected."

"Papa," Cora said, "I have never *seen* you so embarrassed. Why do you not simply say what you brought us here to say?"

"My love," Francis said, "you cannot know how difficult it is for a man to say such a thing. You ladies have no idea."

Helena was smiling at her aunt, who was attempting to remove a particularly stubborn—and invisible—speck of lint from her skirt.

"Neither Cora nor I covet your property or your wealth, Papa," Edgar said. "We love *you.* We would rather have you with us forever. Certainly while we do have you, we want nothing more than your happiness. Do we, Corey?"

"How foolish," she said, "that I am even called upon to answer that. Papa! Could you ever have doubted it?"

"No." Their father actually look sheepish. "I loved your mother dearly. I want all here present to know that and not to doubt it for a moment."

There was a chorus of protests.

"Your children never have, Joseph," Mrs. Cross said, looking up at last. "Of course, they never have. Neither have I. You loved Mrs. Downes just as I loved Mr. Cross."

Mr. Downes cleared his throat again. "This may come as a great surprise—" he began, but he was halted by another cry—of hilarity this time. He frowned. "Mrs. Letitia Cross has done me the great honor of accepting my hand in marriage," he said with an admirable attempt at dignity.

There was a great clamor then, just as if they really had all been taken by surprise. Cora was crying and demanding a handkerchief of Francis, who was busy shaking his father-in-law's hand. Helena was hugging her aunt tightly and shedding a tear or two of her own. Edgar waited his turn, wondering that it had never happened before. His father, with a huge heart and a universe of love to give, had mourned his wife for almost thirty years and lavished all his love on his children. But they were both wed now and paternal love was not enough to satisfy a man's heart for a leftover lifetime.

Mrs. Cross was a fortunate lady. But then, Edgar thought, his father was probably a fortunate man, too.

His father turned to him, damp eyed—and frowning ferociously. Edgar caught him in a bear hug.

Chapter 18

Helena had worn her scarlet gown to the Christmas ball. It was perhaps a little daring for an entertainment in a country home, especially when she was a matron of six-and-thirty. More especially when she was fast losing her waistline. But it was not indecent—and the soft folds of the high-waisted skirt hid the slight bulge of her pregnancy—and it suited her mood. She felt brightly festive.

And desperately unwilling for the day to be over. It almost was. It was already late in the evening, after supper.

Tomorrow Christmas would linger, but in all essentials it would be over. Just as it always was. The great myth lifted one's spirits only to dash them afterward even lower than they had been before. She had feared it this year and sworn to resist it, but she had given in to it. Christmas!

But having given in, she would take from the celebrations all she could. And give, too. That was an essential part of it, the giving. And it was that she had shunned as much as the taking—more. She was terrified of giving. Once upon a time she believed she had had a generous spirit. Despite the disappointment of a lost love at the age of nineteen, she had put a great deal into her marriage with Christian. She might have settled into unhappiness and bitterness and revulsion, but she had not done so. She had set out to make him happy and had succeeded, God help her. But she had focused the largest measure of her generosity and the sympathy of her loving heart on Gerald. She had tried to help him overcome the setbacks of his mother's desertion and his father's dislike. She had tried to help him gain confidence in himself, to realize that he was a boy worthy of respect and love.

And then she had destroyed him.

But not forever. She had perhaps overestimated her own importance. She had harmed him. She had made him suffer, perhaps for a long time. But he had recovered. And she dared to believe that he was now happy. He was still gentle, quiet Gerald, but he was at peace with himself. She did not know all the circumstances surrounding his strange marriage, but there was no doubt of the fact that he and Priscilla were devoted to each other and suited each other perfectly. And their son, little Peter, was a darling. Today there was an extra glow of happiness about all three of them. Peter must have been starved for the company of other children. He had steadfastly made up for lost time. Priscilla had been accepted at Mobley just as if she had never been anything but a lady. Helena guessed that her happiness was as much for Gerald's sake as her own. He would no longer feel that he must absent himself from society for her sake. And Gerald's happiness doubtless had a similar unselfish cause. His wife need no longer hide away from the company of her peers.

Helena watched them dance a cotillion as she danced with her father-in-law. Though they were not the only ones she watched. There were Edgar and her aunt—dear Letty. She was quietly contented. She would have a home of her own again at last and a husband who was clearly very fond indeed of her—as she was of him. And never again would she find herself in the position of being dependent upon relatives.

If she had not married Edgar, Helena thought, her aunt would not have met Mr. Downes and would never have found this new happiness. Neither would he. If she had not married Edgar, Fanny Grainger would not now be dancing with Jack Sperling and looking as glowingly happy as if she expected her nuptials within the month. She would instead be dancing with Edgar and wearing forced smiles. If Helena had not married Edgar, Gerald and Priscilla would be at Brookhurst, alone with their son, trying to convince themselves that they were utterly happy.

Really, when she thought about it, very cautiously, so that she would not jump to the wrong conclusions, nothing very disastrous had happened lately for which she could blame herself. Except that she had forced Edgar into marrying her—though he was the one who had done the actual forcing. He did not seem wildly unhappy. He claimed to love her. He had said so several times. She had refused to hear, refused to react.

She had been afraid to believe it. She had been afraid it was true.

It was as if a door had been held wide for her for several days now, a door beyond which were bright sunlight and birdsong and the perfumes of a thousand flowers. All she had to do was step outside and the door would close forever on the darkness from which she had emerged. But she had been afraid to take that single step. If she did, perhaps she would find storm clouds blocking out the sunlight and silencing the singing and stifling the perfumes. Perhaps she would spoil it all.

But she had not spoiled anything yet this Christmas. Perhaps she should dare. Perhaps she could take that step. If all turned to disaster, then she could only find herself back where she expected to be anyway. What was there to lose?

It seemed suddenly that there was a great deal to lose. The cotillion had ended and her father-in-law was kissing her hand and Edgar was smiling and bending his head to hear something Letty was saying to him. Cora was laughing loudly over something with one of Edgar's friends, and Francis was smiling in some amusement at the sound. The Duke of Bridgwater was joining Gerald and Priscilla—and addressing himself to Priscilla. He must be asking her for the next set. The smell of the pine boughs and the holly with which the ballroom was festooned outdid the smells of the various perfumes worn by the guests. There was a very strong feeling of Christmas.

Oh, yes, there was a great deal to lose. But the sunlight and the birdsong and the flowers beckoned. Edgar was coming toward her. The next set was to be a waltz. She longed to dance it with him. But not this one, she decided suddenly. Not yet. Later she would waltz with him if there was another before the ball ended. She turned and hurried away without looking at him, so that he would think she had not seen him.

"The next is to be a waltz," she said unnecessarily as she joined the duke and Gerald and Priscilla.

"Yes, indeed," his grace said. "Lady Stapleton has agreed to dance it with me."

It seemed strange to hear another woman called that, to realize that the name was no longer hers. She was not sorry, Helena thought. *Mrs. Downes* sounded a great deal more prosaic than *Lady Stapleton,* but the name seemed somehow to give her a new identity, a new chance.

"Splendid," she said. "Then you must dance it with me, Gerald. It would never do for you to be a wallflower."

He looked at her in some surprise, but she linked her arm through his and smiled dazzlingly at him. They had not avoided each other since that first meeting in the library the day before, but they had not sought each other out either.

"It would be my pleasure, Helena," he said.

And so they waltzed together, smiling and silent for a few minutes.

"I am glad we came," he said stiffly after a while. "Mr. Downes and your husband have been extraordinarily kind to Priss and to me. So has everyone else. And Peter is ecstatic."

"I am glad," she said. She was aware that she wore her mocking smile. It was something to which she clung almost in terror. But it was something that must go. She stopped smiling. "I really am glad, Gerald. She is charming and delightful. You have made a wonderful match."

"Yes," he said. "And I might say the same of you, Helena. He is a man of character."

"Yes." She smiled at him and this time it was a real smile. He smiled back.

"Gerald." She was alarmed to find her vision blurring. She blinked her eyes firmly. "Gerald, I am so very sorry. I have never been able to say it because I thought my sin unforgivable. I thought its effects permanent and irreversible. I was wrong. I was, was I not? It is not a meaningless indulgence to say I am sorry?"

"It never was," he said. "It never is, Helena. There is nothing beyond forgiveness—even when the effects are irreversible. We all do terrible things. All of us. For a long time before our marriage I treated Priss as if the label of her profession was the sum total of her character. If that is not an apparently unforgivable sin, I do not know what is. I had to lose her before I realized what a precious jewel had been within my grasp. You do not have a monopoly on dastardly deeds."

"If I had asked forgiveness at your father's funeral," she asked him, "would you have forgiven me, Gerald?" Had she been responsible, too, for all the wasted years?

He did not answer for a while. He took her into an intricate twirl about one corner of the dance floor. "I do not know," he said at last. "Perhaps not. I felt terribly betrayed, the more so because I had loved you more than I had loved anyone else in my life since my mother. But in time I believe it would have helped to know that at least you had a conscience, that you regretted what had happened. Until a few days ago I assumed that you felt no guilt at all—though Priss has always maintained that you must. Priss has the gift of putting herself into other people's souls and understanding what must be going on deep within them even when the outer person shows no sign of it. And she did not even know you."

"I am hoping," she said, "that I can have the honor of a close friendship with my stepdaughter-in-law. If you can say again what you said yesterday, Gerald, and mean it. Can you forgive me? Will you?"

He smiled at her, all the warm affection and trust she had used to see in his face there again. "Priss was right," he said. "She so often is. The one flaw to my peace of mind has been my enduring resentment of you. I have accepted my father for what he was and am no longer hurt by the memory of his dislike. I like the person I am, even though I am not the person he would have had me be. And I have the memory of my mother back. She did not desert me, Helena. She was banished—by my father—and forbidden to see me or communicate with me in any way. I visited my aunts and found out the truth from them."

"Oh, Gerald—" Helena said, feeling all the old pain for his brokenness.

"Sometime," he said, "perhaps I could tell you the whole story. It brought pain. It also brought ultimate peace. She loved me. And you loved me. I have thought about it during the past few days and have realized that it is true. You were very good to me—and not for ulterior motives as I have thought since. You did not plot. You were merely—young and lonely. But even if all my worst fears had been correct, Helena—about my mother, about you—they would not be an excuse for the failed, miserable life to which you thought you had doomed me. I am an individual with a mind and a will of my own. We all have to live life with the cards that have been dealt us. We all—most of us—have the chance to make of life what we will. You would not have been responsible for my failed life—I would have been."

"You are generous," she said.

"No." He shook his head. "Just reaching the age of maturity, I hope. Have you really denied yourself happiness for thirteen years, Helena?"

"I did not deserve it," she said.

"You deserve it now." He twirled her again. "And happiness is yours for the taking, is it not? I believe he is fond of you, Helena. I do not wish to divulge any secrets, but you must know anyway. He told Priss and me when he came to Brookhurst that he loves you. We have both seen since coming here that it is true. He is the man for you, you know. He is strong and assertive and yet sensitive and loving. It is quite a combination. You must be happy to be having a child. I remember how you used to share your disappointments with me when you were first married—because you felt you could not talk to my father on such a topic, you said. How you longed for a child! And how good you were with the children you encountered—myself included."

"I have been afraid of being a mother," she told him.

"Do not be." Their roles had been reversed, she realized suddenly. He was the comforter, the reassurer, the one to convince her that she was capable of love and worthy of love. "All the little children here adore you, Helena, including Peter, who is shy of almost all adults except Priss and me. He fought with the rest of the children this afternoon to be the one to hold your hand in their circle games. You will be a wonderful mother."

"I am so old," she said, pulling a face.

"God—or nature if you will—does not make mistakes," he said. "If you are able to be a mother at your age, then you are not too old to be a mother. Enjoy it. Parenthood is wonderful, Helena. Exhausting and terrifying and wonderful. Like life."

"Gerald," she said. But there was nothing more to say. Some feelings were quite beyond words. And hers at this particular moment ran far too deep even for tears. "Oh, Gerald."

He smiled.

"You want to do *what*?"

Edgar bent his head closer to his wife's, though he had heard her perfectly clearly. The ball was over, the guests who were not staying at the house had all left, the house guests had begun to drift away to bed, the servants had been instructed to leave the clearing away until morning. And he was eager to get to bed. Helena had glowed all evening—especially after the waltz which he had wanted, but which she had danced with her stepson. She looked more beautiful even than usual. Edgar was feeling decidedly amorous.

"I want to go skating," she told him again.

"Skating," he said. "At one o'clock in the morning. After a dizzyingly busy day. With a mile to walk to the lake and a mile back. In arctically cold weather. When you are pregnant. Are you mad?"

"Edgar," she said, "don't be tiresome. It is so bourgeois to feel that one must go to bed merely because it is late and one has had a busy day and it is cold outside."

"Bourgeois," he said. "I would substitute the word *sane*."

But she whirled about and with a single clap of the hands and a raising of arms she had everyone's attention.

"It is Christmas," she said, "and a beautiful night. The ball is over but the night is not. And Christmas is not. Edgar and I are going skating. Who else wants to come?"

Everyone looked as stunned as Edgar had felt when she first

mentioned such madness. But within moments he could see the attraction of the idea take hold just as it was doing with him. The young people were almost instantly enthusiastic, and then a few of the older couples looked at each other doubtfully, sheepishly, inquiringly.

"That is one of the best ideas I have heard today, Daughter," Mr. Downes said, rubbing his hands together. "Letitia, my dear, how do you fancy the thought of a walk to the lake?"

"I fancy it very well, Joseph," Mrs. Cross replied placidly. "But I hope not just a walk. I have not skated in years. I have an inclination to do so again."

And that was that. They were going, a large party of them, with only a few older couples wise enough to resist the prevailing madness. At one o'clock in the morning they were going skating!

"You see, Edgar?" his wife said. "Everyone is not as tiresome and as staid as you."

"Or as bourgeois," he said. "I should not allow you to skate, Helena, or to exert yourself any more today. You are with child. Can you even skate?"

"Darling," she said, "I have spent winters in Vienna. What do you think I did for entertainment? Of course, I skate. Do you want me to teach you?"

Darling?

"I shall escort you upstairs," he said, offering his arm. "You will change into something *warm.* We will walk to the lake at a sedate pace and you will skate *for a short while* with my support. You are not to put your health at greater risk than that. Do you understand me, Helena? I must be mad, too, to give in to such a whim."

"I said I would lead you a merry dance, Edgar," she said, smiling brightly at him. "The word *merry* was the key one." She slipped her arm through his. "I will not risk the safety of your heir, never fear. He—or she—is more important to me than almost anything else in my life. But I am not yet willing to let go of Christmas. Perhaps I never will. I will carry Christmas about with me every day for the rest of my life, a sprig of holly behind one ear, mistletoe behind the other."

She was in a strange mood. He was not sure what to make of it. The only thing he could do for the time being was go along with it. And there *was* something strangely alluring about the prospect of going skating on a lake one mile distant at something after one o'clock of a December morning.

"The holly would be decidedly uncomfortable," he said.

"You are such a realist, darling," she said. "But you could kiss me beneath the other ear whenever you wished without fear that I might protest."

He chuckled. *Darling* again? Yes, life with Helena really was going to be interesting. Not that there was just the future tense involved. It *was* interesting.

She had married a tyrant, Helena thought cheerfully—she had told him so, too. The surface of the ice was, of course, marred by an overall powdering of snow which had blown across it since it had last been skated upon. And in a few places there were thicker finger drifts. It took several of the men ten minutes to sweep it clean again while everyone else cheered them on and kept as warm as it was possible to keep at almost two o'clock on a winter's night.

Edgar had flatly refused to allow Helena to wield one of the brooms. He had even threatened, in the hearing of his father and everyone else present, to sling her over his shoulder and carry her back to the house if she cared to continue arguing with him. She had smiled sweetly and called him a tyrant—in the hearing of his father and everyone else.

And then, as if that were not bad enough, he had taken her arm firmly through his when they took to the ice, and skated with her about the perimeter of the cleared ice just as if they were a sedate middle-aged couple. That they were precisely that made no difference at all to her accusation of tyranny.

"I suppose," he said when she protested, "that you wish to execute some dizzying twirls and death-defying leaps for our edification."

"Well, I did wish to *skate,* Edgar," she told him.

"You may do so next year," he told her, "when the babe is

warm in his cot at home and safe from his mother's recklessness."

"Or hers," she said.

"Or hers."

"Edgar," she asked him, "is it horridly vulgar to be increasing at my age?"

"Horridly," he said.

"I am going to be embarrassingly large within the next few months," she said. "I have already misplaced my waist somewhere."

"I had noticed," he said.

"And doubtless think I look like a pudding," she said.

"Actually," he said, "I think you look rather beautiful and will look more so the larger you grow."

"I do not normally look beautiful, then?" she asked.

"Helena." He drew her to a stop, and four couples immediately zoomed past them. "If you are trying to quarrel with me again, desist. One of these days I shall oblige you. I promise. It is inevitable that we have a few corkers of quarrels down the years. But not today. Not tonight."

"Hmm." She sighed. "Damn you, Edgar. How tiresome you are."

"Guilty," he said. "And bourgeois and tyrannical. And in love with you."

This time she heard and paid attention. This time she dared to consider that perhaps it was true. And that perhaps it was time to respond in kind. But she could not say it just like that. It was something that had to be approached with tortuous care, something to be crept up on and leapt on unawares so that the words would come out almost of their own volition. Besides, she was terrified. Her legs felt like jelly and she was breathless. It was not the walk or the skating that had done it. She was not that unfit.

"If we are not to skate even at a snail's pace, Edgar," she said, "perhaps we should retire from the ice altogether."

"I'll take you home," he said. "You must be tired."

"I do not want to go home," she said, looking up to see that the stars were no longer visible. Clouds had moved over. "We are going to have fresh snow. Tomorrow we will probably be housebound. Let us find a tree behind which we can be somewhat private. I want to kiss you. I want you to kiss me. Quite wickedly."

He laughed. "Why waste a lascivious kiss against a tree," he asked, "when we would be only *somewhat* private? Why not go back home where we can make use of a perfectly comfortable and entirely private bed—and do more than just kiss?"

"Because I want to be kissed *now,*" she said, wrestling her arm free of his grip and taking him by the hand. She began to skate across the center of the ice's surface in the direction of the bank. "And because I may lose my courage during the walk back to the house."

"Courage?" he said.

But she would say no more. They narrowly missed colliding with Letty and her father-in-law. They removed their skates on the bank. They almost chose a tree that was already occupied—by Fanny Grainger and Jack Sperling. They finally found one with a lovely broad trunk against which she could lean. She set her arms about him and lifted her face to his.

"You are quite mad," he told her.

"Are you glad?" she whispered, her lips brushing his. "Tell me you are glad."

"I am glad," he said.

"Edgar," she said, "he has forgiven me."

"Yes, love," he said, "I know."

"I have loved during this Christmas season and have been loved," she said, "and I have brought disaster on no one."

"No," he said and she could see the flash of his teeth in the near darkness as he smiled. "Not unless everyone comes down with a chill tomorrow."

"What a horrid threat," she said. "It is just what I might expect of you."

He kissed her—hard and long. And then more softly and long, his tongue stroking into her mouth and creating a definite heat to combat the chill of the night.

"You have brought happiness to a large number of people," he said at last. "You are genuinely loved. Especially by me. I do not want to burden you with the knowledge, Helena, and you need never worry about feeling less strongly yourself, but I love you more than I thought it possible to love any woman. I do not regret what happened. I do not regret marrying you. I do not care if you lead me a merry dance, though I hope it will always be as merry as this particular one. I only care that you are mine, that I am the man honored to be your husband for as long as we both live. There. I will not say it again. You must not be distressed."

"Damn you, Edgar," she said. "If you maintain a stoic silence on the subject for even one week I shall lead you the *un*merriest dance you could ever imagine."

He kissed her softly again.

"Edgar." She kept her eyes closed when the kiss ended. "I have lied to you."

He sighed and set his forehead against hers for a moment. "I thought we came here to kiss wickedly," he said.

"Apart from Christian," she said, "I have never been with any man but you."

"What?" His voice was puzzled. She did not open her eyes to see his expression.

"But I could not *tell* you that," she said. "You would have thought you were *special* to me. You would have thought me—*vulnerable.*."

"Helena," he said softly.

"You were," she said. "I was. You are. I am. Damn you, Edgar," she said crossly, "I thought it was *men* who were supposed to find this difficult to say."

"Say what?" She could see when she dared to peep that he was smiling again—grinning actually. He knew very well what she could not say and the knowledge was making him cocky.

"I-love-you." She said it fast, her eyes closed. There. It had not been so difficult to say after all. And then she heard a loud, inelegant sob and realized with some horror that it had come from her.

"I love you," she wailed as his arms came about her like iron bands and she collided full length with his massive body. "I love you. Damn you, Edgar. I love you."

"Yes, love," he said soothingly against one of her ears. "Yes, love."

"I love you."

"Yes, love."

"What a tedious conversation."

"Yes, love."

She was snickering and snorting against his shoulder then, and he was chuckling enough to shake as he held her.

"Well, I do," she accused him.

"I know."

"And you have nothing better to say than that?"

"Nothing *better,*" he said, putting a little distance between them from the waist up. "Except a tentative, tiresome, bourgeois suggestion that perhaps it is time to retire to our bed."

"Tiresome and bourgeois suddenly sound like very desirable things," she said.

They smiled slowly at each other and could seem to find nothing better or more satisfying to do for the space of a whole minute or so.

"What are we waiting for?" she asked eventually.

"For you to lead the way," he said. "You will start damning me or otherwise insulting me if I decide to play lord and master."

"Oh, Edgar," she said, taking his arm. "Let us go *together,* shall we? To the house and to bed? Let us make love together—to each other. Whose silly idea was it to come out here anyway?"

"I would not touch that question with a thirty-foot pole," he said.

"Wise man, darling." She nestled her head against his shoulder as they walked.